THE VANISHING

ALEX SCARROW

Copyright © 2024 by Alex Scarrow

All rights reserved

This book is a work of fiction. Names, characters, places and incidents are either the product of the author's imagination or are used fictitiously, and any resemblance to actual persons, living or dead, business establishments, events or locales is entirely coincidental.
No part of this book may be reproduced in any form or by any electronic or mechanical means, including information storage and retrieval systems, without written permission from the author, except for the use of brief quotations in a book review.

Published by GrrBooks

Dedication...

1

She didn't know it, but from the moment Audrey Hincher got up from her desk she was on a countdown.

'I'm off for my lunch break,' she said, turning to her colleague. 'Just popping out to get a sandwich. Do you want me to pick anything up for you?'

Tracey shook her head and tapped the Tupperware container beside her monitor. 'I'm catered for, thanks.'

Audrey grabbed her jacket from the back of her chair and picked up her bag, then headed down the stairs, through the small lobby of Sextus and Co. Accountancy and out on to Havelock Road.

She had a mercifully short list of errands to fit into her half-hour break. First and foremost she had to go to Tesco Express to pick up some Coco Pops for Liam. He'd moaned last night that he was one breakfast away from being completely out. (Never mind that he had a pair of perfectly functioning legs and was, in theory, more than capable of going out to buy them himself.) After that, she needed to pop to the post office to pick up some stamps and envelopes for Mum. She also had a cheque to pay in for Andy. She had to remember to pay it in today or she'd be in for one of his talks later on.

Finally, on her way back from Queens Road, she'd nip into Costa Coffee to grab a frothy coffee and a sandwich. Perhaps, she thought, she'd have a cappuccino today instead of a latte. And maybe a wrap instead of a sandwich.

By the time she picked up Liam's Coco Pops and an extra bottle of milk (because Andy got through a *lot* of it... and she'd rather not face his wrath at finding a half-empty carton in the fridge when he got home) the silent countdown on her invisible ticking clock was at five minutes.

Audrey walked briskly down Havelock Road and popped into Tesco Extra for her sandwich and Liam's Coco-Pops, then headed across the pedestrian area in front of John Lewis. It was busy with dozens of people just like her, rushing to get their chores done and grab their lunch. She nipped into Costa, noticing that there was no queue, and swiftly – for once – got her takeaway coffee, then she turned onto Queens Road and halfway down stopped outside Hassim's corner shop, which had a post-office counter.

It was 12.23 p.m.

She dug into her shoulder bag for Andy's cheque and her purse, as the bell on the door tinkled and she stepped inside.

Five minutes later, she exited in a hurry. Passers-by might have noticed a slightly plump, short, middle-aged woman looking frantic, worried even, pacing back and forth on Queens Road. Moments later, she'd simply vanished into thin air.

2

'It's been weeks, though,' said Okeke, her phone on speaker mode.

'How many?' replied Karl.

Okeke signalled right and waited for a gap in the morning traffic. 'It's been four weeks since he left, and I know your brother took that flight over to the States a week ago, Karl.'

'How do you know?' he asked her.

'He still had his phone's location switched on,' she replied. 'He parked at the long-stay at Gatwick.' Okeke saw her gap and took it quickly before the driver who'd flashed his lights changed his mind. 'He switched it off somewhere in the airport.'

'Then I guess we have to assume he took the job?' Karl said.

She sighed. The last time she'd spoken to Jay he'd been uncharacteristically firm with her. As though he was still on some sort of mission to prove to her that he was his own man. That he was perfectly capable of running his own life and was more than ready to go to the States to become a PI for hire.

He'd sounded so different on the phone then. Not his usual laid-back, bumbling self but in 'pro' mode – all clipped sentences, almost as though he was cosplaying some shady character from a fifties film noir. She'd almost been able to picture him in a trench coat and trilby, with a rolled-up newspaper in one pocket ready to whip out and hide behind at a moment's notice.

'He's not called once since then, Karl. And just one bloody text from him saying he was far too busy and would try and catch up later,' she said. 'Has he not reached out to you at all?'

'I haven't heard a thing,' Karl replied. 'I mean, when I last spoke to him he said he had his ticket booked and was set to go.' Okeke heard him take a deep breath. 'He was still pretty pissed off with you, Sam.'

She rolled her eyes. She thought they'd got past that. 'Why?' she demanded.

'For telling him not to do it, obviously. For telling him he wasn't up to the job,' Karl said.

Okeke swung onto Bohemia Road. 'I didn't say he wasn't up to it. I just said it all sounded a bit dodgy.'

'Yeah, well... whatever, really. He's got it in his head that he needs to do this. I think this is about him proving a point rather than anything else,' said Karl, echoing her thoughts.

'Did he tell you about the money?' she asked. 'How much he's been offered?'

'He said it was quite a lot,' Karl replied.

'It's about a hundred K, Karl,' Okeke told him. 'And this is for three months of snooping around. Oh, and it's cash in hand as well.' She sighed. 'What part of that *doesn't* sound dodgy?'

'Jesus,' Karl muttered.

'*Cash in hand*,' Okeke repeated. 'So that kind of money *and* working in the States when he *shouldn't* be... when he's got no work visa...'

There was no reply from Karl.

'Don't you think that sounds incredibly dodgy?' she pressed.

'There's a lot of people who work like that over there,' he said eventually. 'Off the radar, cash in hand. No green card, no visa. No paper trail for the IRS to follow. It's a migrant economy.' She heard him chuckle. 'The US would grind to a halt without them.'

'You think this is funny?' Okeke snapped. 'You think this is some sort of joke?'

'No,' he replied defensively. 'But... Jesus, look – he *is* a big boy now, Sam. Cut him a bit of slack, eh?'

'A hundred grand, Karl. Who gets that kind of money handed to them in a brown envelope unless they're trafficking drugs or –'

'He's not that stupid, Sam,' Karl cut in.

'He can be,' she said.

She drove past the fire station on her right and signalled to turn into the police station, again waiting for a gap in the traffic. Maybe she was being too hard on Jay. Too ready to believe he was a lumbering idiot, just waiting to be taken advantage of by someone.

'Look, Karl,' she said as she turned into the station car park, 'if he gets caught working over there by US immigration, he'll be in big trouble.'

'Let's assume he knows that, shall we, Sam? Give him a little credit, eh?' Karl said.

'And even if he gets his job done without getting jumped on by the Feds,' Okeke continued, 'what about that amount of cash? What's he going to do? Smuggle it home in his underpants?'

Karl chuckled.

She hadn't mentioned the fact that Jay's name was on an MI5 watch list. She was, in fact, surprised that she hadn't already had a home visit from them to ask why Jay had left the country last week.

She found a space in the car park and slid her beat-up Datsun into the narrow slot. 'And let's not forget... if Jay ends up in big trouble, that also affects me too. You do realise that, right? It'll have a direct impact on my career.'

She switched the engine off.

'He'll be fine,' said Karl. 'He's not as –'

'Don't say "dumb". Because I've never actually said that. Never.'

'He's not as naive as you think.'

She tutted. *You should try living with him*, she thought.

'He's actually proven to be pretty resourceful,' added Karl. 'Given what happened last year...'

'Yeah, you stop right there, Karl. We don't talk about that, okay?' she said.

Okeke looked out of her side window at the station, still wrapped in flapping sheets of orange plastic tied to a lattice of rattling scaffolding. She was going to be late.

'All right – I've gotta go. I'm at work now. If he calls you...'

'Of course I'll let you know. Likewise.'

'Yeah.'

She was about to end the call when Karl cut back in. 'You know he's crazy about you, don't you?'

'Yeah,' she replied quietly. 'I do.'

'This isn't him bailing on you,' Karl said. 'This is him... on some stupid quest to prove himself to you.'

She sighed. 'Christ. A bunch of flowers would have done.'

3

Boyd turned off the tap and paused in front of the mirror as he shook the water from his hands. Nine weeks on from his last dreadful course of drugs and the hair on his head was – thank God – beginning to make a courageous comeback. Baldness suited some men but not him. His head looked fat without hair. His face was nothing but a big doughy mess without stubble and eyebrows to break it up.

He ran his hand across the short carpet of bristles that had restaked a claim on where his hairline had once been. Another couple of months and he'd, hopefully, look normal again.

He'd managed to shed some of the weight that he'd put on too. The puffiness – a side effect of the drugs – had given him a distinct moon-face for the last six months. It was a relief to see the corner line of his jaw again.

His belly, however, was a battle yet to be won. The waistline of his trousers hung low to allow some spill-room for his gut. Muffin-top was too kind a word for it. There was enough of it there that he now preferred wearing his tie long, so that it covered his paunch, Trump-style.

He gave his hands one more shake over the sink, pulled the door to the gents open and stepped back into the amber-hued twilight of the CID bullpen.

The floor was a lot larger now that the Operation Rosper partition wall had been taken down. The disbanded task force had staked a claim on square footage that had vastly exceeded the need for their headcount. The absence of that row of partitions was striking and would take some time to get used to.

The desks were still there, though, along with the potted plants and the jokey printout of Ned Flanders stuck to a whiteboard, but everything with operation-sensitive information on it had been taken down.

Flack's desk was also still there.

That poor bastard. Boyd instantly amended that in his head. That 'poor bastard' had been corrupt. He'd been on the take and he'd groomed his team into following his lead. O'Neal had been one of them. And now O'Neal – young enough and definitely stupid enough not to know any better – would be facing serious time behind bars once the IOPC got their act together. He was suspended for now... coming clean to Okeke at the last moment and allowing her to arrest him had spared him jail time while he awaited his day in court. Last-minute atonement aside, between the expected charges of conspiracy to commit murder and perverting the course of justice Boyd would be surprised if O'Neal got away with anything less than ten years.

Jeff Flack had been old and wise enough to know that ten years or more as a copper in prison would have been unbearable. Possibly even unsurvivable.

What a mess, though. Flack had left his family behind. His wife and two kids left high and dry, marooned on a sandbank of guilt, shock and grief.

As Boyd approached his own desk, he switched gears to something more uplifting. He'd decided to book a holiday in the sun this year for himself, Charlotte, Emma and Maggie. It would be the first time in six years that he'd been away. He was torn between something cheap-as-chips or an all-inclusive ring-fenced job, complete with watered-down drinks, a paddling pool and karaoke in the evenings.

Charlotte and Emma had yet to discover his plan, and that was something else he was pondering: should he surprise them both with whatever he chose or let them have a say in the matter?

'Boyd?' He turned to see DSI Sutherland's perfectly spherical head teetering between the black shoulder pads of his suit. 'Have you got a moment?'

Boyd followed him into his fishbowl of an office and closed the door on the CID floor behind him.

'What can I do you for?' Boyd asked.

Sutherland sat down behind his desk and gestured for Boyd to take the seat opposite.

'As you know, Boyd,' he began, 'Her Madge has decided that Operation Rosper is to be completely shelved. All the intel that that ruddy team accumulated over the last four years has got to be treated as tainted goods. Quarantined, so to speak.'

'All of it?' Boyd asked.

Sutherland nodded. 'I mean, we're not going to flush it *all* down the toilet. Some of it may bear scrutiny and be worth keeping, but a lot of it – most of it – will have to be rigorously questioned before it can be used as reliable intelligence.' He sighed. 'It's a ruddy shame is what it is. A ruddy waste.'

Boyd nodded.

'She wants to launch a brand-new task force to deal with the local county-lines problem we've got this end of Sussex. I mean, it stands to reason that while we have absolutely no one watching them, those wily young buggers will undoubtedly be making hay, won't they?'

Boyd began to get a sense of where this might be heading.

'The Chief Super has managed to secure some additional funding from East Sussex's reserve pool to start a new operation,' Sutherland continued, 'and your name came up as the obvious first choice for the top job.'

'Ahhh,' Boyd murmured.

Sutherland looked as though his own bottom had just been smacked. 'Ahhh? What's that supposed to mean?'

'It means, uh... it means, well, it's quite a big ask,' Boyd answered lamely.

'Well, it is a big deal, certainly.' Sutherland paused, clearly a little disappointed that Boyd hadn't sounded a tad more enthusiastic at the prospect. 'To be honest, Boyd, I was expecting you to bite my hand off to have a crack at something like that.'

Boyd ran his hand over the fuzz on his scalp.

Sutherland frowned. 'It's a no-brainer. You'd have full autonomy. Get to hand-pick your own team. Brand-new office furniture... your very own coffee machine...'

Boyd smiled at that. 'Tempting though that sounds, sir, it's just –'

'It's just what?' Sutherland spread his arms wide. 'What's the problem?'

'It's just that it's an open-ended commitment, isn't it? It's an operation without an exit strategy. Without an end goal,' Boyd said.

'The end goal, Boyd, is to squash the local drug economy,' Sutherland said, wobbling his head from side to side.

'Well, we both know that's not going to happen, don't we?' Boyd said. 'The best I can hope for is to try and keep a lid on it. I'm never going to squash it, am I?'

'Well, come on now, sunshine,' Sutherland replied, 'that's policing in general. It's what we do.'

Boyd had been giving serious consideration, since coming back after his cancer treatment, to taking early retirement. He was fast approaching fifty and, while cashing out early would bite into his pension, he'd done very well on the value of his London house and now his Hastings one too. He'd been extremely lucky, in fact. He reckoned he was looking at four hundred-odd thousand, plus about three-quarters of his full pension. He'd be able to sell and downscale, or sell and move abroad, or not sell at all and live off his pension, perhaps supplemented by some side hustle or other. Jay's foray into PI work and the money that he could make doing essentially the same job as Boyd felt somewhat tempting.

And Jeff Flack's suicide had forced him to focus a little more acutely on what the important things in his life were. Namely Charlotte, Emma and Margot. He was 'Grandpa Bill' now. And unless Danny suddenly decided to forego his budding rock-star lifestyle, move in with them and become a full-time hipster dad, complete with topknot and caboose strapped to his chest, Boyd was expecting – no, *hoping* – he was also going to have to step up and become something of a father figure to little Maggie as well.

Slipping into Flack's old role would mean signing up to an open-ended commitment, one that would undoubtedly keep him busy with unpredictable hours and late nights for the next five to ten years, one way or another. It was the kind of role better suited to a younger, keener DCI looking for a career-builder of an opportunity.

'All right,' sighed Sutherland. 'I can see you're not wildly excited by the prospect, but why don't you mull it over for a while? The Chief Super wasn't expecting a firm answer out of you this morning.'

Boyd nodded. 'Okay. I'll do that.'

'Talk it over with... uh...' Sutherland floundered.

'Charlotte.'

'With Charlotte, right. See what she thinks about it, hmm?'

BOYD EMERGED from Sutherland's office to see Okeke sitting at her desk. She was staring listlessly across the floor at the windows and the orange plastic sheeting outside, snapping and fluttering like a washing line of high-vis laundry.

'You all right over there?' He sat down at his desk, logged onto LEDS, then craned his neck round the monitor. 'Sam?'

She was a million miles away.

'Sam?' he repeated.

Okeke stirred from her thoughts with a shake of her head. 'Huh?' She turned to look at him. 'Sorry,' she said. 'Just... gathering wool.'

Pining over Jay, more like, Boyd thought. He was well aware that the two of them had had a bust-up of sorts. Okeke had told him that Jay had moved out and taken himself off somewhere to 're-evaluate his life goals', or something like that.

Not that Boyd could blame him. He was feeling pretty

much the same way. It was coming up to three years since he'd transferred to Hastings and the glut of cases and incidents and near-misses had left him little time to reflect on much outside work. Even during his six months of sick leave, while dealing with the all-encompassing side effects of chemotherapy, he had been rudely interrupted with work that had spilled off the CID floor and into his life.

It certainly felt like the right time to take stock, to take a leaf out of Jay's book and do some evaluating. Not just focusing on what was important to himself but on a broader scale – what was right for his newly reconstituted family.

With Flack's death, not to mention his own bowel cancer, throwing the issue of mortality into sharp relief, it was most definitely the time to put what mattered into some kind of running order. He'd missed out on pretty much most of Noah's short life, and most of the first two decades of Emma's. Maggie, the little rug rat, was not going to escape him so easily.

His meandering thoughts were interrupted by DC Yates, loitering in front of Boyd's desk and holding his notepad up as if it was a winning lottery ticket.

'Yup?' Boyd said.

'Sir,' Yates began excitedly, 'I just took a missing persons call.'

'And?' Boyd prompted.

'It's a woman. A local woman. She went missing yesterday,' Yates said.

'Who reported her missing?' Boyd asked.

'Her mother did.'

'How old is she?' Boyd asked, feeling very much as though he was pulling teeth.

'I'm not sure,' Yates replied, looking slightly confused. 'She sounded pretty old.'

'No, you muppet.' Boyd rolled his eyes. 'The missing woman. How old is the missing woman?'

'Uh… oh, right,' Yates said, blushing slightly. He checked his notepad. 'Fifty-nine.'

Boyd nodded towards Okeke, who was listening in. 'Take it to Detective Sergeant Okeke; she'll show you the ropes.'

4

Okeke spun the wheel and turned her car left, onto Bohemia Road.

'Your first misper, is it?' she asked.

Yates nodded. 'I mean, I've attended a misper interview before. But not, you know, investigated one.' He smiled. 'Obviously.'

'Well, don't get your hopes up. Seventy per cent of adult mispers resolve themselves,' she told him.

'Right.' He paused, then: 'Really? That many?'

'Yeah. More often than not it's a domestic and one partner or the other has stropped off somewhere for a few days.' She looked at him. 'Honestly? If you weren't a noob, you could probably have handled this one by yourself.' She sighed. 'This visit is more of a courtesy thing at this point. We'll take some details, offer some reassurance, but that's about it.'

'Shouldn't we have brought a family liaison officer with us?' Yates asked.

Okeke shook her head and smiled. 'That's a bit premature, Yates, don't you think? Our person's missing, not dead.

If we rock up with a FLO, the old dear will think we've found a body.' She glanced at him. 'We don't want to frighten her any more than she already is.'

'Right.'

'I mean, if the misper was a minor,' she continued, 'then, yeah... there'd be family support, some hand-holding straight off the bat.'

Okeke followed White Rock Road, then turned left at the theatre, onto the seafront road. She fumbled in her side pocket for her cigarettes.

'So,' she asked. 'How're you finding it so far? Out of uniform?'

Yates nodded thoughtfully. 'It's a lot to take in, I guess. I'm used to handing things over at the end of my shift.'

'Right.' She pulled a cigarette from the box. 'That's the biggest difference you'll notice. There's none of that passing-stuff-on crap. You're stuck with whatever lands in your in-tray until you get a result. Which nine times out of ten ends up as "no further action".'

'Really?' Yates asked.

'Maybe I'm exaggerating a bit,' she admitted. 'But more often than not. The biggest bloody hurdle is getting enough evidence together, in a nicely gift-wrapped parcel, for the CPS to bother getting off their arses to take forward.' She sighed. 'They can be real prats about that sort of thing.'

They drove past the amusements arcade, which was looking forlorn and pointlessly open, its lights blinking away for no one in particular.

'What they want is a guaranteed win. Every time,' Okeke continued.

'Sounds frustrating,' Yates said.

She shrugged. 'You can say that again.' She sparked up

and took a deep puff, blowing the smoke out of the window. 'Sorry... do you mind?'

He shook his head. 'No – go for it.'

'There's far less paperwork than with uniform work, though,' she added. 'That's a bonus.'

'Right. Tell me about it,' Yates agreed. 'The hand-over shite at the end of a shift is definitely something I won't miss.'

TEN MINUTES LATER, they arrived outside the address that Yates had taken down. Fairlight Avenue, Ore, was tree-lined and flanked on either side by large detached houses with tidy front lawns and weed-free driveways. It wasn't exactly a 'millionaires' row', but Okeke guessed the average price along the avenue took the folks here over the halfway mark.

'Righty-right,' she said, pulling the handbrake on and turning the engine off. 'Just remember we're here to take some details, offer some reassurances and hand over a reference number.'

They got out of the car and Okeke led the way up the driveway of Number 36 to the front door. She pressed the doorbell and shortly afterwards it opened to reveal a slim silver-haired woman with a pronounced Punchinello chin and nose. She was wearing a three-quarter-length dark blue cardigan and holding a dishcloth in one hand.

'Mrs Davitt?' Okeke asked.

The woman nodded.

Okeke held up her lanyard for the woman to see. 'I'm Detective Sergeant Okeke and this is Detective Constable Yates. We're from Hastings CID.'

Mrs Davitt's face sagged with relief. 'That was quick. I

wasn't expecting to see someone so –' Her face tightened. 'You haven't found...'

Okeke shook her head. 'No, not at all. We're here so promptly because, for once, we're not completely inundated.' She smiled. 'Can we come in?'

Mrs Davitt led them inside, down a hallway and into her kitchen. She flipped the kettle on. 'Tea?' she asked.

'Thank you,' said Okeke automatically. 'But could we have two coffees?'

'Yes... yes, of course,' said Mrs Davitt, reaching for the cupboard door.

'Actually, it's tea for me,' said Yates. 'If that's no problem?'

Mrs Davitt turned to pull a box of teabags out from the cupboard.

Okeke glanced at Yates with her brows raised.

'I can't stand coffee,' he said quietly.

'Oh dear,' Okeke tutted softly. 'That's strike one.'

A couple of minutes later, they were sitting at the island in the centre of the kitchen, with their mugs of tea and coffee and a plate of Bourbons and custard creams.

'Right then,' began Okeke, pulling out her notebook. 'Your daughter's called Audrey, isn't she?'

'Yes,' Mrs Davitt said. 'She's Audrey Hincher.'

Okeke scribbled that down. 'And she's fifty-nine?'

'That's right,' Mrs Davitt confirmed.

'And you called earlier this morning to report her missing?' Okeke said.

Mrs Davitt nodded. 'She was meant to visit me yesterday after work. But she didn't turn up. I've tried to call her a number of times, but there's been no answer. It's not like her.'

'Does she live alone?' Okeke asked. 'Or is there someone else at home with her?'

'She lives with her... *husband*, Andy,' Mrs Davitt said.

Okeke looked up, her interest piqued by the dismissive tone in Mrs Davitt's voice. She checked her notes again. Hincher. 'So he's Andy Hincher?' she said.

Mrs Davitt nodded again. 'Yes. He's an awful man. Just awful.'

'What makes you say that?' Okeke asked.

'He's vile to her,' Mrs Davitt replied. 'Absolutely vile. And his kids are too.'

'How do you mean?' Okeke prompted.

Mrs Davitt sighed. 'He married Audrey for her money. She can't see it, of course. But it's obvious to anyone else. He married her so that she could be his wretched piggy bank.'

Okeke flicked a look towards Yates. 'Does she have significant money?' she asked.

'Yes,' replied Mrs Davitt. 'She's got a sizeable trust fund.' She wagged a finger. 'The first time she introduced him to me I knew he was up to no bloody good. He didn't *love* her. Not a bit of it. He never has.'

'How long have they been together?' Okeke asked.

'Nearly ten years.'

Okeke jotted that down. Ten years. If they'd been together for a significantly shorter period of time, then Okeke might, at this point, have considered indulging Mrs Davitt's suspicions. But ten years was a long time for a gold digger to sit and wait for a pot of gold, if that *was* his game.

'You said he was... *vile* to her?' Okeke said. 'Do you mean abusive?'

'He controls her,' Mrs Davitt replied. 'He controls everything about her. Where she can go, what she can do, what friends she's allowed to have, what clothes she can wear. He's a bloody bully. A vile, nasty bully.'

'Is he violent?' Okeke glanced up from her pad. 'Would you say?'

'I think he is,' Mrs Davitt replied. She paused for a moment. 'I think he's hit her, yes. I think he's actually hit her a number of times.'

5

Audrey Hincher lived in a modest two-storey terraced house in St Leonards. The houses on either side of the narrow road loomed like prison walls, throwing permanent shadow onto the parked cars that were rammed bumper to bumper on either side.

The front door opened after about a dozen rings of the doorbell.

The young man standing barefoot in the doorway wore pyjama bottoms and a hoodie. In one hand he held a bowl of cereal. 'Police?' he asked.

Okeke held out her lanyard. 'I'm DS Okeke and this is DC Yates. Is Audrey Hincher in?'

'Uh, nerr, don't think so,' the young man replied.

Okeke peered round him. She could hear the thump of music playing loudly from somewhere inside. 'Are you her son?' she asked.

'*Step*son,' he corrected her. 'Liam. Why?'

'Can we come in?' Okeke asked.

Liam frowned and remained where he stood. 'Why do you want to come in?'

'We're concerned for the welfare of your stepmum,' said Okeke. 'Your gran reported her missing this morning.'

'She's not me fuckin' gran,' Liam replied.

'Fine. Well, can we come in anyway?' she asked again, trying and failing to keep the irritation from her voice.

Liam Hincher met her eyes, seemingly up for a game of Who's Gonna Blink First, but quickly crumbled beneath Okeke's withering gaze.

He shrugged and backed up. 'Suit yerself.'

Okeke led the way inside, with Yates closing the door behind them.

'So she's not home?' Okeke asked again.

Liam put his cereal bowl down on a small shelf for keys and cupped his hands theatrically round his mouth. 'Audrey!' he bellowed loudly. 'Yo! Aud! You got visitors!' He waited a moment, then turned to look back at Okeke. 'Nerr. It's a weekday, right?'

'It's Friday,' replied Okeke.

Liam nodded. 'She'll be at work, then.'

'And where does she work?' Okeke asked.

'Some place in town,' Liam said.

Okeke glared impatiently at him.

'In an office,' he added. 'An accountants' place, or something.'

'And has her workplace got a name?' Okeke pressed.

Liam's face wrinkled with some effort. 'Sex-something...'

'Sextus Accountancy?' offered Yates.

Liam nodded. 'Yup. That's the one... yeah, mate.'

'Where's your dad?' asked Okeke.

He shrugged again. 'Away. Some work thing. For a few days, like.'

'And your sister?'

'She don't live here any more.'

'So it's just you here at the moment, Liam?' Okeke said.

Liam nodded.

'Do you have a number for your dad?' Okeke asked.

'S'on me phone.' Liam patted the pocket pouch of his hoodie. 'Back in the kitchen.'

'Well, let's go and get it, then, shall we?' replied Okeke.

Okeke and Yates followed him through the messy front room. There was some zombie game or other paused on the large wall-mounted TV, the source of the thumping music. A pizza box sat open on the coffee table beside an Xbox controller and several cans of Red Bull.

They entered the kitchen, which was equally messy with a sink full of crockery, in dishwater that looked as though it was growing a skin.

Liam huffed irritably as he made a show of moving things around on the cluttered counters. 'So why's that stupid old bitch gone and called the police?' he asked.

'Her mother's concerned,' replied Okeke. 'She was expecting a visit from Audrey yesterday after work. Is this it?' she said, picking up a phone that was beside the microwave.

Liam took it from her and swiped his screen absently. 'Scatty cow must've forgot to visit her mum, then. I'm not surprised. She's a total bubblehead. Why don't you just call her phone?'

'She's not answering her phone, *mate*,' replied Yates tersely.

'Hence the concern,' added Okeke.

Liam shook his head. 'Call her work, then!' He glared at Yates. 'I'm not gonna do yer bloody job for you, *mate*.'

Okeke nodded at Yates, who took out his phone to google the accountancy firm's number.

'Here,' said Liam. 'This is Dad's mobile. You got a pen?'

'Why don't you just call him for me right now?' Okeke smiled. 'Then I can speak to him directly.'

Liam shook his head. 'Fuck it. You do it on your phone.' He read out the number for her. She jotted it down, then called the number on her phone. As it rang, Yates looked up from his own phone. 'Okay. I've got her work number.'

'Call them while I try to reach the husband,' said Okeke as she waited for Mr Hincher to pick up.

Yates wandered out of the kitchen and through the lounge to the front door, in a bid to escape the music pumping away from the TV.

Okeke let the call for Andy Hincher ring a few more times, then ended it. 'There's no answer,' she said.

'He's probably busy. He's at some conference or something,' replied Liam.

'I'll give it a couple of minutes and try again,' she said, glancing around the kitchen. It looked like the kind of a chaos only a young lad living alone for a day or two could create – the sink was piled high and the counters were littered with open jars of Nutella and peanut butter.

'Are you usually this messy?' she asked. 'Don't your mum and dad mind?'

'I'll clean up before Dad comes home,' he said, wrinkling his nose. 'I told you: Audrey's not my mum. I never call her that.'

Okeke wandered back into the lounge and Liam followed her.

'So, when did you last see Audrey?' she asked.

'Yesterday morning, maybe,' he offered.

'Maybe?'

Liam shrugged. 'Or the night before. I don't remember. We don't talk much.'

'You don't get on?' Okeke asked.

'I keep sayin'... she's not me mum. So, no, not really,' Liam said.

'Do you know if she went to work yesterday morning?'

He hunched his shoulders. 'I guess so. I really dunno.'

Okeke looked at him. 'And what about last night?'

He shrugged.

'You didn't see her? Speak to her? She definitely didn't come home?'

Liam shrugged again. 'She might've come in. I didn't hear anything, though. I was up in my room.'

Okeke shook her head. 'All night? All evening? It's a small house, Liam. What do you mean you don't know? If she'd come home, you would surely have seen her or heard her come in.'

He shrugged yet again.

The mess in the kitchen and here in the lounge suggested to Okeke that he was telling the truth.

'The scatty old cow does her own thing,' Liam said suddenly. 'And I do my own thing.'

Okeke, ignoring him, tried Andy Hincher's number again. The call went to voicemail.

'Why don't *you* try calling him, Liam?' she said.

'What?'

'You heard me. Try calling your dad on your phone,' she said, nodding at it. 'Maybe he doesn't answer calls from unknown numbers.'

They heard the front door shut and a moment later Yates stepped back into the lounge, pocketing his phone. 'They said they've not seen her since yesterday lunchtime. She went out for lunch... and never returned.'

Okeke turned back to Liam. 'Call him.'

'He'll be busy,' Liam complained.

'Call him,' she repeated. 'Now. This could be serious.'

Her eyes flicked to the TV. 'And can you turn that thing down, please?'

Liam reached for a remote on the couch and muted the noise. He shook his head and muttered to himself, 'So stupid. She's probably... This is just...' He thumbed his phone's screen. 'He probably won't answer me either,' he added.

'Let's just give it a go, shall we?' Okeke said.

Liam raised the phone to his ear.

'Put it on speakerphone,' said Okeke. 'So we can both talk to him.'

Reluctantly he thumbed the speaker icon and made the call. The phone rang several times and Liam was about to disconnect when the call was answered. 'Liam? What's the —'

'Dad it's me,' Liam said quickly. 'I got the police here with me.'

There was a pause.

'At the house,' he added.

'Is that Andy Hincher?' asked Okeke.

'Yeah. Who's that?' Hincher replied.

'This is Detective Sergeant Samantha Okeke from Hastings CID,' she told him.

'What's going on?' Hincher replied. 'I'm busy. For fuck's sake, what's Liam gone and done now?'

'Nothing,' Okeke replied. 'Your wife's been reported missing.'

There was another pause. '*What?*'

'Your wife, Audrey. She's been missing for —' she glanced at her watch — 'just over twenty-four hours now.'

'Well, she'll be at her mum's probably,' Hincher said.

'It was her mother who called us,' Okeke told him.

'Audrey was supposed to drop by yesterday afternoon and she didn't turn up.'

'Oh... I don't know, then,' Hincher said. 'Maybe she took herself off somewhere. For a break?'

Okeke glanced at Yates. Hincher didn't sound like a worried man. 'Is this like her?' she asked. 'Does she usually "take herself off for a break"?'

There was a longer pause this time. 'Not... no, not really,' Hincher admitted.

The lack of concern from him was starting to needle her. 'Look, you'll need to come back from wherever you are... and into the station,' she told him. Technically, this wasn't true. Audrey was an adult and had only been missing for twenty-four hours. But Okeke wanted to test his response.

'She's probably... just, I don't know, visiting a friend or something,' he told her.

'All the same,' Okeke pressed, 'we need to ask you for a few details about her. Who her friends are... what, if any, family she might have contacted... that sort of thing. We'll need to do this as soon as possible, Mr Hincher.'

Hincher gave a long sigh.

'Right. All right. Fine. Which station should I come to?' he asked.

'Hastings,' Okeke said. 'The one on Bohemia Road.'

'The big one?' he asked.

'That's it. Ask for me, DS Okeke.'

'DS... O'car – what?'

'*Oh-car-key*,' she said for what felt like the millionth time in her life. She fished into her jacket, pulled out a business card and handed it to Liam. 'I've given your son my card. If you can come in this afternoon or tomorrow, that would be very helpful.'

'Right. Yes... I suppose...' he began.

'And of course, in the meantime, if you do hear from her...' Okeke looked at Liam. '*Either* of you... You let me know straight away. All right?'

'Yes... Yes, of course,' replied Hincher.

Liam nodded.

6

'Well? What did you make of that?' asked Okeke, pulling out of their tight parking space and into the narrow road.

Yates started fidgeting in his seat and went to pull his notebook from his back pocket.

Okeke chuckled. 'Old habits, eh?'

'Huh?' Yates seemed confused.

'I'm not asking to read your notes like a bloody robot,' she told him. 'I'm after your opinion.'

'Ah, right,' Yates said. 'Well, um... I didn't get the sense that either the dad or the son were that concerned about her welfare.'

'Same here,' Okeke agreed. 'Zero shits given, as far I could see. So, then you ask yourself the obvious questions, don't you?'

Yates looked at her, hoping for a prompt.

'First: *why?*' she continued. 'Why did Audrey suddenly disappear? Why don't either of them appear to be the slightest bit concerned?'

'Because they don't care much about her?' he volunteered.

She nodded. 'That, or they're overplaying it.' She glanced at him. 'That's a mistake people often make... They overdo it.'

'You think there's something dodgy going on there?' Yates asked her.

Okeke pressed her lips together as she mulled it over. Even if you don't particularly care for a person, you would at least show some morsel of concern over their unexplained disappearance. Neither father nor stepson seemed to give a damn. And Liam's bollocks about not knowing if she came in last night because he'd been in his room? Well, Okeke wasn't buying that.

'What did they say at her work?' she asked Yates.

'Just that she stepped out to grab a sandwich for lunch and never came back to work,' he replied.

'Nothing more?' said Okeke. She sighed. 'Go on, you can get your security blanket out.'

Yates struggled to pull his notebook out of the back pocket of his trousers – they were slim fit and tight. 'I'm used to having it tucked into my tac vest,' he mumbled as he wrestled it out. 'Got it.' He opened the bent cover and flipped through several dog-eared pages.

'So... I spoke to the office manager, Linda Hayes. She said Audrey was usually reliable. She'd been working there for about six years. Linda was surprised that she'd not called to say she was sick or unable to come back to work.'

'Did *she* sound concerned in any way?' Okeke asked.

'She sounded slightly annoyed, if anything,' Yates said.

'Did you speak to any of Audrey's colleagues?'

'No, only the office manager,' he replied.

Okeke signalled right to turn onto the seafront road. 'It

might be a good idea to call them again tomorrow and arrange to go in and chat with whoever she sits next to,' she said.

They sat in silence for a while as they passed the amusement arcade once again.

'You think she's likely to turn up this evening?' he asked.

'Maybe. I hope so.' Okeke had a nagging, hectoring feeling about the two men she'd spoken to. Liam had seemed slightly on edge. Arguably understandable given that they'd turned up on his doorstep without warning. But it was the way he'd behaved over calling his dad that had struck her as odd. He'd been very twitchy about handing his phone to her. She checked the clock on the dash. 'Let's have a late lunch break when we get back.'

'Cool.' Yates grinned. 'I'm starving.'

'Then maybe we'll have a little background look at Audrey, Andy and Liam this afternoon. See if there's anything on LEDS for any of them,' she continued.

Yates sighed. 'Right. Yeah. LEDS... I'm still trying to get my head around that. I'm used to Holmes.'

'Cheer up. If you were still in uniform, you'd be form-filling and typing this up all afternoon,' Okeke pointed out. 'And then you'd be moved on to something else.' She looked at him. 'And that's the difference... right there. We're not on a conveyor belt of call-outs and half jobs.'

He nodded. 'So what happens now? Do we open an action log?'

'Not yet,' Okeke told him. 'She's an adult and entitled to bugger off for a break if she wants one. Honestly, given the total lack of shits given by the men in her life, I can't say I'd blame her if she had.'

'How long do you leave it until you open up a log on a case like this, then?' Yates asked.

Okeke hunched her shoulders. 'After three days we'll have to log it for the Misper Unit. They'll open a file and put her up on their website. Then we wait to see whether someone spots her, or she just turns up somewhere. But...'

'But?'

'If we come across anything that gives us cause for concern... then –' she smiled – 'it's our case to look into.'

7

Boyd tossed the cubes of tofu into the pan, to join the sizzling onions and garlic. Tonight was sambal night. Formerly known as *Chicken* Sambal Night, but since Emma seemed to be back on the vegan bandwagon and busting his nuts about factory farming and imports of American chlorine-saturated chicken, tofu cubes it was.

Charlotte brought his glass of wine in from the dining room and handed it to him. 'Smell's good,' she said.

'It would smell even better if it was actual chicken instead of condensed fungal matter,' he muttered.

'Oh, you grumpy neanderthal,' she replied, nudging him. 'Once you dollop that chilli paste in, that's all we'll taste anyway.'

'It's sambal paste. Not chilli paste. There's a difference, you know?' He took a slug of his wine. 'Chef Bill insists on working with authentic indigenous spices, not plebby substitutes.'

'Good grief. I suspect Chef Bill has been watching too much *MasterChef*. Please... don't turn into Greg Wallace.'

He ran a hand over his fuzz. 'You ever seen the both of us in the same room at the same time? Hmm?'

She laughed and watched him as he stirred the tofu cubes around the pan in an attempt to get some colour on them.

'Two things,' he said after a while.

'Uh-huh?'

'Thing one. I was thinking...' he began.

'Uh-oh,' she said, smiling.

'I was thinking,' he continued, 'about booking a holiday for us all this summer.'

She raised a brow and sipped her wine. 'Oooh,' she said. 'A holiday? That sounds good. Where are we going?'

He shrugged. 'I hadn't actually got that far,' he admitted. 'So, at this point, the world is our oyster. I started out thinking maybe somewhere hot, sunny and sandy?'

'Oka-a-y,' Charlotte said.

'But then, this afternoon, I thought why don't we take a holiday to somewhere like Disneyland? Now that we've got a little 'un to impress?'

'Ooh, what's this about a holiday?' Emma appeared in the doorway, gently bouncing Maggie in her arms and patting her back gently in an attempt to induce a hearty belch.

Boyd grinned. 'Disney? What d'ya think?' He nodded at Maggie, who was burbling contentedly on Emma's shoulder. 'She'll love it. And not the crappy Paris one. I mean the one in Florida. With guaranteed sun.'

'Dad, she's not even six months old!' Emma pointed out.

'Yeah, but she'll be ten months if we went in, say, September,' he replied.

Emma shook her head. 'Ten months old, eh?' She laughed. 'Dad, just think about it. She won't even be toddling by then. Can you imagine Goofy or Mickey Mouse looming over her buggy? They'd scare the crap out of her. You ever seen *Five Nights at Freddy's?*'

He shook his head. He'd not even heard of it.

'It's a freaking, gaudy-coloured horror show! That's what Disney would be like to her,' said Emma.

Charlotte nodded. 'Maybe it's a bit too soon, Bill? Eh?'

'And... good God, America?' Emma rolled her eyes. 'During election year? Are you crazy?'

'Maybe somewhere closer to home?' Charlotte suggested. 'Dorset?'

Boyd frowned. 'Well, there'll be sea and sand, I guess.'

'They do get some sun down there, Bill. If you pick the right week,' Charlotte said.

He pulled a face. In truth, he had actually set his heart on somewhere abroad. 'How about somewhere like Turkey?' he suggested.

Emma pulled a face. 'You're on the Black Sea there, aren't you?'

He shrugged. 'So?'

'Russian navy,' she replied. 'And drones. I'm just saying.'

Boyd shook his head. 'What about Greece?' he tried.

Emma sucked air between her teeth. 'I don't know how I'd feel sitting on a lounger on a beach knowing there's boats out there on the horizon full of desperate people,' she said.

Boyd raised his hands in exasperation. 'Well, *where*, then?'

Emma grimaced. 'I'm not sure how I'd feel flying anywhere now, to be honest.'

Maggie let out a satisfyingly fulsome belch and Emma stopped patting her back. 'Job done. I'll go and put her down.' She walked out of the kitchen, murmuring to Maggie as she went.

Charlotte sipped her wine. 'It's not so easy organising a holiday these days, is it?'

Boyd resumed stirring the pan. 'Not if you're going to worry about everything that *might* happen,' he grumbled.

'I can't say I blame her,' she replied. 'It feels like a very topsy-turvy world out there.' She watched him stir the onions and tofu for a while. 'You said two things, Bill. What was the other?'

'Oh, yeah,' he said. 'Sutherland offered me Flack's old job.'

Charlotte set her glass down. 'The chap who drove his car off a cliff?'

Boyd nodded. He'd not shared much about Flack with her. She didn't know that he'd been on the take and indirectly responsible for the death of an informer and for the attempted murder of a minor. He, and everyone else in CID, were on orders not to discuss it with anyone.

'They need to set up a new drugs-busting team and Sutherland asked if I wanted to lead it,' he told her.

'And? What do you think about that?' she asked.

'I'm not too keen,' he said. 'I don't want to get sucked into an open-ended commitment.' He looked at her. 'I'm not even sure I want to keep doing this job as it is for too much longer.'

'Really?' This was news to her.

He nodded.

'Are you beginning to lose your love of policing?' she asked.

He snorted. 'I've never exactly *loved* it, Char... It's a job. You know? It keeps the shekels coming in. Keeps me busy.'

He sighed and looked at her. 'Too busy. It's been pretty much full-on since I moved down here.'

She nodded and took his arm. 'It has been a somewhat "eventful" couple of years, hasn't it?'

8

Okeke and DC Yates led Andrew Hincher into Interview Room 1.

'So you lot work Saturdays, then?'

Okeke ignored him. 'Take a seat, please,' she said as she closed the door on the noisy corridor.

Okeke had pulled up Audrey's Facebook profile this morning and found herself looking at a very plain woman with short greying hair that, in her opinion, did no favours, and the heft to her face and neck suggested that Audrey was moderately overweight. She was fifty-nine years old, but the photo – or perhaps it was the dowdy clothes she wore – made her seem ten years older.

Mr Hincher, on the other hand, was not what Okeke had been expecting.

She'd pictured someone who vaguely mirrored Audrey in the way most middle-aged and older couples invariably mirrored each other – a shared lifestyle led to a shared weight, a shared 'look' and occasionally even matching cardigans. Given a room of strangers to pair into couples, she wouldn't have matched them on first impressions alone.

Andrew, at fifty-one, was of course younger. But he looked ten years younger than that. He obviously took great care of himself, hitting the gym and putting in the miles. He was slim, and, she noted, very attractive for a silver fox. His short hair was speckled salt and pepper, and his jawline sported a carefully moderated line of clipped bristles that accentuated the fact that he actually still had a jawline.

'Thanks for coming in this morning, Andrew,' she began. 'I presume you've not heard anything from Audrey since we last spoke?'

He shook his head. 'I've not heard from her since I left on Wednesday afternoon.'

'At this stage it's still early doors,' Okeke told him. 'We won't action anything until seventy-two hours have passed, because most of the time this kind of situation tends to resolve itself.'

Andrew nodded. 'I'm sure she'll be back soon,' he said.

Okeke glanced at Yates, again noting his complete lack of concern. 'Can you describe your last interaction with Audrey?' she asked. 'When that was and how she was the last time you spoke with her.'

'Sure – she was her usual self,' Andrew replied.

'Which is what?' Okeke asked.

'Well, she was busy getting herself ready for work,' he said. 'She didn't seem to be worried about anything in particular. She was just her usual self. We had breakfast. I reminded her I was going to be away at this work thing for a couple of nights, then I gave her a kiss and said I was off.' He shrugged. 'That was it.'

'What was this business thing?' asked Okeke. 'What do you do?'

'I install home-security systems. It's a franchise business.'

'How does that work?'

'You buy into the business,' he said. 'They set you up with the training, the kit you need, their branding, their sales leads and all that stuff. Then you're your own boss. You can take on as much work as you want.'

Okeke jotted that down. 'And this conference you went to – what was that for?'

'They organise a couple of them a year. They like to keep us all up to date on tech developments, marketing, customer relations,' He sighed. 'You have to go to at least one of them.'

'We spoke to Liam,' said Okeke, changing tack. 'He doesn't seem to get on particularly well with Audrey.'

'What do you expect?' Andrew replied. 'He's her stepkid. She's not his mum, is she?'

'Yes, he made that very clear,' Okeke said.

'They don't get on. But it's not like they're at each other's throats,' he clarified. 'He puts up with her; she puts up with him.'

'Liam described her as...' She looked at Yates. 'What's the term he used?'

'A "scatty old cow",' Yates said, glancing down at his notebook.

Andrew shrugged. 'Yeah, well, she is a bit. She can be a bit muddle-headed. Forgetful. It's more than a bit annoying having to organise her all the time.'

'Organise her?' repeated Okeke. 'What do you mean?'

'She forgets to pay bills. She loses bank statements. She forgot to re-insure my van last month. I was driving around illegally for a couple of weeks, you know?'

'Does she have any friends you know of?' Okeke asked.

Andrew shook his head.

'Does she have friends at work maybe? Does she go to any clubs? Classes?' Okeke tried.

'Not really,' Andrew replied. 'She doesn't socialise. She doesn't really mix that well.'

'Why not?' Okeke asked.

'She's... I don't know... She's insecure.' He shrugged. 'She's prone to depression, mood swings. She's a bit anxious, that kind of thing. She doesn't like mixing with people if she doesn't have to.' He shook his head. 'It's hard work living with her, to be honest.'

'She's fifty-nine,' said Okeke flatly.

Andrew frowned for a moment, trying to work out whether that was a statement or a question. 'Yeah. That's right,' he said at last. 'She's fifty-nine. What's that got to do with anything?'

'Well, she's almost certainly post-menopausal?' offered Okeke.

He shook his head. 'How would I know? How am I supposed to know about that kind of thing? I mean, probably. Yeah.'

'What I'm getting at...' continued Okeke, 'is that it can get quite bad. And some of the things you are describing would fit in with that.'

He shook his head. 'Right. Well, I do know she's difficult and argumentative. Sometimes she's just a bloody nightmare to live with.' He sighed. 'Like I said. Hard work.'

Okeke settled back in her seat. She wasn't getting a scintilla of concern for Audrey from this man. He seemed to be a complete empathy vacuum.

'Ok, so the impression I'm getting from you is that things aren't great between the two of you at the moment. Is that fair to say?'

'Yeah, it's not great,' he admitted. 'We've argued a lot. That's why Becca moved out.'

The Vanishing

'And Becca's your daughter?' Okeke said.

Andrew nodded.

'What do you argue about?' she asked him.

'Money,' he replied. 'Bills. Housework. The usual sort of things, I suppose.'

Money and bills were a flashpoint for most people nowadays. But housework? Okeke felt herself bristle. What was he expecting? A meal on the table when he got home, his clothes laundered and his socks paired?

'We spoke to Audrey's mother yesterday,' she said conversationally. 'She voiced some concerns about her, actually.'

'Like what?' Andrew said, sitting up.

'She seemed to think that you were controlling,' Okeke said. '*Abusive* was the word she used, I think.'

'She said *what?*' He slapped the table with the palm of his hand. 'Well, there's a shocker. That old cow's never liked me.'

'Why not?' Okeke asked.

He snorted. 'I dunno... probably because she thinks I'm too common.' He leant forward. 'She's a right stuck-up cow, that one. Well and truly up herself.'

Okeke decided to push him a little harder. 'She told us she suspected that you might have hit Audrey...'

'*What?*' Andrew stood up.

'On more than one occasion,' Okeke continued. Then: 'Sit down, please, Andrew. This is not an accusation.'

'Fuck! What?' He sat back down in his seat and shook his head vigorously. 'I've *never* hit her! I'd never fucking hit a woman, for Christ's sake!' He clenched his jaw angrily. 'That's... that's what's the word? Slanderous, right? That's *actionable*! I could sue her for that!'

Okeke shook her head and looked down at the list of questions she'd scribbled down to ask. 'Is it possible Audrey might have... a "friend" you don't know about?'

'You mean, what... a *boy*friend?'

'*Any* friend,' Okeke replied.

Andrew's face flexed into a tight smile. A fleeting glance of incredulity, which he quickly smothered. 'I doubt it. Like I said, she's not a people person. When she's not at work, she's at home.'

'Does she have any interests? Any hobbies?'

He laughed. 'Not really...' Then he gave it a moment's thought. 'She likes musicals.'

'You mean shows?'

'Films. She doesn't go to any shows.' He let out a deep breath. 'She watches them on TV. Over and over. *The Greatest Showman, Mamma Mia...*'

Okeke considered mentioning the other thing Mrs Davitt had said – that Audrey had a trust fund, but decided to hold that piece of information back for now. The probability that Audrey was alive and well somewhere may have just shot up a few percentage points. Maybe she'd decided to take herself up to the West End to spoil herself and just not told him. An act of rebellion. A 'fuck you' to her less-than-caring husband.

She clicked her pen and tucked it back into her jacket. 'All right then, I think that's all for now.'

'That it?' Andrew glanced from Okeke to Yates.

She nodded.

'So what happens now?' he asked.

'Well, if Audrey doesn't turn up or make contact with you or anyone else by the end of tomorrow, we'll log her onto the missing persons database,' Okeke said.

'And what does that mean in terms of, you know, you people actually doing anything?' Andrew asked.

At last, thought Okeke, something from him that sounded almost like a shred of concern.

'We wait and see,' she said. 'If anything else turns up –' she smiled thinly at him – 'we'll be in touch.'

9

Boyd stared less than enthusiastically at the to-do pile stacked in his in-tray. Coming in to work on a Saturday while they were short-staffed was beginning to feel like an endurance challenge. The majority of the pile was related to a number of complaints from residents in the Silverhill area about 'TikTok bikers'. Apparently the online fad of young lads nicking motorbikes and driving them recklessly around while live-streaming to earn 'ticks' from their followers had taken a foothold in Hastings. And the epicentre of those complaints seemed to be, unsurprisingly, clustered around Cottle Street.

Checking the most regularly flagged names against their social media accounts was the kind of low-grade detective work that ate up man hours for little benefit. Since most of the offenders were minors, the best that CID could hope for was to issue a few cautions and criminal behaviour orders... which, in Boyd's mind, were every bit as useless as they sounded.

He looked up from his desk to see if he could spot any of his DCs staring into space. Yates, he knew, was busy with the misper, but Warren and Rajan seemed to be gassing endlessly about something over by the printer.

He decided to eeny-meeny one of them for the task and had just raised a finger to begin mentally reciting the playground rhyme when he spotted Okeke staring at him from her desk. She seemed troubled.

'Something up?' he asked her.

She nodded. 'You got a minute for me, guv?'

He checked his watch. It was coming up to eleven, coffee time – or elevenses, as Charlotte liked to call it. 'I'm heading up to the canteen if you want to tag along...'

Okeke got up from her desk as he did the same, and they headed towards the double doors to the stairwell.

'What's on your mind?' he asked.

'That misper Yates picked up yesterday,' she replied.

He pushed one of the doors open and waved her through. 'Isn't that Yates's problem?'

'Well, it's *his* paperwork, for sure...'

They took the stairs up to the second floor.

'I'm sensing a "but" ambling its way towards me,' he said.

'But,' she complied, 'I've got a nagging feeling about it.'

'Okay,' he said, beginning the final flight of stairs. 'Let's hear it.'

She explained to him what they had so far: a mature woman missing for two days now, what they'd been told by her mum, and the conversations with Andrew and Liam Hincher. By the time she was done, they were standing at the back of the queue in the canteen.

'I'm concerned for Audrey's welfare,' she finished.

Boyd glanced at her. 'When you say concerned for her welfare...'

Okeke clucked her tongue absently. 'There are a couple

of things Andrew, her husband, said that are worrying me.' She paused. 'He gave me the impression that she's... I dunno... in a vulnerable state of mind. That she could even be a risk to herself.'

'What things? Did he imply she's suicidal?' Boyd asked.

Okeke nodded. 'I mean, he didn't say the word. But that's the impression I got from talking to him. They seem to have a pretty cold relationship. It sounds like he swans around and does what he wants, and she's the drudge who has to keep things ticking over in his life.'

Boyd grabbed a tray and they shuffled along in the queue. 'That's not so uncommon,' he pointed out.

'Maybe. But this was... He was cold, Boyd. I mean really cold.'

'So are you saying you've got concerns about *him*?' Boyd asked.

Okeke nodded slowly. 'I think I do. It's not just how little he seemed to actually care; there were some other things too.'

'Like?' Boyd prompted.

'The mismatch between them, for one.'

'What do you mean?'

'Well, he's... younger,' Okeke said. 'Eight years younger, so a *lot* younger, really. He's physically fit, he looks after himself. I mean... he's *fit*.'

Boyd raised a brow at her.

'Yeah, exactly that,' she said. 'And he's a looker. A bit of a silver fox. A bit like Paul Hollywood, if he lost a few stone. And she's... well, she's matronly. You know, sort of plain, frumpy.' Okeke winced as she said it. 'And she seems old for her age. She could almost pass as his mum. I'm not getting the whole "we fell in love at first sight" vibe from him, that's for sure.'

'Maybe she's fantastic in bed?' he said with a smirk.

Okeke glared at him. 'Wow. Of course, that must be it. How insensitive and sexist a comment was that?'

'You're right,' Boyd conceded. 'Sorry.' He slid his tray along and then pointed out a Danish pastry to the canteen lady. 'Can I have one of those, please?'

Okeke nudged his arm. 'Aren't *you* meant to be keeping fit?'

'Sort of,' he admitted.

'He'll have one of those muesli yoghurt pots,' she said on his behalf. The canteen lady looked at Boyd; he reluctantly nodded and she dug one out from the cooler and put it on his tray.

'The point is...' Okeke continued, 'I got the feeling that there's something else going on there.'

'An affair?' Boyd suggested.

'Maybe...' She sighed. 'I wouldn't be surprised. But I think it could be about money.'

'Is she rich?' he asked.

'Well now, there's the thing. Her mother mentioned something about a trust fund. So maybe, yeah.'

'Right, so he's a silver fox who's bagged himself a sugar mummy?' Boyd smiled. 'If that's a thing.'

Okeke nodded. 'And there's no love there for him, from the mother-in-law. I think she sees him as a gold digger. And there's one other thing she said...'

'A cappuccino, please?' he said to the server at the drinks counter, then he turned to Okeke. 'You want a frothy milky one, or black?'

'Black,' she replied. 'The other thing,' she continued. 'Her mum said she thought he was abusive.'

Boyd looked at her. 'She said that?'

'She said she suspected he'd hit her. On several occasions.'

'Ah...' Boyd sighed. 'That's the bit that you should have begun with.' He hated DV cases. They were so incredibly difficult to get over the prosecution line. He looked at her. 'Are we talking visible bruises?'

'We didn't get that far.' Okeke sighed. 'Maybe I should have pressed her mum on that a bit more. I'm thinking I should have now.'

'Well, you're on... what? Coming up to two days missing?' he asked.

'Seventy-two hours tomorrow lunchtime,' she said.

'So then, once you've filed the misper, you can justify logging some hours on this, if you're sure there's grounds?' Boyd said.

'I do. I really do.' She looked at him. 'The more I've thought about that interview, the more concerned for her I've become, guv.'

~

OKEKE TOOK her coffee back to her desk and considered making a start on the backlog of low-grade cases she still had to finish up. But her mind kept circling back to Audrey and Andrew Hincher. In many ways they were a trope, a cliché. The bullying husband and his mousy, downtrodden wife. The man who clearly thought he could have done better and the poor woman who was stuck with him. Her thoughts drifted sideways to Jay and how different a man he was: gentle, kind, humble... His radio silence had started to make her suspicious, though. She'd begun to entertain the notion that Jay had flown over to the US to be with this

Ronni person. That there was no actual job going on, just a lot of shagging.

But then that didn't fit with the man she loved. He was unfailingly loyal, unfailingly in love with her. *But...* he'd been suspicious of *her*, hadn't he? He'd thought that there was something going on between her and Marcus. And to be fair, she admitted to herself, Jay had been right to question her. She was almost certain that their row about Marcus had tipped the scales in his head into accepting this job. If she was going to have a guess at what was going on, to try and put her 'Jay hat' on and think things through from his perspective... *Would he?*

Nope. She shook her head. Not even if he wanted to prove a point would he be cheating on her. That just didn't compute. He might be hoping that she'd think that, though. Deliberately blanking her texts and calls... just to make her think that he could find someone else if he wanted to.

Stop it. She shook those circular thoughts out of her head and decided to busy herself with work. And sod it... the menial to-do list could wait.

She logged into LEDS and typed in Andrew Hincher's name. She wasn't at all surprised to find it in their system. She stared at his mugshot for a moment, at an image taken twenty years ago. He'd been thirty-one then and not quite as wiry as he was now. There was a little more muscular bulk, but he still looked the athletic type. His hair had been light brown with no early outliers of silver showing. The expression on his face radiated irritation or perhaps it was smugness.

She checked the notes. He'd been accused by his girlfriend at the time of assault and battery. Her statement made for sadly predictable reading – a relationship that had started out, well, with one or two red-flag moments that the woman had considered forgivable one-offs and had explained away as due to stress brought on by money problems and work pressure.

There were even some pictures of bruises on her abdomen – which he'd explained as her being drunk on a night out with mates and falling over on the way home.

Reading on, it became depressingly clear that Andrew Hincher was the classic stereotypical abuser: a man with a short temper and a fragile ego.

The recorded interview with him was even more depressing to watch. He and the male detective seemed to be chatting like two good ol' boys over a pub table. His assertions that the victim was a 'nightmare to live with', 'difficult', 'unpredictable' and 'hard work', echoed what he'd said yesterday about Audrey.

The record showed that there'd been insufficient evidence to charge him and he'd been let go.

Fortunately, the woman in question had regarded the incident – *...repeatedly punched me in the stomach and torso area, then kicked me in the small of my back as I lay on the floor in our kitchen...* – as her clear warning to pack her things and get the hell out.

There was nothing else on file.

Okeke could well imagine that if Andrew Hincher was ever brought to book again for something similar a defence barrister would argue that that one 'alleged' incident so many years ago clearly indicated that this kind of behaviour was not habitual for him. That a man with an anger problem and a tendency towards violence was more than likely to have attracted more than one allegation across his adult life.

'Excuse me, sergeant?'

Okeke glanced up from her monitor to find Yates standing there. 'Yeah?'

'So I rang up Sextus Accountancy and I've managed to arrange an interview with one of Audrey's work colleagues for five o'clock,' he said. 'She works Saturdays.'

Okeke checked her watch. It was half-past three. She realised she'd invested a hour and a half on Hincher that, technically, she shouldn't have. She glanced over at Boyd's desk and saw that he wasn't there to overhear.

'Sod that,' she replied. 'Let's go and have a chat with her right now.'

'What?' Yates looked back at his desk. 'Should I call them back and –'

Okeke stood up and grabbed her jacket from the back of her chair. 'No need. We'll just say we were passing.'

'Do we need to tell –'

'The guv?' Okeke shook her head. 'Nah. Grab your jacket, mate. C'mon.'

10

Havelock Road was double-yellowed on both sides, with just a couple of marked-up parking spots available. All of them, predictably, were occupied. Okeke rolled her Datsun up behind the last parked car in the row, so that at least her front wheels were technically within the painted box and made Yates give her his warrant card to put on the dashboard in case some diligent traffic warden decided the rear half of the car was worth ticketing.

They climbed out, crossed the pavement and walked up to the glass door for 39 Havelock Road. A brass plaque indicated that several businesses were located in the same building. Sextus and Co. Accountancy was on the first floor. Okeke and Yates stepped inside and began to climb the stairs.

'By the way, I looked up Andrew Hincher on LEDS,' Okeke said. 'He's been accused of DV previously. About twenty years ago.'

'Really?' said Yates. 'Was he convicted for it?'

She glanced at him. 'Have a guess.'

Yates seemed as though he was actually giving that some thought.

'The answer is no,' Okeke said, rolling her eyes. The referral rate to CPS was bloody pitiful. Less than five per cent, in fact. And of those, less than one per cent ever led to a conviction. It was no wonder that women on the receiving end of a fist from their partner often felt that reporting such a thing to the police was a complete waste of time.

She pushed open the glass door for Sextus Accountancy, approached the receptionist, and raised her lanyard. 'I'm Detective Sergeant Okeke of Hastings CID. This is Detective Constable Yates. We're here to speak to...' She turned to him.

'Tracey Robbins,' Yates supplied.

The receptionist's eyes widened. 'Is this about Audrey?' she asked.

Okeke nodded. 'My colleague here made an appointment to chat with Ms Robbins at five, I think, but...' She shrugged. 'Since we were passing, we thought we'd pop in on the off-chance that she might be available now.'

The receptionist nodded. 'I'll go and get her.' She gestured towards a small, glass-walled room with a small round table and some seats. 'Do you want to make yourselves comfortable in the consultation room?'

Okeke nodded and led Yates in. There were only two chairs; she took one of them. He had younger legs; he could stand. A moment later, the receptionist returned with a young woman by her side. She gestured towards the room and Tracey Robbins pushed the door open and stepped inside to join them.

'Are you the police?' she asked.

Okeke waggled her lanyard again and pointed at Yates. 'You spoke to my colleague on the phone earlier?'

Tracey looked at him. 'Didn't we arrange this for five o'clock?' she asked.

Yates nodded. 'We did. It's just that –'

'We were passing and thought we'd pop in on the off-chance that you could talk to us now,' completed Okeke. She smiled. 'Take a seat, Tracey.'

Tracey sat down.

To Okeke's eyes, Tracey Robbins seemed the complete opposite to Audrey in every way. She was much younger; she had an enormous trout pout going on and those implausible, thick wedged eyebrows that all young women these days seemed to wear and, of course, the obligatory spray tan.

'So, Tracey, I believe you work closely with Audrey Hincher?' began Okeke.

'I sit next to her if that's what you mean,' the younger woman replied. 'We admin for different accountants, though.'

'Right,' Okeke said. 'But is it fair to say that, out of everyone here, you probably know her best?'

Tracey nodded. 'I would think so. Not that she's very easy to get to know, mind.' She glanced at Yates, then back at Okeke. 'She's very shy. Very quiet. She keeps herself to herself, if you know what I mean.'

Okeke nodded. 'I do. So I believe you were the last person to interact with her before she stepped out of the office?'

Tracey nodded.

'Can you take me through it? Tell me what happened?'

Tracey shrugged. 'There's not much to say, to be honest. Aud said she was going out to get a sandwich. She asked me if I wanted anything and I said no, because I'd brought my own in that day.'

'Did she seem off in any way?' asked Okeke. 'Agitated? Upset?'

Tracey shook her head. 'No. Not really. Just, you know, normal.'

'Did she say where she was going specifically?' Okeke asked.

'No,' Tracey replied thoughtfully, 'but, I mean, there's a Costa down at the end that we all normally use. And a Tesco Express.'

Okeke glanced at Yates. He pulled out his notepad and started scribbling.

'Make a note for us to check the CCTVs in both,' she said to him.

He nodded.

'Can you remember what she was wearing?' asked Okeke.

'Yeah. She always wears the same coat. Sort of a... a tan-coloured mac, I guess you'd call it.'

'And her work clothes?' Okeke asked.

Tracey's Lego-brick eyebrows locked together for a moment. 'Um, she was wearing a pale blue work blouse. And I think... yeah, she was wearing a chequered skirt. Tartan-like.'

'Like a kilt?' said Yates.

She smiled. 'Yeah.'

He scribbled that down too.

'Did she have a bag?' Okeke asked.

'Yeah. A shoulder-strap one,' Tracey replied. 'Like a satchel. She only ever uses that one – well, that's the only bag I've ever seen her with at work.'

'Did you ever see Audrey *outside* work? You know, for after-work drinks, that kind of thing?' said Okeke.

Tracey shook her head. 'A few of us girls sometimes grab a drink on a Friday after work. But Aud never comes along.'

'Not her thing?' Yates said.

Tracy pulled a face, as though she had something to say but was unsure as to how to say it. 'Um, I'm not sure if it's for me to...' she began.

'Go on...' prompted Okeke.

'Well, I don't think her Other Half approves of her coming out with us,' she finished.

Okeke's gaze met Tracey's. 'What makes you say that?'

Tracey shook her head. 'It's just... every time I ask her along, she'll say something like "I probably shouldn't" or "I can't be late home"... that kind of thing. Never "I don't want to" or "I have other plans", you know?' She shrugged. 'I get the impression her fella doesn't like her doing that. Going out.'

'Has she ever said that?' Okeke asked.

'Not as such, but...' Tracey leant forward and lowered her voice slightly, 'I think he might be a bit...' She paused. 'Well... a bit of a bastard, to be honest.' She grimaced at the word. 'Excuse the language.'

'That's okay.' Okeke smiled at her. 'I use worse.'

'She gets calls on her phone from him sometimes,' Tracey continued. 'And because my desk is literally right beside her, I can sometimes hear his voice spilling out, you know?'

Okeke nodded.

'And, I know I shouldn't eavesdrop, but he sounds like a right nasty shit.'

'How do you mean?' Okeke asked.

'Shouty. Rude. Arsy. Telling her things he needs, jobs she has to do when she gets back home,' Tracey told them.

Okeke glanced in Yates's direction to make sure he was

getting it all down, then looked back at Tracey. 'Is he controlling, would you say?'

Tracey nodded. 'I wouldn't put up with that kind of shit from my fella, I'm telling you. And something else,' she said, leaning further forward, her voice dropping to little more than a whisper. 'I think he might have *hit* her.'

Okeke found herself mirroring Tracy, leaning in towards her. 'Why do you say that?'

The young woman pressed her lips together. 'I don't want to throw out accusations as such...'

'It's all right,' Okeke replied. 'This isn't going anywhere, Tracey, and it might be important.'

Tracey nodded, then glanced down at her well-manicured hands. 'Well, sometimes she comes in with tummy pains. Like period cramps? And Audrey's not young, right? She's...'

'Fifty-nine,' Okeke said.

'Right. So... it's not *that*. I asked her if she should see a doctor, but she said it was probably stress-related.' Tracey's eyes flicked to Okeke. 'And I don't think it was *work* stress.'

'How do you know it wasn't work-related?' asked Yates.

Tracey turned to him. 'It's not a stressful job. She meant... *home* stress.' She looked back at Okeke meaningfully. '*Him*.'

'Go on,' said Okeke.

'And... there was one time she came into work with foundation on. Concealer. And she never does that. She wears a bit of eyeliner sometimes, but she's not the make-up type. It was put on really heavy on one side. You know? Really slapped on her cheek. I thought at first that she might have been going out and had just applied it badly. But then I kept seeing her wince when she took a sip of coffee. She kept touching one side of her face.'

'Did you say anything?' asked Okeke. 'Did she say anything about that?'

Tracey shook her head, all of a sudden looking away guiltily. 'I reckon... I reckon that was a bruise she was hiding.'

11

Boyd had just got through the front door and acknowledged Ozzie and Mia sufficiently for them to be satisfied and trot back to the dining room – and the possibility of falling scraps from Maggie's high chair – when his phone buzzed in his pocket.

He pulled it out to see it was Okeke calling him.

'All right?' he replied as he hung up his jacket and wandered down the hall to see what was cooking.

'I know it's a day early, but I've filed the misper report for Audrey Hincher,' she replied without preamble.

'And you're ringing me to tell me this because...'

'Because Andrew Hincher has form for DV,' she told him.

He stopped in the doorway to the dining room. Emma was busy trying to fill Maggie's mouth with something mashed-up and she looked very much like a plasterer filling a drill hole.

'As in *convicted*?' he said.

'Nope. Just cautioned.' She sighed. 'Shocker, eh? But that's not all of it.'

'Go on,' he said.

'Her work colleague said Audrey exhibited signs of being in an abusive and controlling relationship. So that's her mother *and* a colleague who've said it.'

'So you want to get cracking on this, then?' Boyd said.

'Yeah. It'll be three days tomorrow,' she replied. 'I want a couple of DCs for legwork.'

'All right. So I'm presuming that's Yates, plus one?'

'That'll do me,' she said. 'And I want to put out a media BOLO for her.'

Middle-aged woman disappears in the middle of the day in the middle of a town, mused Boyd – the kind of puzzle that got Joe Public's telephone finger twitching. 'You'll get a shit ton of useless calls coming in, you know?' he cautioned.

'Good,' she replied firmly. 'The more attention, the better as far as I'm concerned.'

'You might need more than two gophers,' Boyd told her. 'But we can rethink that once we see how things pan out. If you go wide and she turns up after a boozy hen party somewhere, you'll look like a right muppet. You know that, don't you?'

'I don't think she's that kind of woman,' Okeke said. 'Anyway, I'd rather we looked proactive... in case it is a worst-case scenario.'

'Oka-a-y,' he replied. "Well, we'll set that up on Monday, then,' he told her.

'I'd prefer this weekend,' she replied.

He sighed. 'Really?'

'And if she's found dead in a ditch...'

It was a fair point. Letting another forty-eight hours roll by without being seen to be doing anything could come back and bite them hard.

'All right,' he agreed. 'See who you can pull in on my say-so.'

'Thanks, guv.'

Boyd ended the call and tucked his phone back into his trouser pocket.

'What's going on?' asked Emma.

'Missing person,' he replied. 'A middle-aged woman who went missing a few days ago in the middle of town. For no apparent reason. She just seems to have vanished.'

'Like that Nicola Bulley?'

'Christ,' he puffed. 'I hope this doesn't turn into something like that.'

'That was a complete police screw-up, wasn't it?' Emma said.

'The investigation?' he said. 'No. I think they did a pretty good job with that, to be fair. It was the communications bit they botched.' He sat down at the table and watched Emma smear more of the lumpy gunk across Maggie's lips. 'They were too focused on actually doing their jobs and didn't have the time or resources to keep the social-media rumour mill in check.'

With the absence of regular police updates, the information vacuum had been filled with armchair detectives and TikTok 'reporters' throwing out their own increasingly bizarre theories into the void.

'Sam wants to make a public appeal for people who might have seen our misper.' He reached out for one of Maggie's twitching bare feet and absently twiddled her big toe. 'But she'll have to be careful how she manages that, won't she, Maggie? We don't want a repeat of that media shitstorm, do we? Hmmm?'

'Om, wum mlubble,' Maggie replied judiciously.

12

Boyd rapped his knuckles on his desk to get the attention of everyone on the CID floor. Which wasn't saying much. With the eleven remaining members of Team Rosper currently suspended, they were down to just seven bodies. Sutherland was spending most of his time these days looking down the backs of sofas and shaking out old jam jars to find additional funds to fill the many vacant seats in the bullpen.

'Okay, has everyone got their coffees and sweeties?' Boyd began.

He was greeted with a ripple of nods.

'All right then. Let's get started.'

He'd commandeered a partition wall that had once formed part of the Great Divide between Rosper and the rest of the floor. Now with the partition next to his desk, he picked up a printout of an image of Audrey Hincher and pinned it to the board.

'This is Audrey Hincher, aged fifty-nine,' he announced, then he nodded to Okeke to take over.

She stood up. 'Audrey went missing on Thursday at

about 12.30 p.m.,' she told the group. 'She was in the middle of town, on Havelock Road. So, in a busy area at a busy time of day. She left her place of work, Sextus and Co. Accountancy, to grab some lunch and she never returned. By lunchtime today she will have been missing for three days. Her mother reported her missing about twenty hours after Audrey went out for lunch.'

'So, given that the wait-and-see window of seventy-two hours has now expired,' said Boyd, 'we're moving this into investigation mode. This is why you've all been dragged in on a Sunday morning...'

Minter shrugged. 'Fine by me – I wasn't up to that much today, to be honest, boss.'

Okeke reached for another printout and pinned it to the board. 'This is her husband, Andrew Hincher, who was away when she went missing. And –' she reached towards Boyd's deck for another picture and pinned it beside Andrew's face – 'this is his son, Liam, who was at home at the time. I've interviewed them both...'

'And?' said Boyd.

'Oh, yes – me and Yates spoke to Audrey's mother first, then we called round to Audrey's home and interviewed Liam. Later we got a chance to speak to Andrew, and we also spoke to Audrey's work colleague on Friday.' She took in a deep breath. 'So here's what we have so far. Andrew was away on a work conference. Liam lives at home – mostly in his room – and claims he doesn't interact with his stepmum much at all. He claims he wasn't aware that she'd *not* come home on Thursday night.'

'Is that credible?' asked Minter.

Okeke shrugged. 'He seems like most other lads his age, totally self-absorbed, more interested in his belly button than what's going on around him. So I think I can believe it's at least plausible that he didn't notice she hadn't come home. Andrew, however –' she turned to examine his picture – 'gives me some cause for concern. He has some previous form for domestic violence.'

'Was he convicted?' asked Warren.

'No. He wasn't charged at the time. It looks as though CPS didn't think they had enough to bother with him.' She glanced at Warren, then the others. 'Which, as you all know, doesn't mean he's innocent... It just indicates that the CPS couldn't be arsed.'

Warren nodded. 'Right.'

'Audrey's mother said that she suspects her daughter is in an abusive relationship,' Okeke continued, 'as does her work colleague Tracey Robbins. They both mentioned they'd thought she might have been hit by Andrew. Tracey suspected that Audrey had used heavy make-up to cover up a bruise. So... with those things in mind, and given that it's been three days... I think we need to bring Andrew Hincher in.'

'It's a bit premature, isn't it?' said Minter.

She shook her head. 'In my mind, there are three possible scenarios. One: they had an argument that went too far. He hit her too hard and one thing led to another.'

'And he *did* her?' filled in Minter.

She nodded. 'Two: he murdered her for her money.'

'Money?'

'Yeah. Her mother said she has a sizeable trust fund. In fact, she suggested Hincher had married Audrey simply to get his hands on that. And the third scenario is that she's just packed her bags and walked out on him.'

'Which way are you leaning?' asked Boyd.

She looked at him. 'Well, not the third, that's for sure.'

'Why not?' he asked.

'She hadn't brought anything into work with her,' Okeke said. 'No overnight bag, no nothing. She just went out for a sandwich and never came back.'

'Scenario four, then,' said Minter. 'It was some random stranger?'

Okeke gave him a sceptical frown. 'What, and he dragged her off the high street?'

Minter shrugged. 'Perhaps a friend? Or a work colleague? Maybe she went to meet someone for coffee?'

'According to Andrew, she has zero friends.'

'A secret friend maybe?' suggested Warren. 'Or even a Tinder hook-up?'

Okeke handed him the same look she'd given Minter. 'She's fifty-nine, mate.'

'There's Old-Person Tinder,' he replied. 'Match.com... um... and other ones, right? Maybe they met for a lunchtime coffee and... I dunno... things went from there?'

Okeke sighed. 'My money's on Hincher, given that he has a DV caution against his name, and the fact that, having spoken with him, there's a noticeable lack of concern or empathy from him. There was nothing, in fact. He really didn't seem to give a shit about her welfare.'

'Wait, that's not an easy thing to read,' said Minter. 'I mean, you can be called out for not showing any emotion at all or showing *too much* of the ruddy stuff. You're damned if you do and damned if you don't, eh?'

Warren nodded. As did Yates... and Rajan... and Abbott.

Men! Okeke inwardly eye-rolled. The emotional landscape for them appeared to be high peaks or flat plains. There were no rolling hills. No gradient. Absolutely nothing in between.

'I'd like to bring him in,' said Okeke. 'Put some pressure on him.'

'In what way?' asked Boyd.

She looked at him. 'We need to put out an announcement, right? So I think we should ask him to be a part of that. To do the whole "*if you're out there, babes, come home to me*" thing. See how he reacts to that suggestion.' She turned to Minter and the others. 'It's not so much how he performs, whether he gives us tears or not... It's whether he's willing to expose himself to a bunch of cameras.'

Boyd nodded. 'Right.'

'And if he doesn't want to?' asked Minter.

She smiled at him. 'Well, we can't force him, obviously, but... come on, if he says no, that's got to be a red flag right there.'

Boyd nodded. 'Okay. It can't hurt to ask him.'

'I'd like to put that press call together for this evening, guv. If that's all right?' Okeke said. 'See if we can get it on local news? I mean, it's a Sunday. There's bugger all news on a Sunday.'

Boyd nodded. 'Fair enough. If you think you have enough to run with.'

She shrugged. 'There's the couple of interviews. But, yeah, we could do with scraping a bit more together. Some CCTV footage would be nice. Havelock Road must have plenty of cameras. We know where she set out from, so we should be able to get a decent cam-trail to show.'

'Right.' Boyd rasped his fingers across his chin. 'Then let's get started.' He looked at Yates. 'You're on the CCTV treasure hunt. We need the cameras along Havelock Road, and that includes any cameras from the shops she might have gone into.'

'Yes, sir,' Yates replied.

'Warren,' Boyd said, 'we need her phone data. Her

socials. Let's get applications in for those asap. Also, does she have a car? If so, notify ANPR.'

He turned to Rajan. 'You're on the door-to-doors for her neighbours. And, while you're there, check for any neighbour security cameras that point towards her home. Let's see if there was anything odd going on there in the days leading up.'

'Yes, sir,' Rajan replied.

'Also, Yates...' Boyd said, 'just double-check on Andrew Hincher's business-trip alibi, would you? Make sure we have that locked down.'

Yates nodded.

Boyd looked at Okeke. 'I presume you're okay doing the press bit?'

'Of course,' she replied.

'All right, then you'll be SIO-ing this for the moment.' He noticed Minter stirring and Abbott pouting. 'It's a *misper* for now, not a murder case, gents. And since we're short-handed, let's get the young 'uns out there earning their keep, eh?'

He needed to keep Abbott for night shifts. The minimum rank on the floor had to be DI. And Minter, he knew, was already the SIO on several other cases, although they could be parked if needed. He'd be able to take over if... God forbid, Audrey's body did turn up somewhere.

Boyd lifted a hand to dismiss them, then a final thought occurred to him. 'By the way, not a word off this floor about Andrew Hincher being our first port of call. Let's not put him on his guard.'

13

Warren pulled up Audrey Hincher's Facebook page. Not that it was a great deal of use. The page was public and he could see her feed, but in the seven years that she'd been on it she'd posted only a few dozen times – a few reposts of funny cat pictures, a couple of Wordle results, one photo of her on a trip to somewhere sunny.

Her friends list included Andrew, Liam, and Hincher's daughter, Rebecca. And no one else.

It looked like the kind of Facebook page set up by some well-meaning teenager for an ageing relative, with all the basics established – a profile picture, location and a few bland interests – but not a lot else.

Warren moved on to her phone records. Okeke had obtained Audrey's number from her husband. Before using the tracker software on LEDS, Warren tried it again. His call went straight through to her voicemail. Which meant it was off. Or she'd set it to aeroplane mode.

He entered her phone number into LEDS and a few moments later the search returned her provider and account details. He copied those and pasted them into the application form that Sutherland would have to approve before it was sent off to the magistrates for a warrant to unlock her IMSI number and data. He pinged an email to Sutherland with the form attached and then went downstairs for a puff or two on his vape. His mum had been nagging him to quit smoking and switch over... She'd finally had enough of the stink of fag smoke in her house. So far it seemed to be just about scratching his nicotine itch. It was a damn sight cheaper too.

He found Okeke outside practising her press brief and chugging away on a *real* fag. He caught a whiff of the smoke and immediately felt the urge to ditch his vape and blag one of hers. He resisted the temptation.

'All right?' he asked.

'Yeah,' she replied. 'You applied for the phone data yet?'

'Yeah, yeah. All done and with Sutherland,' he said.

'Good. And Facebook?' she prompted.

'Nothing much on it,' he replied. 'She doesn't really use it. Some cat memes and that's about it. She's got a friends list of three. Just Andrew and his kids.'

'Doesn't surprise me,' she replied. 'I'll bet he stalks her page too.'

Warren pulled his vape out and it burbled like a sinkhole as he inhaled. 'Aren't you, you know... kind of jumping to conclusions on this Andrew bloke?'

She glared at him. 'I'm not jumping anywhere, thanks very much. And I'm pretty sure he is an absolute bastard.'

'But, like, a murdering one?' Warren blew out vapour. 'I mean, it's dumb as shit, to murder your own wife and then pretend she's done a runner.'

'Maybe it was a heat-of-the-moment thing,' she said, taking a drag of her cigarette.

'Yeah but *if* he murdered her, then it looks like it *might* have been planned,' he replied. 'If he was away at this business thing... then that's him setting up his alibi, right?'

'Well. there you go, then,' she replied coldly.

'No.' He shook his head 'You're missing my point. Her disappearing at precisely the time he's away, somewhere I guess that's really busy, where he'd have been able to slip out unnoticed for a few hours... Making him look guilty as shit? That's a bloody dumb way to do it, right?'

Okeke rolled her eyes. 'So he's a *dumb*, murdering bastard.' She flicked ash from the tip of her fag. 'I'm hoping Yates will get us some CCTV showing him picking her up in Havelock Road. Well, not *hoping*... but, you know, *anticipating*. By the way, have you checked if she has a car yet?'

'Isn't that something you should have asked Andrew Hincher?' Warren pointed out.

She shook her head. 'Forgot. I'll ask him when I go over. But you can look it up anyway. If she's not DVLA registered, then we won't need to waste our time chasing down cars, will we?'

'Right,' he replied, pulling on his gurgling vape. 'I'll do it after this.'

She looked his way. 'Hold up. When the hell did you switch from ciggies?'

'Uh, last week. I'm trying to quit.' He sighed. 'It costs too bloody much to smoke these days.'

She laughed. 'God, you sound old.'

'Unlike you, I'm still struggling on a DC's wage,' he said.

'Well, you're living at home rent-free,' she said.

'Bollocks. I have to pay Mum five hundred quid a month,' he grumbled.

Okeke stubbed her cigarette out. 'Try paying full whack.'

'I thought you and Jay went halves?' he replied, surprised.

'*Pffft.*' She sighed. 'Not the way things are going.' She pulled out her car keys. 'Right, I'm off to see the delightful Andrew Hincher. See you in a bit, Boy Wonder.'

∼

LIAM HINCHER OPENED THE DOOR. 'Oh, it's you lot again.'

'It's just me,' replied Okeke.

'Have you found her yet?' Liam asked, running a hand through his dishevelled sandy hair.

'No. And I presume she hasn't made contact with you or your dad?' Okeke said.

He shook his head as he backed up to let her in. 'Dad!' he shouted. 'Police are here again!' He turned to her. 'Better go through to the lounge.' He waved her into the empty room, slammed the front door and hoofed it up the stairs. Okeke went in and sat down on the sofa. It was a little tidier than last time, but not much.

She heard an exchange of murmured voices coming from upstairs. As she waited for Andrew, she took in as much as she could of the lounge. On the wall were some framed pictures of kids in school uniforms. She saw a girl, presumably Rebecca Hincher, and recognised a much younger Liam. There was a picture on the mantelpiece with Andrew and his kids together, all of them holding the slippery sides of a fish that he'd presumably caught. Exactly as she'd remembered, there were definitely no pictures of Audrey, though. Not a single one.

She heard footsteps coming down the stairs and a moment later Andrew Hincher entered, dressed, but with wet hair and splotches of damp on his shirt.

'Is it a bad time?' she offered.

'You caught me in the shower,' he replied.

Okeke looked at her watch. It was gone eleven.

Andrew pulled a face as if she'd insulted him. 'I've just got back from a run. I do 5K's every morning if I haven't got a job lined up.' He threw the towel over the arm of the sofa. 'I didn't know coppers worked Sundays.'

'We work all days,' she replied. 'As needed.'

'Right.' He shrugged. 'So is there any news?' The question fell out of his mouth like an after-thought.

'None so far,' she said. 'I came by to ask a few more questions about Audrey, if that's okay?'

Andrew sat down in an armchair. 'Fire away.'

'Does she have her own car?' Okeke asked.

He shook his head. 'She doesn't know how to drive. Never bothered to learn.' He sighed. 'It's me that has to run her around everywhere. Or Liam.'

Okeke made a note. 'Now, I forgot to ask last time... can we have access to her mail? I presume she gets bills... statements. There might be something in her post that will give us a clue as to where she might be.'

'Help yourself,' Andrew replied. He got up out and headed to a filing cabinet in the corner of the room. Okeke noticed him take out a key to unlock it. He pulled open the middle drawer and paused. 'How much of it do you want?'

Okeke got up and joined him at the cabinet. She peered down into the drawer. There was a row of tabbed suspension folders: *'Gas and lecky'*, *'Van'*, *'Insurance'*, *'Statements'*, *'Audrey's stuff'*.

He pulled out the one marked 'Statements'. 'These are hers. Take them all if you need them.'

He handed the folder to her.

'What's in "Audrey's stuff"?' Okeke asked.

'Catalogue stuff, mainly. Some book-club spam. Bits 'n' pieces.' He looked at her. 'You want that too?'

She nodded. He lifted the folder out and dumped it on top of the other.

'What's in the other drawers?' she asked.

'My work stuff. Paperwork. Invoices. Quotes,' he said.

She noted he didn't offer to show her those. She crimped the urge to ask him to open them up. *Let's not put him on his guard.*

She carried the folders back to the sofa, pulled out a large, folded evidence bag and carefully eased them in before sealing it and filling in the label.

'A forensics bag, eh?' he said, nodding at it. 'You gonna dust it all for fingerprints or what?'

'It's just so that we can catalogue what we have so we can return it all to you,' she replied flatly. 'I'm going to reach out to your daughter, Rebecca, today so that I can ask her about Audrey,' she continued.

'Be my guest,' Andrew said with a shrug.

'Your son said that Rebecca left because she was fed up with the rows you and Audrey were having...'

Andrew frowned. 'Becca left because she wanted to live in her own place.'

'But you and Audrey *were* having rows?' she persisted.

He gave her suspicious look. 'No more than any other couple has.'

'What sort of things do you and Audrey row about?' Okeke asked.

He shrugged.

'Money?' offered Okeke. 'That's usually a trigger issue. Or affairs?'

He laughed. 'Audrey wouldn't cheat on me.'

'And how about you?' she asked.

'No.' He smiled. 'Work keeps me way too busy for that kind of shit.'

'So money, then,' she said.

He stiffened. 'What about money? Between me and Audrey, we get by just fine, thanks very much.'

Once again, Okeke found herself tempted to shake him to see if he rattled. The trust fund that Audrey's mum had mentioned could well be the prize he had his eyes on. Boyd's final words echoed again in her head.

Let's not put him on his guard, eh?

'Okay,' she said. 'I think that's it.' She picked up the evidence bag and headed for the door. 'Oh, one more thing.'

'Yeah?'

'We're going to put out an appeal for Audrey, later this afternoon. A shout-out for eyewitnesses, anyone who might have seen her, that kind of thing. Would you be able to come in and help us with that?'

'What do you want me to do?' he asked.

'Just be there,' she said. 'Perhaps make an appeal directly to her? To come home? Or just to make contact?'

She thought she detected a hint of reluctance, but he nodded. 'Sure. Sure. Anything I can do to help. Anything.' He smiled coolly. 'We want her back home. Of course we do.'

14

DC Yates checked the list of CCTV cameras he'd spotted along Havelock Road. There was one beside the entrance to the Tesco Express, another further along outside the Vive Hotel, one above the Flames Grill, and another outside Fox and Sons Estate Agents. Then, overlooking the pedestrian area, there were two mounted on the old Debenhams building, one of them directed towards the market area and the other angled to cover Robertson Street. Between them, he guessed there was an unbroken trail of overlapping coverage as far as Costa Coffee.

Coming out of the coffee shop and into the pedestrian area, there were six routes she could have taken. Either back down Havelock Road, or along Station Road, Queens Road, Robertson Road, Harold Place or Wellington Place; they radiated out from the pedestrian area like six spokes of a cart wheel. He had also logged the cameras covering all five of those possible options.

Yates decided his best bet was to head back to the

station, identify the public space cameras' ID numbers and get started on their downloads. Once he had those, he could begin with Thursday lunchtime and the cameras closest to Sextus Accountancy, pick Audrey out and track her movements from camera to camera.

∽

DC Rajan deployed his widest, friendliest grin as the door opened. 'Mornin', love. Have you got a moment to–'

'No! I *don't* want to buy any bloody squeegees or dishcloths or cheap disinfect–'

The old woman started to close the door on him as he fished out his ID card.

'Police,' he said quickly.

'*You're* police?' She stared suspiciously at his thick black beard, then up at his bog-brush thatch of dark hair.

'It's all there on the plastic, love,' said Rajan, waggling his warrant card for her to see.

Her eyes dipped down and she squinted at it. 'Sussex Police?' She frowned suspiciously. 'What's that accent? You're not from round here?'

'I'm from Newcastle,' he replied, smiling. 'Pet.'

Then, unexpectedly, she smiled back. 'Like Sara Milly-something,' she said.

'Uh-huh... Okay, yes, and Ant and Dec and our grand contribution to global cuisine, saveloy 'n' chips.'

Her smile widened.

'Have you got a moment?' he asked her. 'I'd like to ask you a few questions about your next-door neighbours.' He nodded at the terraced house next to hers.

'The Hinchers?' she replied.

He nodded.

The old woman's bushy grey eyebrows bounced up with surprise. 'Has he finally done her in?' she asked.

That was a little more than Rajan had been expecting straight off the bat. 'Done her in?' he echoed. 'Why do you say that?'

She nodded at the Hinchers' house. 'Awful piece of work, he is.'

'How do you mean?' Rajan asked.

'Well, he's violent. isn't he? He's angry, shouty... and very, very rude.'

'*Violent?*' Rajan repeated.

She nodded. 'The way he is with that poor, poor woman.'

'Audrey?'

'Is *that* her first name?' she replied. 'Do you know I've never actually spoken to her. Not once. And I've been here six, nearly seven years!'

'When you say "violent", Mrs...?' Rajan prompted.

'Mrs Farmer. I'm Gloria Farmer. Yes, he's nasty with her, he is. Really nasty. Always being, you know, *rough*-handed with her. Dragging her around by the arm like she's some dog on a lead.'

'*Dragging* her?' Rajan asked.

Gloria nodded at the street. 'Dragging her to his van when he takes her to work. Ooh, he's so rough. He shoves her into the passenger's seat and slams the door on her.'

Rajan pulled out his notepad and started making notes. 'Have you ever seen him actually strike her?' he asked.

'Strike? You mean, hit her?' Gloria asked.

He nodded.

'Not exactly,' she said. 'But...' She thought for a moment. 'Well, there was something I saw last summer. They were having a barbecue in the back garden. And... I don't know what it was about... maybe she'd burnt his food or something, but he threw his dinner at her.'

Rajan looked down at her. His brows bounced up. 'Threw his...'

'Dinner.' She nodded. 'The plate and the food. The whole lot.'

'Was she injured? Did the plate hit her?' Rajan asked.

'I don't know. I think she might have got burnt a little. The food had come straight off the grill.'

'And you saw this?' Rajan asked.

'From my back window,' Gloria replied. 'Upstairs. I'd heard him starting up on her, you know, shouting at her ,and I was curious.' She shrugged guiltily. 'Being nosy, I suppose you'd call it.'

'Was anyone else with them in the garden?' Rajan asked.

'Just his lad,' Gloria said. 'It was just the three of them. The boy didn't do anything about it either. He didn't even go into the house after her to see if she was okay. As a matter of fact, I think they were both amused by the whole thing.' She tutted. 'Awful man... and his boy's just as bad.'

15

Okeke settled down at her desk, with a tub of hummus, pitta-bread soldiers and a coffee from the canteen, and began to pick her way through Audrey's post. The bank statements showed evidence of what had been a sizeable chunk of money – one hundred and seventy-five grand, to be precise. This had been whittled down to just sixty-seven over the last decade. Presumably this was her trust fund. What was left was hardly worth murdering her for. And it didn't look as though Andrew would have had to go down that route anyway. From the evidence before her, all he had to do was ask... and Audrey would give.

Okeke noticed that the utility bills, council tax, subscriptions – Sky Sport, Netflix, Disney+ et al – were coming out of Audrey's bank account too, all doing their bit to eat away at her nest egg.

'So,' muttered Okeke, 'she really is his piggy bank, then.'

Shocker. The bank statements inked a little more detail into the depressing picture she was painting of the Hinchers' relationship. Audrey worked full-time in an admin role that Okeke couldn't for the life of her imagine that Audrey yearned to rush to every morning. And she was paying for, it seemed, pretty much everything, while her partner swanned around doing whatever he did, and his adult son loafed around at home and played games on his PlayStation.

Okeke picked up the folder marked 'Audrey's stuff'. It was a slim folder, full of miscellaneous bits and pieces – anything that *wasn't* to do with Andrew Hincher. There were some photos of a very pretty girl dressed primly in her school uniform, one of her in a hockey kit in a team line-up and another showed her riding a pony. There were several faded Polaroids of Audrey with her parents, sitting on a towel on a beach, somewhere much too sunny, the water much too blue to be in the UK. In them she was a smiling, slightly chubby little girl of about nine or ten, in an orange swimsuit, wearing a floppy sun hat and holding a spade. Beside her was a lean man with sunglasses, thinning hair and sideburns – presumably her late dad, both of them working on a wonky-looking sandcastle.

The remaining few photos were of Audrey when she was older. A teenager now, the puppy fat had long gone. She was a slim, attractive young woman, smiling broadly and wearing jeans and an Abba T-shirt. Two girlfriends flanked her, one in a Wham! T-shirt, the other sporting George Michael's face. That picture evidenced a girl brimming with self-confidence. Okeke smiled. There she was, proudly wearing an Abba shirt back when, let's be honest, they weren't considered particularly cool, with two girls conforming to what was.

There was also an A-Level certificate. Audrey had earned three A's – clever girl. And in one final picture, taken a few years later, she was in a university gown and mortarboard cap and clutching a degree in something Okeke couldn't quite make out. She was between the same man as in the sandcastle photo, greyer, thinner, older, balder... and a younger Mrs Davitt. They were all beaming at the camera.

'Detective Sergeant?' Okeke looked up from the papers spread across her desk. 'Ah! How'd it go, Rajan?' she asked.

'I spoke to the neighbours either side,' he replied. 'It doesn't sound good for the husband.'

'How do you mean?' Okeke said, sitting up straighter.

'Well, the old woman in the house next door didn't have anything nice to say about Andrew Hincher.' Rajan told her the story of the barbecue in the garden and of hearing Hincher's raised voice coming through the walls on a regular basis. 'The people on the other side said the same about raised voices. Mostly Andrew's.'

'Mostly? Did they hear Audrey too?' Okeke asked.

He shook his head. 'They heard two different male voices. Andrew... *and Liam*.'

Okeke winced. 'So Liam yells at her as well?'

Rajan nodded. 'That's what they thought it sounded like.'

'Jesus,' she muttered. Dreadful though Audrey's situation sounded, it gave Okeke a glimmer of hope. Perhaps Audrey hadn't been abducted by a stranger or murdered by her husband. Perhaps she'd just got up out of her seat three days ago, left her desk and decided that anywhere else would be better? But then, surely, her first port of call would have been to go home to her mother? At the very least, to call her to tell her that she'd finally decided to leave.

'Did you clock any security cameras aimed at the Hinchers' house?' she asked.

'Ah, shit. I forgot that bit,' Rajan admitted.

'Well, that's another trip out for you, mate,' Okeke said.

Boyd, spotting them deep in conversation, wandered over to join them, coffee in hand. 'How's it going?' he asked, taking a sip. 'Did you get Hincher to agree to come in for the press brief?'

She nodded. 'Yeah, he's agreed to do it.' She started to tidy up Audrey's paperwork, putting it back into the correct folders. 'He didn't seem particularly keen. But... he didn't say no either.'

'Hmm,' Boyd replied. 'He doesn't really seem to be helping his case, does he?'

Okeke shook her head. 'Rajan?' she said, glancing at him.

'Yeah?' he replied.

'I need you check out Andrew Hincher's alibi. That conference thing? Double-check he *was* there. You've got the details, haven't you?'

Rajan shrugged. 'Yates is on that.'

'Okay, well, can you check with him, mate? Oh... and have you seen Yates?' she asked him.

'I just saw him walking back up the hill to the station,' replied Rajan. 'With a bag of chips.'

'We'll need the CCTV footage, if there is any, for the press brief,' said Boyd. 'Rope in Minter and Warren to help him.' He checked his watch. 'I've got the press room booked for five. So there's not a lot of time.'

'I'll crack the whip,' Okeke said.

Boyd grinned. 'I've absolutely no doubt you will.'

16

Okeke took a seat at the trestle table that had been set up in the press room and gestured for Andrew Hincher to take the seat beside her.

She poured some water for them both, then twisted in her seat to make sure the screen behind her was on and linked to her laptop and that the first slide was on the screen. She turned back round, leant forward on her elbows and glanced at Boyd, who was standing to one side at the back. He gave her a supportive nod.

'Right then, are we all ready to start?' she called out.

The press room was full. Boyd was right. Sundays were slow and the weekend press and news teams were here, eager for something juicy that they could drop into tonight's news and tomorrow's early editions that *wasn't* about the Wacky Labour Party or the Sleazy Tory party or Bloody Nigel Farage. Britain had had just about enough politics for a while and a newly missing-person mystery would do very nicely.

The noise of creaking seats and murmured conversations quickly died down.

Okeke looked at the brief she'd only finished typing twenty minutes ago. 'Good afternoon, or evening actually, and thank you for abandoning your Sunday roasts and coming in. I'm Detective Sergeant Samantha Okeke, the acting SIO on the investigation into missing person Audrey Hincher.'

She gestured at Andrew Hincher. 'Sitting with me is Audrey's husband, Andrew, and he'll be speaking in just a minute.' She cleared her throat. 'Right, so then, on Thursday a local woman, Audrey Hincher, fifty-nine, went missing.' She pressed the clicker in her hand and Audrey's face appeared on the screen behind her.

'Audrey works at Sextus Accountancy on Havelock Road. She was last seen heading out at midday to pick up some lunch and hasn't been seen since. Her mother reported her missing on Friday morning and, with it now being Sunday evening, we are very concerned for her welfare and safety. With adult missing persons, as a rule, there's a wait-and-see period of seventy-two hours before we open an investigation, but given the vulnerable mental state we believe she may be in... we have already begun to take action...'

She pressed the clicker again.

'We've managed to collate images from various CCTVs along Havelock Road down towards the market area beside the old Debenhams building.'

A low-resolution, jerky video of Audrey stepping out of a glass door and onto Havelock Road appeared on the screen. She'd been circled in red so that it was obvious which figure was her.

Okeke paused the clip. 'Audrey was wearing a tan-coloured coat, dark skirt and carrying a shoulder bag at the time she disappeared. This was at 12.17 p.m.'

She resumed the video sequence that Warren had hastily stitched together. Another camera showed her entering the Tesco Extra further down the road. The sequence leapt forward five minutes to reveal her emerging from the store.

'As you can see, Audrey exited Tesco Express and then walked down Havelock Road towards the pedestrian area...'

Another shot appeared on the screen, Audrey Hincher, once again, circled in red.

'She heads into the Costa Coffee and comes out a few minutes later,' Okeke continued.

The same image jumped forward to show Audrey emerging from the cafe with a paper coffee cup in one hand.

'Now she turns onto Queens Road,' Okeke said, 'and this last image of her was taken from one third of the way down, near Hays Travel.'

Audrey appeared in a jerky shot for just a couple of seconds before she passed beneath the camera and out of view.

'There's a camera at the far end of Queens Road, but we've studied that and there's no sign of Audrey there, nor can she be seen returning to the pedestrian area and back up Havelock Road.' Okeke paused the video. 'So, we have surmised that Audrey Hincher went missing somewhere along the second half of Queens Road. The public-space cameras covering that section are not currently in operation, so we have a blind spot. And... it's in that blind spot that Audrey appears to have completely vanished.'

Perhaps a touch overdramatic, there, she told herself. But if it helped get this onto tonight's local evening news, then what the hell.

'Audrey never returned to Sextus Accountancy and did

not show up at her mother's house as planned after work. We are appealing, therefore, for anyone who might have been in Queens Road between 12.20 and 1 p.m. on Thursday to come forward if they can recall seeing her, or if they recall seeing anything out of the ordinary. We're interested in any incident that looked odd or out of place.' Okeke turned to Andrew Hincher. 'I'm going to hand over to her husband, Andrew, now, who is going to make an appeal to Audrey directly.'

Okeke smiled and gave him the nod to proceed.

'Uh... yeah. Audrey?' he began. 'Wherever you are... you know... you should come home now, love.' He paused and scratched the back of his neck. 'Everyone's really worried about you. Your mum, the kids, the police... and me.' He turned to Okeke. It seemed to her as though he was desperate to hand back to her. She flashed her eyes at him.

I need a bit more than that, mate. FFS.

'Um...' Andrew resumed, 'so we want you back. In one piece, right? Don't be a silly bugger about it. Whatever's upset you, we can sort it out. Make it right. There's all these police people out there spending their time looking for you. We shouldn't be wasting their time and money like this. So come home, love... okay?'

He turned back to Okeke and shrugged.

'Right, okay,' she said, leaning in towards the bank of mics. 'I'll take questions.'

She pointed to a hand raised in the front row.

'Roger Gleve, *Bexhill Chronicle*. You said she was potentially unstable?'

'I said *vulnerable*,' Okeke clarified.

'What did you mean by that?' he asked.

Okeke realised that maybe she'd overstepped the mark.

She had nothing specific to back it up, other than the fact that Audrey was living with the completely nasty piece of shit that was Andrew Hincher.

'By that I mean...' she began, 'I mean, we suspect she may have been in a low swing of depression when she went missing.' *Low swing of depression? What the fuck does that mean?* 'It's possible that something has happened to her, or she'd had some bad news or... or...'

'She was always depressed.' Andrew stepped in to help her out. 'Always. I asked her so many times to, you know, go and see a doctor or to do something about it. But she never did.'

'So she was a suicide risk?' asked Gleve.

Andrew nodded.

'What we're saying is that her state of mind may be a factor here,' Okeke added.

'Steve Harper, *Sussex Online*. Has her phone been recovered?' asked a red-headed man in the second row.

'We're still looking into that,' Okeke replied. 'We're applying to her supplier for the data and once we have that we should be able to get a clearer idea of where she went after the CCTV tracking lost her.'

Okeke pointed at another raised hand.

'Are you concerned that there may be a third party involved?' asked a journalist on the front row.

'At this stage, no,' Okeke said. 'But of course that's not something we've ruled out. We're keeping our investigation and our minds open.'

She pointed to someone else.

'This is a question for Mr Hincher...' the journalist said. 'Had there been a row between you? Or a disagreement before she went missing?'

Andrew frowned, clearly annoyed by the question. 'No! We don't *row*,' he said.

'Is it possible she's just... left you?' the journalist asked.

'Could there be someone else she –'

'No! Of course not,' Andrew cut in. 'Who'd –' He ground to a sudden halt.

Okeke looked at him, trying to hide the shock on her face. He reached for his glass of water and took a quick slug.

'Who... who would she know?' Andrew continued. 'She never went out. She never made any friends. She –'

Okeke turned her attention to the journalists in front of her. 'I'll take one more question,' she said.

~

CHARLOTTE PAUSED the TV with the remote control and looked from Boyd to Emma.

'He's done her in, hasn't he?' she said.

Boyd took a sip of his wine. 'Well, now, that's a bit of a leap, isn't it?'

'Oh, come on,' Charlotte replied. 'He seems like an utterly horrible man.'

Ozzie hopped up onto the sofa beside Boyd and stared at him intently.

'What? You think he's guilty too?' said Boyd. Ozzie's eyes flicked down to the cheese stick in Boyd's hand, then back at his eyes. 'Ahhh, I see where you're coming from...' he murmured as he covered the food protectively with his other hand.

'He did use the past tense at least once that I noticed,' said Emma. 'That's a "tell", right?'

'Hmm...' Boyd pulled a face. 'Not a reliable one. I mean, if an interviewee is constantly doing it, then maybe –'

'He's got killer's eyes,' said Charlotte quite seriously.

Boyd glanced her way. 'And again... that's not entirely reliable, Char.'

'Oh, you can't fake that,' she said. He thought he detected a twinkle in hers. Was she teasing him, he wondered?

'*Predators*' *eyes*,' Charlotte added. 'Intense... staring... unflinching...' She gave him her best unflinching eyes.

It was somewhat unsettling, to be fair, Boyd noted. But then they were both on their second glass of Malbec.

'Well, in that case we probably need to have a word with Anthony Hopkins and Derren Brown too,' Boyd deadpanned.

'I'm serious,' said Charlotte. 'And it wasn't just his eyes. There wasn't one ounce of empathy or concern in the way he spoke about her.' She looked at Emma and then Boyd. 'Did you two not sense that?'

Emma nodded. 'I did. It was like he was just going through the motions.'

'He didn't shed a single tear,' added Charlotte. 'If she *has* run out on him, then I think I could perfectly understand why.'

'Statistically,' said Emma, 'it's nearly always the hubby or the boyfriend who's guilty, isn't it? A row that went too far? Or a jealous-rage thing?' She turned to Boyd. 'Right, Dad?'

Boyd sighed. 'We don't have any evidence of violence. And, anyway, Hincher has an alibi. He was at a business conference the day she went missing.'

'Well, that's a bit convenient, don't you think?' said Charlotte. She sipped her wine. 'That she'd pick that particular day to go missing?'

Boyd shook his head at them both. 'God help me if either of you were jurors at my murder trial.' He lifted his cheese stick up and took a bite from it. It was unexpectedly soggy.

Beside him, Ozzie was licking his lips.

'Ughhh!' Boyd exclaimed as he spat the contents of his mouth out into his hand.

17

'So... everyone thinks he's done it,' said Warren. He was swiping the screen on his phone. 'Everyone on Facebook.'

'Yeah, well, luckily Facebook don't carry out police investigations,' replied Minter.

'I notice the *Mail Online* has picked up the story,' said Rajan. He raised his phone and read out the article.

'... *during his public plea for help, Andrew Hincher, fifty-one, displayed a distinct lack of compassion or concern for his wife, Audrey, fifty-nine, who has now been missing for four days. Indeed many members of the public have voiced the opinion online that his dismissive, cold manner and his careless slip of the past tense was reminiscent of Maxine Carr's similar gaff during the investigation of the Soham Murders...*'

'Right.' Boyd sighed irritably. 'And the tabloid press have got a spotless record when it comes to pinning it on the guilty party.' He shook his head.

'He's got previous form,' said Okeke.

'But no charge,' said Minter. 'And, let's not forget, no clear motive, folks.'

Okeke jerked in her chair as she turned to glare at him. 'No charge on a DV doesn't mean he was innocent! Not by a long way.'

Minter raised his hands apologetically. 'I'm just pointing it out, Okeke, mate.'

'You're aware of the reporting and prosecution stats, right?' she asked him.

'I'm well aware,' he replied, 'but, as I said, there was no *actual evidence* of –'

'Her mother and a work colleague both said they suspected she was being abused by Hincher. And… and we've got a neighbour claiming to have seen an incident!' she argued.

'Again. There's no actual hard evidence, Sam. It's just hearsay!' Minter said.

'Oh, for fuck's sake!' she spat. 'That's how wife-beating bastards like him get away with it all the time!'

Boyd raised his hands. 'Okay, okay. Let's keep things civil, you two.'

'Last night after the press briefing,' continued Okeke, 'he didn't stop to ask me how things were going… or if we had any leads. He just pissed off out of the station. As quick as he could. He –'

'Hey, Sam?' Boyd cut in. 'Let's just…'

Okeke tutted and gave Minter a head-shake. 'No "actual hard evidence",' she muttered, mocking his accent.

'Well,' said Boyd, 'the fact is Minter's right: we don't have any evidence. More importantly, nor do we have any clear motive. It doesn't seem to be about money, does it?' he said, looking at Okeke. 'You were telling me he's well on the way to clearing her out already.'

'Maybe she told him she wouldn't give him any more.'

She shrugged and looked at Yates. 'Did you get around to confirming his alibi?' she asked.

The young man nodded. 'I spoke to the event's organiser. They have a record of Hincher checking in and picking up his pass on the first day.'

'But that doesn't cover him for the whole two days, does it?' she replied. 'He could have checked in, ducked out to come back to Hastings to deal with Audrey, and then returned?'

'Which would imply some degree of planning, Okeke,' said Minter. 'So we're talking premeditated murder, right? And for what? Sixty or seventy grand? That he's *already* helping himself to!'

They sat in silence for a moment. Boyd gazed across the mostly deserted bull pen, bathed in the sickly amber glaze of daylight through the plastic sheeting outside.

He looked at Warren. 'Have we had any calls come through on the tip line?'

'None yet,' Warren said.

'*Nothing?*' Normally they'd get something, at the very least the obligatory time-wasting call from Hector the Hoaxer.

'Not a sausage,' Warren replied.

Boyd laughed. 'There's a saying handed down from your mum if ever I heard one!'

'Guv,' said Okeke, 'I think he did it.'

'Why?' cut in Minter. 'Because he didn't break down in floods of tears during your press conference?'

'Because I think he's a narcissist,' Okeke said. 'Because he clearly has no empathy or feelings for Audrey. Because he's clearly controlling and coercive. Because there are three different people who believe he was violent towards her. Have you been listening to a word I've said?'

Minter shook his head. 'So, isn't it just as likely she's taken herself off? Waited until Andrew was gone for a few days, and then, you know, packed her bags and buggered off?'

Okeke ignored him and turned to Boyd. 'If Hincher's responsible for her disappearance, guv, we're wasting valuable time not gathering forensic evidence. If there's traces of blood in his house, we're giving him all the time he needs to have a thorough clean-up.'

Boyd was well aware of that. 'I can probably get Sutherland to agree to knock up a warrant application for the magistrate, but whether a magistrate would agree that your... *instinct*... was grounds enough to grant one, that's another question entirely.' He shook his head. 'Honestly, Sam? I just think we need something material. Something we can put on the application, other than she sometimes wore heavy make-up. We'd probably have more luck if we could point to some suspicious online activity, messing with her bank account, that sort of thing... What about her phone? Who's on the phone data?'

Warren put his hand up. 'Me. I've applied. Still waiting to hear back.'

'Well, chase that, please,' Boyd said.

'Sir,' Warren replied.

'There's also Hincher's daughter,' said Okeke. 'I haven't reached out to her yet.'

'Same again, then. Chase it up,' Boyd said. He felt the need to throw her a bone. 'And, Sam... I watched the press conference last night and I got the same feeling as you. He really doesn't give a shit.'

'And he did use the *past* tense, sir,' offered Yates.

Boyd suppressed a sigh. 'That's... not really a thing,

Yates. It's great for *Hetty Wainthropp Investigates*, but not for an action log. Look, Okeke, just give me something, anything that doesn't stack up, other than his demeanour, and I'll make sure you get your warrant.'

∼

THE PHONE WAS ANSWERED after the first ring. 'Is that Rebecca Hincher?' Okeke asked.

'Yes. Who's this?' came the reply.

'I'm DS Samantha Okeke from Hastings CID,' Okeke told her.

'Oh, thank God. I've tried calling you lot this morning, but somebody put me through to the wrong station, then I got put on hold and eventually disconnected,' Rebecca said.

'I'm sorry about that,' Okeke replied. 'Did you call the hotline number?'

'I called the Hastings station number. Is that the same one?' Rebecca asked. She sounded harried. Or perhaps it was just frustration. 'I saw the news about Audrey on my phone this morning. She's been missing since Thursday?'

'That's right,' Okeke told her.

'Where? How? What happened?' Rebecca asked.

Okeke gave her the gist. 'The last sighting we have of her was along Queens Road. She seems to have effectively vanished in a blind spot between two CCTV cameras. You know where Queens Road is?'

'Yeah, yeah. I've lived in Hastings all my life. It's always busy there,' Rebecca said.

'Right. Well, we were hoping last night's appeal might throw up some sightings of Audrey there. Maybe give us an indication of where she went next,' Okeke said.

'Do you think she's alive still?' Rebecca asked.

Okeke drew a breath, and hoped Rebecca didn't infer anything from the micro hesitation. 'Yes. Obviously we're concerned for her welfare, but there's no reason, yet, to think that she's come to any harm.' She paused. 'Can I ask you why you were trying to get through to us this morning? Not that that's a problem, Rebecca. It was first thing on my to-do list to give you a call...'

'I *am* worried about her. About her welfare,' Rebecca replied. 'I'm worried something *has* happened to her.'

'Okay. Why would you think something has happened to her?' Okeke asked.

There was a pause from Rebecca's end. Then finally: 'Dad.'

'Okay.' Okeke tried to keep her voice calm. 'What can you tell me about your dad?'

'I think... Oh God, this is going to make me sound totally mental...' Rebecca said.

'It's all right, go on,' Okeke said in what she hoped was a reassuring voice.

'I think...' Rebecca began, 'I think... look, this is from a long time ago. I think I witnessed him kill my mother.'

Okeke stifled a gasp as she fumbled for her pen. 'Okay... you think you saw–'

'I'm not sure, though,' Rebecca said, her words suddenly tumbling over themselves. 'That's the thing, I'm not sure if I saw it or not. I was just, like, five at the time. And it's something I always thought was a really bad nightmare, you know? Just a nightmare, that was just really, really... vivid.' She paused.

'All right, so what do you recall?' Okeke asked. 'What do you think *you* saw?'

'Mum's feet. Sliding along the carpet,' Rebecca whispered. 'One of her slippers coming off...'

'Sliding along?' Okeke cut in. 'Do you mean, as if she was being dragged?'

'Uh-huh,' Rebecca said. 'What I remember was... standing on the stairs in our house. I was meant to be in bed. Asleep, right? But I couldn't. I was scared. I didn't like the dark, so I'd come down the stairs. But only halfway because I didn't want Dad to see me out of bed – he'd have been fucking furious if he had. He'd have smacked me hard. So... I was on the stairs and I was looking down into the lounge. The door was open, just a bit... and I remember seeing Mum's feet sort of sliding out of view, then the door closed.'

'Did you see anything else?' Okeke asked her.

'No,' Rebecca replied quietly.

'And your mum?'

'The next morning, Dad told me that Mum had run off with another man. Just left us.'

'Okay,' Okeke said. 'That must have been terrible for you. But you're not a hundred per cent sure if that's something you saw... or...'

'Dreamed. Yeah,' Rebecca paused. 'I've always thought it was a really bad dream because Mum was gone. I never saw her again... and I've always thought that memory was my imagination, if you see what I mean. Trying to make sense of it afterwards or something...'

'Can you remember what happened immediately afterwards? Do you remember any police or social workers visiting?' Okeke asked.

'No. I can't. It's... all a bit blurry. I was only five,' Rebecca reminded her. 'Liam was, you know, just a baby.'

'So...' Okeke was quickly doing the maths. 'This happened – your mum disappearing in what – 2004, 2005?'

'2004.'

Okeke jotted that down. 'Rebecca... you don't live with your dad and brother any more, right?'

'I don't see them. Either of them. At all,' Rebecca said.

'How long ago did you move out?' Okeke asked.

'Five years ago,' Rebecca said. 'I'm not gonna lie – I left as soon as I could.'

Okeke scribbled that down too. 'But, for a while, you did live in the same house as Audrey?'

'Yeah, for three or four years, I did. It's the same house that Dad and Liam are in now.'

'And why were you so keen to leave?' Okeke asked.

'Because of how bloody awful it was at home,' Rebecca replied.

'How do you mean?'

Rebecca took a deep shuddering breath. 'I didn't like how Dad treated Audrey,' she said. 'Liam started copying him and treated her like shit too. They treated her like a... like a servant. Like a slave. Like a dogsbody.'

'Was your dad ever violent towards her?' said Okeke. 'Did he ever hit her?'

'He was abusive, yes. I saw him grab her hair and drag her into the kitchen once. He shouted at her a lot. I've seen him throw things at her too.'

'Right,' Okeke said. 'So I would call that violent domestic abuse, Rebecca.' She paused. 'Did either of them – your dad or Liam – abuse you?'

'They were abusive. But no... they weren't violent towards me. All the same, I couldn't cope with watching it happen to her. I left. And I wanted Audrey to leave with me,' said Rebecca.

The Vanishing

'You *asked* her to leave?' Okeke said.

'Yeah. But she wouldn't.' Rebecca paused. 'Audrey was the closest thing I've had to a mum, you know?'

'What did she say when you asked her? Did she say why she wouldn't come?'

'No.' Rebecca sighed, her breath fluttering. 'Why do women always refuse to leave an abuser, huh? Denial? Hope that they'll change one day?' And now Okeke could hear the tremor in her voice, not just her breath. 'I really, really hope... she's done the right thing and walked out on him.'

'Me too,' Okeke said.

'I want to know she's okay,' Rebecca continued. 'Will I be kept up to date? Are you the main police person in charge of this?'

'Yes, I'm SIO,' Okeke replied. 'At the moment. And yes, Rebecca, I will keep you informed. In fact, if you're okay with this, I'll probably need you to come into the station so we can discuss this a bit more.'

There was a pause.

'Rebecca?'

'I'm... I'm not sure.'

'Or I could come to you?' Okeke said. 'Where are you based?'

'Hailsham,' Rebecca answered.

Not too far away, then. It was just north of Eastbourne. 'I could come over today. This afternoon? How would that be?' Okeke asked.

'I'm working today. Two shifts. I've got a break between them at three,' Rebecca told her. 'I work at the Wetherspoons in Hailsham.'

'Would you like me to meet you during your break?' said Okeke.

'O-okay. Yeah. All right,' Rebecca replied.

Okeke jotted that down. She had one more question, though, that she wanted to ask quickly, before Rebecca Hincher hung up. 'Before you go, Rebecca, what's your mother's name?'

'Carol,' Rebecca replied. 'Carol Docherty.'

18

Okeke drew up in the small car park behind the Wetherspoons pub The George.

She'd had time before she set off from Hastings to look up Carol Docherty on LEDS. The only thing recorded under her name was a misper file opened in 1994 and there had been no follow-up. She noted that: it was Andrew Hincher who'd called the police; a DC Grant had been sent out to respond to the call; and that the address was the same as it was now. Andrew Hincher, it seemed, had been living in the same terraced house for the last three decades at least.

The notes suggested that DC Grant hadn't considered it necessary to properly interview Hincher. Reading between the lines, Hincher had gone with the same characterization for Carol as he had for Audrey. Allegedly, she too, had been 'always moody', 'depressed' and 'batshit crazy'. DC Grant had added in brackets 'Post-natal depression?' and further down his notes: 'Drug habit?'

Okeke stepped inside The George. The lunchtime rush had thinned out – if, indeed, there had ever been one. She spotted a couple of lingering customers and behind the bar a woman in her twenties placing pint glasses on a shelf.

She wandered over. 'Rebecca?' she asked.

The woman looked up. 'DS Okeke?'

Okeke nodded. 'Are you due your break yet?'

Rebecca finished what she was doing and dried her hands on a tea towel. 'I can make us a coffee,' she offered.

Okeke smiled. 'That would be nice.'

Rebecca pointed to a table by a window that looked out onto the car park. 'Grab a seat. I'll bring it over.'

A couple of minutes later, Rebecca joined her with a couple of cappuccinos and a tray of sugar sachets. 'I've got twenty minutes,' she said as she sat down.

Okeke pulled out her notebook and placed it on the small round table. 'So I looked into your mother's misper case,' she began.

'Misper?' Rebecca asked.

'I mean, "missing persons".' Okeke smiled apologetically. 'Work lingo is a bad habit of mine. Your mother – she was your biological mother, right?'

'Yeah,' Rebecca said.

'I'm afraid hers is an outstanding file. I couldn't find any result,' Okeke told her.

'Well, I didn't think there would be,' Rebecca replied. 'Like I said earlier... I think he did her in.'

'So why are you coming forward with this now?' Okeke asked.

Rebecca had a pierced brow and blonde hair, which was stained pink and pulled back tightly into a bun. On her left forearm were busy-looking tattoos that – Okeke suspected – hid a ladder of self-harm scars.

'Because I've never been that sure about it,' Rebecca said.

'But you seem to be now?'

Rebecca nodded. 'With Audrey going missing like this? Yeah, I'm definitely more sure now.'

'What can you remember about your mum?' said Okeke.

Rebecca huffed. 'Not much.' 'It says in the notes that she might have been suffering from depression. There's a query about her being a drug addict...'

'Well, I wouldn't know. I was five. But Dad's always said she was a druggie. That she did the right thing "walking away" and leaving us with him.'

'Right.' Okeke sipped her coffee. 'And you were saying you left home because of the way your dad was with Audrey?'

'Yeah. It was toxic at home. He treated her like shit.'

'They've been together...'

'About twelve years,' Rebecca said. 'I was fifteen when Dad started seeing her. Liam was eleven.'

'And was he always like that with her?' Okeke asked.

Rebecca thought for a moment. 'Right at the beginning, no. You know how it is... He was putting his best foot forward. The so-called honeymoon period. But I'd say for most of the time following that he was a bastard towards her.' She leant forward. 'I saw your police-appeal thing earlier this morning. I watched it on YouTube.'

Okeke tilted her head. 'And?'

'Dad... ' she began. 'He made me want to throw up.'

'What do you mean?'

Rebecca shook her head. 'He doesn't give a crap about her. All that "please come home, love" shit? That was just vomit-inducing.'

'Crocodile tears?' Okeke suggested.

Rebecca nodded. 'Did he even manage any?'

Okeke hadn't seen any. He'd done a fair bit of eye-rubbing while she spoke to the press, so by the time the cameras settled on him the rims of his eyes had reddened. But there had been no tears. Not that she could offer that little insight up to the action log. Some people cried at events like that; others held their shit together.

'So you remember seeing your mother's body being dragged out of sight by your dad?' Okeke said.

Rebecca nodded again. 'I saw her feet disappearing out of view. Like she was being dragged across the carpet.'

'Did you see that it was your dad doing the dragging?' Okeke asked.

Rebecca shook her head.

'And do you think she was... unconscious? Or dead?'

'Well, she was unconscious, for sure,' Rebecca said.

'And you're certain this happened in the same house he lives in now?'

Rebecca nodded once more.

'Do you recall any police searching the house after your mum disappeared? Were there any people in forensics gear?'

'You mean those white... space-man suits?'

Okeke smiled and nodded.

'No. But... remember, I was five. It's, like, really foggy.' Rebecca frowned. 'I think... I *think* me and Liam might have stayed with Gran for a few days afterwards. Dad's mum.'

Okeke jotted that down. 'When would this have been?'

Rebecca shook her head. 'It's a bit jumbled. After Mum went missing, definitely.'

'Immediately after?' Okeke asked.

Rebecca's frown deepened for a moment, then she finally shook her head. 'No, I don't know how long after. It's all jumbled up. Really.'

Okeke clicked her pen. 'Can you give me your gran's details?'

'She passed away,' Rebecca said. 'During Covid. She was in a home at the time.'

Okeke took another sip of coffee. She glanced again at Rebecca's tattoos. Yes, she could see gentle ridges hidden there, almost camouflaged by a pattern of Celtic swirls.

'Rebecca... can I ask, did your dad ever hurt you?'

Rebecca quickly dropped her arm out of sight. 'No. I told you that already,' she said.

'Are you sure?'

'What do you mean, *Are you sure?*'

Okeke sensed there was something there. Something she was hiding, or perhaps simply denying. 'And what about Liam?' she asked.

Rebecca shook her head. 'He smacked us both. He got angry, right, but nothing else...'

'Okay,' Okeke said, tucking her pen and notebook away in her jacket.

'Becks!' a male voice called from the other side of the empty pub. 'Kitchen! Please!'

'I'd better get back to work,' Rebecca said.

'Look, one more thing,' said Okeke. 'You told me on the phone that your dad killed Audrey. You seemed so certain. Why?'

'Why?' Rebecca breathed out slowly. 'Honestly?'

Okeke nodded. 'Honestly.'

The young woman sighed. 'I think he was done with her. Done *using* her. He wanted a skivvy, didn't he? He wanted a child-minder... A cash cow. She had money, you see – well, to start with anyway.'

'A trust fund,' Okeke supplied.

Rebecca nodded. 'He dipped into it all the time. I'd be surprised if there's any left at all.'

'There's still a fair sum,' replied Okeke. 'I can't imagine he'd have murdered her for that, though.'

Rebecca nodded. 'I think he just wanted rid of Audrey. He was fed up with her.'

'So why not just split up with her?' asked Okeke.

Rebecca shrugged. 'Then there'd have to be a settlement, right? She'd get half his house... That's the only thing he actually owns and he wouldn't want that to happen.'

19

Boyd thumbed his chin absently as he processed what Okeke had just told him.

'So, this first wife...'

'They weren't married,' Okeke clarified.

'Carol Docherty...' he continued. 'There was absolutely no follow-up on her misper?'

'None that I can see on LEDS.'

Boyd shook his head. It didn't necessarily mean that nothing had actually been done, but – given that the misper dated back to 2004 when a lot of police intel was still on index cards stuffed in filing cabinets – it was possible any records of further efforts to locate Carol Docherty had been lost along the way. That might also explain why this DC Grant might not have been aware that Hincher had previous DV form before her case and thus not been more rigorous about following through.

'And his daughter claims she saw him dragging her mother's body in the house that he's currently in?' Boyd said.

Okeke nodded. 'But she did say she didn't see who was

doing the dragging. And, to be fair, she couldn't have known if her mum was, you know, actually *dead*.'

'Because she might just have been passed out?' Boyd asked.

'What?' She bristled at that suggestion. 'Simply because Andrew claimed she was doing drugs at the time?'

'Because,' he replied, 'that's a question a defence barrister would ask. *My client*,' he began with a courtroom drawl, '*was merely moving her onto a seat or sofa so that her daughter wouldn't find her sprawled on the floor in the morning.*'

'Come on, guv,' said Okeke, 'there's enough for a warrant now, surely?'

There probably was. It would be a pretty easy sell to Sutherland and probably an easy sell to the magistrate, but, once news got out that there was a police van and possibly a CSI van parked outside the Hinchers' house, the press and social media would launch into a feeding frenzy and Andrew Hincher would be the prey.

The man had DV against his name, a previous partner who'd 'disappeared' and a wife who was now a missing person – the tabloids would go full tilt at him. Not that Boyd could blame them. The press loved a hate figure to plaster over their websites... and the pressure would be on Sussex Police to bring Andrew Hincher in and bang him up.

Which was all well and good, until some other lead turned up that proved Andrew innocent, at which point Sussex Police would get it in the neck for caving in too readily to the barking red tops and be accused of 'lazy policing' and 'tunnel vision'. He sighed.

'She's been missing four days now,' Okeke prompted.

'All right then,' Boyd replied. He looked at his watch. It was gone three o'clock. 'Let's get the paperwork sorted by end of play.'

'Thank you,' she said, getting up from her seat.

'A word of caution, though, Sam,' Boyd cut in. 'If we find any suspicious forensics for Audrey and this is elevated to a murder enquiry...'

'I know... Minter gets SIO.'

He nodded. 'I just want you to be aware.'

20

Boyd waited beside his car. He'd decided to let Okeke have her moment – to knock on Hincher's front door and waggle the freshly inked Section 8 warrant in his face. It was her shout, her legwork and her case...

... for the moment.

The door opened, revealing a young man in the doorway. Okeke whipped out her warrant for him to see, while the accompanying uniformed officers and DCs Yates, Warren and Rajan waited patiently behind her.

Andrew Hincher appeared beside his son and, after a few terse words had been exchanged, they backed away to allow Okeke to enter, then the rest of the crew piled in behind her.

Boyd looked around. The blue lights on the police van had prompted a fair bit of curtain twitching and curious faces. Another few minutes and there were sure to be neighbours out on their doorsteps with their phones swinging around. Give it fifteen minutes and there'd probably be some local press snapping away too.

He glanced down the narrow street. One of Sully's CSI vans was parked up. He couldn't see if it was Sully or Magnusson in the front seat, or one of their suited-up forensic minions. The driver-side door swung open and he recognised the intimidating height of Magnusson emerging. The passenger side opened and Sully got out too. The Full Monty, then. Presumably it had been a slow day in forensics and they'd both fancied a field trip.

~

OKEKE TURNED TO WARREN. 'I want every bit of digital tech you can find. Phones, laptops, tablets.'

'On it,' replied Warren.

'You can't just grab all our stuff!' complained Liam.

'Just your dad's,' Okeke replied.

'This is fucking ridiculous!' snapped Andrew. 'What the fuck's going on?'

'You'll get it all back in one piece – don't worry, Mr Hincher.' She handed him the warrant. 'This is for you. And we'll be taking you in for interview,' Okeke told him, as he scanned the paper.

'You're arresting me?' Andrew said incredulously.

'Under the Police and Criminal Evidence Act 1984, Section 8, you're going to be arrested for interview as a detained suspect in the disappearance of Audrey Hincher,' Okeke said.

'What the fuck!' he spat.

She turned to the uniformed sergeant behind her and nodded at him to begin the required cautions before removing Andrew from the house.

'He's all yours, sergeant,' Okeke said, then she turned to Liam. 'We're going to be searching the house, room by room.

So I'm going to have to ask you to step outside until we're done with the lounge.'

'I'm not under arrest, am I?' he asked warily.

She managed a calm smile. 'No, I'm just asking you to step outside for a bit, that's all.'

Okeke waited until both men had been led out through the front door, then reached into her jacket pocket and pulled out several pairs of nitrile gloves.

'Gloves on, both of you,' she told Rajan and Yates.

'What are we looking for?' asked Rajan.

'Indicators of recent violence. Possible forensics locations. Signs of recent cleaning, scrubbing, moving of furniture. Basically anything you think seems suss. Start with the bathroom and the kitchen. And any other room that has a tap and a sink in it.'

They headed off in different directions, leaving her alone in the lounge. A moment later, Boyd entered.

'Andrew Hincher's on his way to the station to be signed in. Your clock will start ticking in about half an hour's time,' he said to Okeke. 'You know what you're checking for?'

'Not specifically,' she admitted.

'Let's pretend I didn't hear that.'

'Okay... well, signs of a struggle would be helpful,' she said. 'But given Hincher's had four days to tidy up, I'm after anything that looks like a recent spring clean.'

'You were here not long ago, right?' Boyd asked.

She nodded.

'Anything look like it's been moved around?' he said.

She shook her head. 'It seems pretty much as it was.'

'You know, if Andrew did do something to her, he almost certainly wouldn't have done it at home.' He nodded over his shoulder at the open front door. 'Not with his lad hanging around here all the time.' He started to walk away, then stopped. 'Oh, you might also want to have the boys check out Hincher's work van.'

She sucked in air through her teeth. 'That's covered under the Section Eight, is it?'

'It's parked right outside,' Boyd said with a shrug. 'So not too much of a stretch to argue it's technically part of the home search.'

She nodded. 'Fine. I might have them start with that, actually.' She headed out of the lounge into the hallway, muttering, 'Keys, keys, keys,' under her breath.

Okeke was about to step outside and ask Liam where his dad would normally keep the keys to his van when she paused and turned to look up the stairs. She could hear Warren up there, clattering around, searching for tech.

The stairs.

The same stairs that Rebecca had, supposedly, been standing on when she'd witnessed her mother being dragged out of view.

She took the first couple of steps, turned round and sat down.

'Uh... what're you doing?' asked Boyd.

Okeke could see into the lounge through the open door, and the bay window looking out onto the street. It was perfectly plausible that young Rebecca Hincher could have seen her mother's feet disappearing slowly from view if she'd been perched right here at the bottom of the stairs. Her mother's slippered feet being tugged across the...

'She said... carpet.'

'Sorry?'

'Rebecca said she saw her mother being dragged out of view *across the carpet*,' Okeke replied.

Boyd turned to look back into the lounge. The floor was wooden and covered by a large patterned rug.

Okeke got up off the stairs and stepped back into the lounge. The rug was large enough that it covered most of the floor. The sofa, the armchair, the filing cabinet in the corner were all on top of the edges, holding down the rug to stop it from being easily rucked up.

She squatted and lifted the corner closest to the door. The boards beneath the rug were a shade or two lighter, cleaner, less scuffed from years of foot traffic.

'Can you give me a hand with the sofa?' she said. 'Just lift that end so I can pull the rug out.'

Boyd did as she asked. She tugged the rug from beneath the sofa's raised legs and rolled it back, up to the side of the armchair, exposing about a third of the lounge's wooden floor.

They both noticed it at the same time – the faintest outline, just a fraction darker than the rest of the freshly exposed timbers. Its edge seemed blurred, as if someone had made an effort to scrub it out of existence.

'We'd better get Sully and Magnusson in,' said Boyd.

21

'Oh yes,' replied Magnusson. 'It's definitely blood. And a fair dollop of it too.'

She looked at the team gathered round the conference table. Now they had some blood, they had a potential murder investigation... and, with it, the Incident Room.

They also had Hatcher. Clearly, she'd read the tea leaves and could see that this case had the potential to turn into one that would catch national attention, particularly if they mishandled the comms side of things.

Magnusson continued: 'We also found what look like cast-off specks beneath one of the upper cabinets in the kitchen.'

Boyd nodded. 'And would you say they're also old deposits? From around the same time as the blood in the lounge?'

'It's hard to say,' Magnusson replied. 'The spray dots are too small to make any sensible colorimetric assessment of exactly how old they are.'

'They're not a few days old, though?' Boyd pressed.

She shook her head. 'Oh God, no. If I was a gambling woman, which I'm not – it's a filthy habit – I'd wager that the specks in the kitchen and the stain on the lounge floor come from the same time, same incident.'

'Can we get any viable DNA from it?' Boyd asked.

'It's perfectly possible.' She sucked air in. 'Expensive, though.'

She glanced at Sutherland, who was also sitting in on this morning's meeting. Boyd did the same. Sutherland's face, unsurprisingly, had shot to bright red at the mere mention of money.

'Just say if you want me to send them off to Ellessey for mRNA profiling,' Magnusson said.

'Carol Docherty has been an unresolved misper since 2004, sir,' Boyd said to Sutherland.

'And if we receive a viable profile on the blood, do we have anything of Docherty's to compare it against?' Sutherland asked.

Boyd shook his head. 'Probably not.'

'Well, it's a bit bloody pointless, then, isn't it?' he grumbled.

'The profile might match with something on the NDNAD,' replied Boyd. 'We could also take a sample from either of Hincher's kids to check for a familial match.'

Sutherland puffed his cheeks as he considered that.

Hatcher nodded. 'Let's have that done,' she said.

'If the blood can be attributed to Carol Docherty,' continued Boyd. 'Then we've got forensics matched to a disappearance, and also testimony from the daughter, Rebecca. That's robust enough for the CPS, right?'

Hatcher nodded. 'Lesley, I think, would bite your hand off for that one.'

Boyd looked at Okeke. 'And if Hincher's appearing guilty

with regards to Carol, it puts him under greater pressure to talk about Audrey.'

'Or makes him even more guarded,' Okeke countered. 'If he *is* guilty of her disappearance.'

'You really think he knows what's happened to her, Boyd?' asked Hatcher.

Boyd glanced her way and nodded. 'It's looking more likely, ma'am. I think the evidence is stacking up.'

Sutherland pressed his lips together as he mentally weighed up the budgetary sting. 'All right then, send the samples over to Ellessey and they can fleece us as per usual. I suppose... and if we do get a match...'

'We resolve an outstanding misper *and* a murder,' Minter chipped in. 'A BOGOF – buy one, get one free.'

'Of course,' said Hatcher, 'if Audrey suddenly turns up alive and well, we'll look like –'

'Then we'll look like we've acted proportionately in bringing him in last night, ma'am,' cut in Boyd. 'Just on the Docherty evidence alone.'

She nodded. 'True.'

'It's only been five days,' said Okeke. She looked at Boyd and then everyone else. 'She *could* still be perfectly fine.'

'Five days, Okeke,' said Minter. '*And* it's been on the telly.' He shook his head solemnly. 'Doesn't bode well, does it? If she'd seen herself making the news... she'd have contacted someone, right?'

'It doesn't bode well,' agreed Boyd. 'But for the record, as far as anybody outside this room is concerned, this is still an active missing persons. Docherty aside, we have every reason to hope that Audrey might still turn up safe and well.'

Boyd turned to Magnusson. 'Where the hell's Sully?'

'He rang and said he's going to be late in this morning,'

she replied. 'His car's broken down. But don't you worry – I've already got our digital whizz working on Hincher's tech. Jules reckons he'll have it all cracked open and retrieve a data dump for me by lunchtime.'

'Boyd?'

Boyd looked at Hatcher. 'Ma'am?'

'When are you planning to bring Hincher up to interview him?'

Boyd checked his watch. It was gone nine thirty. He'd been processed by eight last night, which meant they'd used up thirteen of their twenty-four hours. However, given the discovery last night of the blood in the lounge and the kitchen, applying for another twelve hours would – should – be a no-brainer.

'I'm going to bring him up after this,' Boyd said. 'He's had a whole night to sweat on it. Minter?'

'Boss?'

'You and I will interview him.' He glanced at Okeke. 'Sorry, mate, but...'

'I know, I know...' She sighed. 'I knew it was coming.'

'Minter's SIO on Carol Docherty,' said Boyd. 'But Audrey Hincher's still a separate misper. So that remains your case.'

'Unless Hincher suddenly – miraculously – decides to confess to her murder,' said Sutherland.

Boyd hunched his shoulders. 'He might. Stranger things have happened.' He turned to Minter. 'But let's launch the interview softly-softly. Let him think we're on his side and just box-ticking. Buddy up with him. You're pretty good at that.'

'Righto,' Minter said.

'Let's get him to say as much as we can before he feels the need to call in a solicitor. We'll take a break over lunch, and hopefully there'll be something on his phone or laptop we can hit him with this afternoon.'

'And if not, boss?' Minter asked.

'Then we'll throw Carol Docherty's blood at him.' Boyd turned to Warren. 'Where are we with Audrey's phone?'

'I was going to tell you. I got the records from her service provider this morning. We've got a "last signal" location for the phone.'

'Bloody hell – where?' Boyd exclaimed.

'Harold Street.'

'That's just a couple of streets away from her house,' said Okeke.

Boyd spread his hands. 'Warren, what're you waiting for? Move!'

'Huh?'

Boyd nodded at the door to the Incident Room. 'Go and see if it's been dumped!'

'Oh right.' Warren got up. 'Now, sir?'

'Yes, *now*!' Boyd clapped to chivvy him towards the door. 'The sooner we have it, the sooner we can crack it.'

Warren hurried out and Boyd went over to close the door.

'Should we consider looking over Hincher's back garden?' said Magnusson.

Boyd wandered back to his seat and stood behind it. 'Yup. That's probably not a bad idea.'

'Discreetly, if you please,' said Hatcher. 'There'll probably be press lingering outside his house this morning.'

Boyd shrugged. 'I'm sure word has spread that he's in custody. Yates,' he said, 'pop over and take a look, will you?' He glanced Hatcher's way. 'Discreetly.'

'Uh, I'm looking for what, guv? A fresh grave?'

'That, or... anything else that seems suss. Just have a

poke around,' Boyd said.

'Check for any decking,' Minter said darkly. 'Or a patio. That's always a good sign.'

Okeke shook her head. 'I peered out. It's just lawn. Some flower beds.'

'I could tag along with a methane detector,' offered Magnusson.

Boyd nodded. 'All right. Yes. Do that.'

'But go in a CID pool car, please,' said Hatcher. 'Not a CSI van. And suit up inside the house. Away from any windows.'

Magnusson nodded.

Boyd turned back to Yates. 'Hincher's alibi – you were going to look into that a bit more? Does the venue have CCTV on their main entrance? Can we catch Hincher leaving the place with time enough to overlap with Audrey's disappearance on Thursday? Yates... actually, you're doing the garden, so, Rajan, can I leave that with you?'

'Yes, sir,' said Rajan.

'And Hincher's van. Did anyone look that over last night?'

'I did,' replied Magnusson.

'And...?'

She shook her head. 'Nothing.'

'Did you check thoroughly?'

She gave him a stare that would have withered any unfortunate potted plant sitting between them.

'All right,' Boyd said. 'We have jobs to do.' He glanced at Sutherland, then Hatcher. 'Is there anything you want to add, ma'am?'

Hatcher pushed her chair back and stood up. 'No. Just let's make sure we don't overfocus on Docherty and forget Audrey. She's the one in the news at this point.'

22

Andrew Hincher sat down at the interview table, looking worse for wear. Boyd had the feeling that he was the kind of man who usually took his time in the bathroom on any given morning: a thorough trim of his silvery, close-clipped beard, a once-around with nasal tweezers, a tweak of hair gel and a splash of something scented.

Right now he seemed as though he'd been on a pub crawl the night before and not made it home.

'Did you sleep okay?' asked Boyd.

'No. I didn't,' Andrew grumbled. 'The pillows're too thin. Worse than a fuckin' Travelodge.'

'How was the breakfast?' said Minter.

'I ate it,' Andrew replied. He looked at Boyd. 'Where's the copper who had me locked up last night? The black one?'

'Detective Sergeant Okeke, you mean,' Boyd replied. 'She's on other business.'

'Why the fuck did she have me arrested?' asked Andrew. 'Why was my name on that –'

'You've been detained for questioning,' Boyd cut in.

'So, what does that mean? Do you lot actually think I did Audrey in?'

Boyd shook his head. 'Not at all. It means we have some things we're not too sure about and we'd like you to help us clear them up.'

'So why fucking arrest me? Why not just ask me what you want to know?' Andrew persisted.

Boyd had two pages of notes in a folder in front of him. One was headed 'BE NICE'. The other: 'GO FOR THE KILL'. He opened the folder and glanced at the first sheet.

'I want to start by getting a clearer picture of Audrey. I'd like to go over again what kind of person she is, what state of mind she was in last time you saw her, and your thoughts on where she might have gone.'

Andrew narrowed his eyes suspiciously.

'Look, your name was on the warrant,' continued Boyd. 'We can't search a premises without the named person being relocated and supervised.' He was talking bollocks, of course. 'I'm afraid the quickest, easiest and cheapest way to do that is to offer you a room at our place.' Boyd smiled apologetically. 'Hastings Hilton.'

Andrew glared at him.

'Fine,' Boyd said. 'So the last time you saw Audrey was...'

'Wednesday afternoon. Had a job to do on the way up to the conference. Then I booked into Travelodge on Wednesday night, ready for the next day.'

'For this business conference of yours,' said Minter.

'Right,' Andrew replied.

'What was this conference for?' Boyd asked. 'In fact...' He shuffled some papers in his folder for effect. 'I'm not sure I'm clear on what it is you do.'

'I install home security,' Andrew replied.

'Burglar alarms? Door cams? That sort of thing?' asked Minter.

Andrew nodded. 'Interior and exterior cameras, panic buttons, motion sensors. The whole solution.'

'And this conference you were at...' Boyd prompted him.

'I'm a Berkley Security franchisee,' he said. 'They like to keep us all up to date on their product range and...'

Boyd let him go on for a bit. He had the notes from Okeke's interview so he knew this already. He just wanted Andrew relaxed and talking.

'And you were going away for how long?' he asked.

'For four days,' Andrew replied. 'From Wednesday morning to Saturday. So three nights away from home.'

'Was Audrey upset about that?' asked Minter. 'Perhaps, I dunno... jealous? Suspicious, maybe?'

'You mean, did she think I was cheating on her with someone?' Andrew asked.

Minter nodded.

'Yeah, I think she probably did. She was always checking on me. Asking where I was going, what I was up to.'

'Well, I'm not surprised,' said Minter affably. 'You're not a bad-looking bloke, are you, Andy?'

Boyd couldn't help glancing up from his notes and locking eyes with Minter for a moment. *I said butter him up! Not* chat *him up.*

'I've done all right,' Andrew conceded. 'Kept me hair. Managed to keep fit.'

'You've done pretty well, mate. You're fifty, aren't you?' Minter continued.

'Fifty-one,' Andrew said.

Minter stroked his beard thoughtfully. 'So... your Audrey's significantly older, I believe?'

'She's fifty-nine. Eight years older, yeah, but I wouldn't call that "significantly",' Andrew replied.

'No. Fair play, mate. But she *is* a little bit older.' Minter stroked his beard again. 'So tell me, how did the two of you first meet?'

∼

WARREN QUITE ENJOYED this kind of task, truth be told. There was an element of Jack Sparrow about it – a pirate making his way to 'X' on an old crinkly map and hoping he was close enough to the exact spot to find the treasure. The 'X' in question was the best-guess triangulation of three nearby phone masts that had collectively agreed that the last known location of Audrey Hincher's phone was roughly halfway down Harold Street.

He checked his location on his phone against the map that they'd received from the phone company. He noted a caveat beside the printed-out map, that the location was an approximation with a granularity of about fifty metres. Which, of course, didn't sound that much on paper. But that radius, when applied to a narrow residential road flanked by front gardens, bushes, wheelie bins and parked cars rammed nose to tail on either side, made for a challenging treasure hunt.

Magnusson had given him a handy tip on his way out – take a torch. That hadn't made much sense to him immediately, given that it was the middle of the day. He was searching outside, why would he want a flipping torch? But, as Warren panned it around now, in broad daylight, beneath the bushes and in the shadowy voids beneath each parked vehicle, it made perfect sense: every shard of broken glass, metal ring pull and foil wrapper glinted back at him as he swept the torch beam across the ground.

He stood up straight and peered into the front garden beside him. It was full of clumps of nettles and a gone-wild lawn. He swung his torch over it, the light picking out the reflection from a broken bottle and a coin.

The next garden along was separated by an ivy bush that spilled out across the pavement. He ducked down into the narrow space beneath the branches and leaves, he was boxed in on one side by a Bedford van and the other by a low and practically hidden stone wall. There, in the almost twilight gloom, he panned his torch back and forth.

The phone company's 'last location' pin-drop didn't necessarily mean the phone would still be on Harold Street. The pin simply marked the last place that the phone had been detected. It could have been turned off here, which meant that all his snuffling around on hands and knees could quite possibly lead to nothing.

'Hey! What you up to there, boy?'

Warren backed out of the narrow space between the van and the ivy and looked up at an old man who wore a battered bowler hat, a stained old blue tracksuit top and yellow Marigold gloves. *Of course he was. Normal for Hastings*, Warren thought. The man also had a traditional smoking pipe bouncing from one corner of his mouth to the other.

Warren got to his feet, produced his warrant card and held it out. 'I'm police,' he said.

'Police?' The old man didn't appear to be convinced by the flimsy piece of plastic. 'Buy that on the interwebs, did ya, son?'

'No. I'm actually police. For real,' Warren tried again.

'Ya don't look old enough for yer balls to 'ave dropped yet,' the old man cackled.

'Yeah, well,' Warren assured him. 'They have. Fully. Down.'

'Wotcha looking for down there, son?' the man asked.

'A phone,' Warren said, wondering if he really wanted to invest time and effort explaining himself to the daft-looking old bugger. 'You live on this street?'

The man smiled. 'Aye.'

'Which house?' Warren nodded at the front doors either side of the explosion of ivy.

'Neither, lad. I live *on* this street... literally,' the man said.

'You mean homeless? You're a rough sleeper?' Warren asked him.

'I'm not homeless, lad,' the man replied. 'There's a perfectly comfortable shed down the way that I've made my own.' He smiled again. 'And I patrol Harold Street from there. That's me headquarters, so to speak.'

'You...'

'I'm the neighbourhood watchman,' the man said cheerily. 'Here day and night, I am. Always on duty. Providing round-the-clock service.'

Warren realised that chatting to the eccentric old fart might not be such a waste of his time after all. 'Would you have been here on this street five days ago? Round about midday?' he asked.

'Five days ago, eh?' The old man's eyes narrowed. His crinkly face folded up on itself and his heavy-bowled pipe bobbed precariously. 'That would be...' He reached deep into the pocket of his tracksuit top.

'Last Thursday,' Warren supplied.

The old man pulled out a small, dog-eared black notebook.

Warren couldn't help smiling. 'You really *do* "police" this street.'

'Oh, aye, son. I have done for thirty years or more. Now... last Thursday, you say?' He leafed backwards through his notebook until he settled on the right page. His eyes widened. 'Ah...'

'What?'

'Yes. I made an entry here, in the afternoon. It was a funny thing...'

~

RAJAN WAS surprised and impressed at how quick the receptionist at Ferryman's Lodge had been with locating and uploading the data from their foyer's CCTV. She'd told him it might take a few hours, but that she'd get on it straight away and come up with the goods.

And now he was back down from Greater London, at his desk and looking at the zipped files on the memory stick. He double-clicked on the one with Thursday's date appended and it quickly unpacked itself to reveal one large media file. He opened the file and after watching it for a few seconds he was relieved to see from the digital timestamp that it wasn't real-time footage that he was going to have to laboriously sift through but a sequence of motion-sensor triggered captures. The camera was aimed across the hotel's foyer towards the main entrance and was, for once, a decent high-resolution image running at 30 frames per second, rather than the usual stop–start 6 fps of the older security cameras. Watching those gave him a headache.

The timestamp flicked rapidly forward through the early-morning hours until half eight, then slowed right down to virtually real time as a flood of people began to enter the hotel and clog up the foyer – they were the Berkley Security attendees. Rajan watched a queue form beside a trestle table as attendees signed in and collected their name badges.

Yates had called the hotel yesterday and had been able to confirm, via Berkley Security, that Andrew Hincher had signed in at 8.47 a.m.

Rajan sped the video forward to just before and began to study the crowd of heads in the foyer. He quickly spotted Hincher's close-cropped silver hair and designer beard, leaning over the table and entering his details on to an iPad.

Andrew lingered at the table for a moment, chatting to the woman sitting behind it. She handed him a badge. He moved on and out of shot as the next attendee started tapping in his details.

'All right then,' muttered Rajan. 'So, confirmation that he *did* turn up to school, like a good boy.' He fast-forwarded to a point where the foyer was clear of attendees and watched as the woman who'd been manning the check-in table cleared everything away and moved the Berkley Security banner stand back against the wall.

The conference was underway and the only people now triggering the foyer's CCTV were the receptionist and a couple of cleaners, going about their daily tasks.

He glanced at the timecode in the corner: 9.37 a.m.

Given that Audrey Hincher went missing in Hastings just after midday, there wasn't much of a window left on the video timeline for Hincher to leave the conference and make his way back home. It was a good two-hour drive from there to Hastings – and that was with a clear run on the M25 and A21.

Rajan was about to give up when a solitary figure strode quickly across the foyer and headed for the main doors. He paused the video as the man pulled the glass door open and glanced back into the foyer.

'Motherfucker,' whispered Rajan.

The image was blurred because the man was moving quickly, and the more Rajan zoomed in, the worse it got. But... the slim, silver-haired man at the door did look a hell of a lot like Andrew Hincher.

∽

MAGNUSSON TURNED round to answer the young man's question. 'It's a methane detector.'

Liam Hincher frowned. 'Looks like a metal detector to me.'

'Nope,' she replied irritably. 'It's a methane detector... Now, would you mind if I crack on?'

'Come on, mate.' The police sergeant standing beside the back door stepped towards the young man. 'Let's have you back in the house. Let the lady get on with her job, eh?'

'I wanna watch,' Liam replied. 'It's interesting. It's like one of the Netflix true-crime thingies.'

'He shouldn't be in the garden,' Magnusson called over her shoulder. 'Get him inside, please.'

The sergeant spread his hands as though he was herding sheep and shepherded the reluctant Liam Hincher through the open door and into the house.

Magnusson resumed sweeping the nose of the detector back and forth, inching her way along the patchy lawn.

Yates, meanwhile, was at the end of the long, thin garden, poking around inside the shed. He emerged from the creaking doorway and shrugged. 'Nothing going on in there.'

Magnusson paused and looked his way. 'You were in there for less than a minute. That was hardly a *forensic* search.'

'Well, there's not much in there,' said Yates, shrugging once more. 'A lawnmower, a strimmer, a barbecue thing. Definitely no body.' He grinned. 'You'd have heard me screaming.'

Magnusson straightened up and sighed. 'Do it again, Yates. And this time move things and look behind them,'

'I thought I'm not meant to touch or move anything,' he replied.

She nodded at his gloves. 'Which is why you're wearing those. Have another go, please. And keep in mind that it's not just a whole body you're looking for. You're looking for spots, stains, smears... Even if you think a mark is just an oil stain, you give me a shout, all right?'

Yates nodded and headed back into the shed.

She turned to the sergeant standing guard beside the back door. He was shaking his head. 'Kids, eh?' he said, smirking.

Magnusson resumed shuffling her way along the lawn, gently teasing the sensor's nose to and fro until she approached the fence and the bushes at the edge. As she prepared to turn round and do the return length, the detector let off a soft buzz.

'Hello there,' she muttered, sweeping back over a patch of ground where the shaggy grass had pretty much given way to a bed of stones and dirt.

The detector buzzed again.

23

'Good evening, Andrew,' said Boyd, nodding as he entered the interview room for the second time that day. He set his coffee and his notes down on the table. 'How's your afternoon been?'

'Fucking boring,' replied Andrew. 'Look, when do I get to go home? Because this is getting beyond a joke. I've been kicking my heels down there for –'

'Twenty-two hours,' supplied Minter. 'And we've still got another couple of hours to enjoy your wonderful company.'

Andrew looked at Minter. 'Then I can go?'

Minter nodded. 'Indeed you can. Unless we have sufficient grounds to apply for another twelve hours of your precious time.'

'There aren't any *grounds*,' Andrew said tersely, 'because I don't know where Audrey's fucking well gone!'

Boyd took a sip of coffee and nodded at Minter to start the interview.

'For the record,' Minter began, 'this is the second interview with Andrew Hincher. The date is Tuesday the twenty-first of April; the time is 5.35 p.m. Present are interviewing officers DCI William Boyd and DI Steven Minter and interviewee Andrew Hincher.'

'Well now,' began Boyd. 'I've had a fascinating afternoon, Andrew.' He spread out his notes on the table. 'A number of bits of interesting information have drifted in while you've been kicking your heels downstairs.'

'You've found her?' Andrew replied.

'Unfortunately, no. But... let's run through what we *did* find, shall we?' Boyd said.

Andrew sighed. 'Christ... Fine. If we have to.'

This was not the response Boyd had been expecting. He'd been hoping to see a flash of panic dart across the man's face. Instead, he just looked irritated.

'So, let's start with Carol Docherty...'

'Don't tell me... you've finally found that crazy old bitch?' Andrew said, sitting up.

'No. But we have found her blood in your house,' Boyd replied. He was aware that he should have said that they'd found *someone's* blood. They weren't entirely sure if the faint stain on the floorboards was going to deliver a viable chromograph. But Hincher didn't need to know that.

'Where?' asked Hincher.

'On the floor of your lounge, under the rug. It appears that someone, a long time ago, had a jolly good go at trying to scrub the floor clean. Can you explain why her blood would be there, Andrew?'

He shook his head.

'Did you have a fight perhaps?' Boyd asked.

Another shake of the head.

Andrew hunched his shoulders. 'Carol and me had plenty of fights,' he said. 'She was a drug addict and an alcoholic, for God's sake!'

'We interviewed your daughter,' continued Boyd. 'She gave us a statement saying that she witnessed you pulling her mother's body across the lounge floor.'

'*What?*' Andrew exclaimed.

'She believes that you are responsible for Carol's disappearance,' Boyd added calmly. Now the bastard was finally starting to look uneasy.

'That's fucking crazy!' Andrew's eyes narrowed. 'She was five when Carol left us.' He shook his head in disbelief. 'She was *five*! Maybe she's misremembering. Or maybe it was a stupid nightmare!'

'And yet we have Carol's blood... in the very same room, and in the very same place that Rebecca claims to have seen you dragging Carol's body,' Boyd mused.

'Christ! If I *had* been dragging her, it would have been because she was smashed out of her skull!' Andrew countered. 'I can't tell you how many times I had to pick her up off the floor and –'

'Rebecca also claims,' Boyd cut in, 'that the day after she witnessed you dragging her mother... Carol left. And that she never saw or heard from her mother again.'

Andrew sighed. 'Little five-year-old Becca *claims* that, does she?' He laughed humourlessly. 'Silly little cow is messed up in the head, you know that, right? She's just as fucked up as her mother was.'

Okeke had briefed Boyd on her interview with Rebecca. She'd told him that she did seem quite fragile. That there were self-harm scars on her arms. Boyd knew that this detail, combined with the fact that the memory of her mother being dragged was from when she was five, made it unlikely that the CPS would deem it admissible evidence.

Boyd moved on. Magnusson was in Hincher's back garden right now, digging up a section of dirt in the corner.

His phone could buzz at any moment with news that she'd unearthed a body. In which case, Boyd would get his extra twelve hours and Hincher would almost certainly end up behind bars for Docherty's murder.

Until then, though, while the clock ticked down, there were other things for them to discuss.

'Let's talk about your alibi, Andrew,' said Boyd. 'You claimed you were at the Berkley Security conference at the same time that Audrey went missing.'

Andrew nodded. 'I was there.'

'That's great,' said Boyd, 'except we have CCTV footage of you ducking out of the event at just before ten a.m. Which, although it would have been tight, would have given you enough time to drive back down to Hastings and cross paths with Audrey. Wouldn't it? Did you plan this? Did you decide to use the conference as a good opportunity for an alibi? Did you murder Audrey?'

Andrew laughed. 'Are you fucking serious? I didn't duck out! I was there the whole fucking day!'

'But we have footage of you leaving,' said Boyd. 'And no footage of you returning.'

Hincher shook his head. 'Well, obviously, *mate*, it isn't me on your bloody footage! I was there all day Thursday and all day Friday... Right up until I got that call from your police sergeant!'

Boyd had studied the CCTV footage. Annoyingly, the quality wasn't that good. What he'd seen was the blurred image of a man who looked as though he *could be* Hincher – slim, silver haired, a trimmed beard. But it wouldn't hold up in court. They would need a CCTV trail that showed a clear, in-focus shot of Andrew's face, or an ANPR hit triggered by his van on the way down to Hastings.

Boyd sighed inwardly. An ANPR hit would also give him grounds for those extra twelve hours. He willed his phone to buzz.

'Moving on...' Boyd looked down at his notes. This one was the biggie. And if Hincher *was* involved in Audrey's disappearance, this was the piece of information that almost certainly would have him bleating for a solicitor. 'We've managed to recover Audrey's phone,' he said.

Andrew's eyes rounded. 'Her...'

'Her phone. We've found it. It was switched off and it was dumped,' Boyd told him.

'Huh?'

The expression on Andrew's face was one of genuine surprise. Boyd had witnessed enough fake-surprised faces in interrogation rooms over the years to recognise the real deal.

'Her phone was found tossed into the front garden of a house on Harold Street,' he said.

'That's the street just next to ours,' said Andrew.

'Quite,' replied Boyd. 'It was found very close to home. A witness claims to have seen a car stop very suddenly and observed somebody getting out and throwing something.' Boyd shuffled through his papers for Warren's notes.

'... *about one o'clock. I saw a blue vehicle come down my street and stop for a moment. A person climbed out, wearing some sort of hood and flung something. They did it quickly, then climbed back into the car...*'

'Jesus fucking Christ! That wasn't me!' Andrew replied.

'Because you were at that conference still, right?' offered Minter.

'Right!' Andrew said, now slightly panicked.

Boyd checked his watch. Their two hours were whittling

down. If Andrew didn't say something incriminating soon, they'd have to let him go. He was beginning to have a horrible suspicion they were barking up the wrong tree. He decided to go for one last hard push.

'Andrew,' he began, 'I'm going to tell you what I think happened. I think you planned this. I think you used the conference as an opportunity to set up an alibi. You stepped out as soon as you could and returned to Hastings and then I think you caught sight of Audrey on her way back to work, picked her up and drove her somewhere, where you murdered her and disposed of her body.' He sat back in his seat, watching Andrew intently.

Andrew once again did a sterling job of looking utterly astonished. '*What?* That's fucking crazy! Why the hell would I do that?'

'You tell me,' replied Boyd. 'Maybe she discovered something about Carol? Maybe you let something slip about Carol? Is that it? And she'd threatened to take it to the police?'

'I didn't do anything to Carol!' Andrew barked. 'And I didn't murder Audrey, for fuck's sake!'

He was looking rattled now.

'Or maybe it was simply for money?' said Minter. 'Is there a life insurance policy on her somewhere, mate? Is that it? Is she worth more to you dead than alive?'

Boyd felt his phone buzz in his pocket.

Ah... thank Christ, here it is. The clincher.

'We'll have to pause this for a moment,' he said, pulling his phone out of his pocket. 'Something's just come in.'

Boyd got up and headed for the door. He stepped into the hallway, closing the door behind him. He walked a few yards away and answered his phone.

'Evening, Boyd.' It was Sully. He sounded rather pleased with himself.

Boyd glanced down the hallway at the double doors to the stairwell and the CSI department beyond. The lazy arse was calling from there. 'What is it?'

'The Hinchers' PC,' replied Sully. 'Our Julian has just made a ver-r-r-y interesting discovery...'

∽

'My God,' Boyd muttered as Sully swiped through the various images he'd pulled up on the screen. 'That's... that's Audrey Hincher, isn't it?'

'No,' Sully replied. 'Those are AI *renditions* of her. Hincher used a dodgy bit of software called Unsafe Diffusion. Basically you train it up with photographs of your subject, then you can ask it to make pictures of them doing anything you want them to do.'

Sully enlarged one of the thumbnails. 'I mean, not only is that a truly unpleasant pose but it's anatomically impossible, I'd say.'

'But that looks... real,' said Minter, tilting his head to better study it.

'Until you examine the way those legs are articulating.' Sully glanced at the DI. 'Audrey Hincher's fifty-nine, right?'

Boyd nodded.

'And let's count those fingers, shall we?' Sully leant forward. 'I make it thirteen.' He turned to Minter. 'Unless she's a double-jointed mutant who's been moonlighting as a porn contortionist all her life, I think it's safe to say that's one hundred per cent a fake image.'

Boyd had seen enough. He gestured at Sully to close the picture. 'And you think this is *Liam's* handiwork?'

'That's my guess,' Sully said. 'These images were generated and stored on the family PC, which is located in the lounge if I remember correctly.'

Boyd nodded.

'And the timestamps on them are during the working day... when I presume both Audrey and Andrew Hincher are out working.'

Boyd couldn't help feeling decidedly queasy. 'But that's his *stepmum*, for Christ's sake,' he said.

Sully shrugged. 'To each his own.'

'She's nearly sixty and he's just...'

'Some lads his age have, shall we say, a thing for older ladies. Cougars, gilfs... call them what you will.' Sully glanced at Boyd. 'I presume you're familiar with the term *gilf*?'

'Yeah, yeah, yeah.' Then Boyd shook his head. 'Jesus.'

'I haven't shown you the worst ones,' added Sully. 'Some of his images I would describe as torture porn. Really quite unpleasant. I'm no psychologist, Boyd,' he continued, 'but if he was getting kicks out of this, then I'd say he's a pretty messed-up chappie.'

Boyd stroked his chin absently. He'd been hoping for a slam-dunk on Andrew this afternoon: a body in the back garden, an ANPR hit on his van racing back down to Hastings. A done deal. Neither of those had arrived and the clock had just about reached piss-or-get-off-the-potty time.

'Nothing from Magnusson yet?' he asked, without much hope.

Sully shook his head. 'They're still digging around the garden. They haven't found anything yet as far as I know. She said the methane detector had picked up something, but quite honestly that could be anything from a dead cat to a bag of kitchen waste.'

It was decision time. Andrew Hincher would be returned to his cell for dinner and, unless something earth-shattering turned up in the next hour, he'd be free to go by the time he'd scraped the plastic tray clean.

'I'm not a gambling man,' said Sully, raising a brow, 'but I'd put a tenner down that you've got the wrong Hincher.'

24

Andrew Hincher pushed his way past the pair of paps who were still lingering outside his house. 'Fuck off!' he snarled as he pulled his door keys out.

'Andy?' one of them called out as Andrew stepped up to his front door. 'Did you do it, mate? Did you murder your wife?'

'I said, *Fuck off!*' Andrew barked over his shoulder as he shoved the key into the lock and pushed the door open. He slammed it quickly behind him.

'I'm home!' he shouted out of habit. It was his muscle-memory response on closing the front door. Only this time there was no sound of crockery being set down, no oven door slamming shut, no swish-slap, swish-slap of slippers on lino as Audrey bustled through from the kitchen into the hallway to dutifully greet him.

The old girl was usually eager to see him. She'd peck him on the cheek and ask him how his day had been. She'd listen to him grumble about customers and installation jobs that had taken longer than he'd bargained for.

Though she quickly became annoying, he had to admit he missed those first few minutes of walking into a house with the smell of dinner on the go and someone eager to listen to him prattle on about his day. She was like a well-behaved Labrador.

Audrey might not be the most stimulating of company – her eyes were always cast down to her hands or her feet, her conversation was limited, her opinions on everything were little more than a softly spoken echo of his – but she did a passable job of making his house feel like a home.

She'd been gone for nearly a week now and the place was starting to look, and smell, like a shithole. He could hear the thump of his son's music upstairs and he could smell the earthy, meaty odour of weed.

Andrew gritted his teeth. 'LIAM!' he yelled. 'How many bloody times have I told you? Keep the smoking to your room!'

Liam's bedroom door cracked open and the thump of music spilled out. The door closed again, locking away the awful sound, and Liam appeared at the top of the stairs in his olive-coloured hoodie and grubby baggy jeans, the crotch almost down to his knees.

'You're back?' he mumbled.

'Yeah, I'm back, thank fucking Christ!' Andrew said, wandering away from the stairs and into the kitchen. 'You going to make us a brew or what?'

Liam thumped down the stairs and followed him into the kitchen. He obediently slapped the kettle on and began the hunt for a teabag and some in-date milk.

'Jesus, Liam, you won't believe the fucking questions they were asking me!' Andrew said. 'You know what? They actually accused me of murdering Audrey! Can you believe it?'

Liam pulled the last couple of clean mugs from a cupboard. The rest were in the washing-up bowl, sitting in greasy water that had started to grow a skin at the edges.

'They accused me of sneaking back from the conference, snatching her in the high street, driving her somewhere, murdering her and then dumping her bloody body!'

Liam hunched his shoulders. 'That's crazy.'

'I mean, God knows how that's going to affect my work,' Andrew went on. 'I bet I'm going to lose a whole load of jobs as a result of this. Who wants someone accused of murder round their house to put in a burglar alarm, right?'

'Right,' replied Liam limply.

'Is that all you can say?' Andrew shook his head.

'Dad, they took everything,' said Liam. 'Even the PC downstairs.'

'I know,' replied Andrew, foraging in a cupboard for something to eat. 'We'll get it all back, when they've finished with it... eventually. Sandwich?'

Liam shook his head.

'You all right there, son?' Liam seemed paler than usual, distracted. 'Are you coming down with something?' Andrew asked.

'I... feel a bit sick,' Liam said quietly.

Andrew clamped his lips. 'It's probably that weird shit you keep smoking. I could smell it as soon as I came in. How many times have I told you? Keep it to your bloody room and keep the bloody window open.'

'Dad...'

Andrew uncapped some Marmite and pulled some Flora out of the fridge. 'What?'

'I'm scared.'

'Huh?' Andrew turned to him. He *did* look worried. Liam's normally sullen face had a limited range of expressions: pissed off, bored, sulky... 'Scared' was something Andrew hadn't seen on the boy's face in a long while.

'You're scared? Why?' Andrew asked him.

'I think...' Liam was chewing the side of his thumbnail, a habit that Andrew had thought he'd grown out of. 'I think... the police might be coming for me next.'

'What? Why the hell would they want to do that?'

Liam shrugged. 'I... uh... I've done someth–'

The doorbell rang, swiftly followed by the sound of a muffled voice calling, 'Police!'

'Oh, shit,' whispered Liam.

Andrew saw his son's face blanch even more. 'Liam? What the fuck have you done?'

Liam turned and disappeared out of the kitchen. Andrew thought he'd gone to answer the door, but he heard the utility-room door slam.

Shit. He's run away?

The doorbell rang again, followed by an insistent knocking. Briefly, the faintest trace of paternal defiance held him from answering the door. But then a stronger instinct of self-preservation drove him out of the kitchen. He was damned if these bastards were going to re-arrest him for obstruction of justice.

What the fuck has that stupid idiot boy gone and done now?

He opened the front door to reveal one of the bearded detectives who'd been tormenting him earlier.

'Where's Liam?' asked Boyd.

Andrew Hincher took a step back to let them in. 'He's done a runner out the back,' he said.

Boyd thumbed his radio. 'Minter, Rajan. Target's escaped out the back!'

∽

LIAM SPRINTED to the bottom of the garden, sidestepping the trenches the forensics people had been digging earlier that afternoon. He wrenched the gate open and sped into the rat-run walkway beyond.

His mind was a blur of utter panic and for a second he couldn't figure out which way was the quickest to Harold Street, which was where his tatty old Mini Cooper was parked.

'Police! Stop!'

He checked over his shoulder through the open gate at two plain-clothed coppers – both bearded, one who looked a bit like Rylan off the telly, the other who looked like that comedian Ranga-something... and both charging towards him.

Left. Left. Left! His brain sprang into action. He spun on his heels and scrambled along the cluttered assault course of garden waste, wheelie bins and fly-tipped bric-a-brac, dimly aware that at the far end of the rat run he may well race straight into the waiting arms of another copper.

As he ran, slipping in dog muck that soiled his spotless Sketchers, he could hear the slapping of footsteps on mud behind him, closing in rapidly. He pulled a wheelie bin over to slow them down and carried on towards the far end.

A moment later, he emerged onto Harold Street, relieved to see that the police hadn't figured out his escape route. His Mini Cooper was fifty yards down the street, wedged tightly between two other cars, in the tiny space he'd managed to squeeze into yesterday. As he sprinted towards it, he had a brief moment of earth-opening-beneath-his-feet panic. His car keys! Where were his car keys?

He thrust a hand deep into his hoodie pocket; there was nothing. *Fuck. Fuck. Fuck.* He dug into his jeans pockets, feeling the cylinder of his vape, the case of his earbuds and then, just as he was beginning to despair, he felt the plastic Bart Simpson head of his key fob.

He pulled his car keys out and rammed them into the door of his Mini. At the same time, he heard the police calling his name from up the street, demanding he stay where he was.

Fuck that.

Fuck them arresting him and throwing him in the clink for the rest of his life. Because that's what they were going to do, right? When they found all that stuff on the PC. And he knew they would find it, no matter how well he'd hidden it.

He jumped into the car, rammed the key into the ignition and started it up. In the wing mirror, he could see the two coppers now sprinting down the pavement towards him.

Liam threw his car into reverse, clunking hard against the van parked behind him, then slammed into the Prius in front, spinning the steering wheel into a hard lock and grinding against the rear end of the Prius as he lurched into the narrow road and jerked forward down Harold Street, grateful that there wasn't another vehicle coming the other way. He gunned the accelerator, leaving a plume of exhaust in his wake as he careered to the end of the street and turned right towards the seafront.

Minter and Rajan came to a halt. Rajan was wheezing like a hob kettle. Minter, panting hard, was already fumbling on his belt for his radio.

'Minter!' he began, then sucked in some air. 'Liam's got away in a car. Light blue Mini Cooper, registration BN19 RVF. He's turned right, heading to the seafront.'

25

Okeke could hear the radio chatter coming from her jacket pocket. Minter and Rajan, the muppets, had lost Liam. The irritation in Minter's voice was clear – he was very much pissed off that he'd lost out in a hundred-metre dash to some kid who looked as though he rarely moved from the sofa. That was going to bug Minter big time – and was something she'd enjoy ragging him about later.

At least he'd got the number plate, which would soon be pinging up on the screen of any patrol cars that were out and about in town. And, of course, it would also be pinging away on ANPR as Liam Hincher whizzed past the many cameras in the area. They'd have him soon enough.

'Ewww, that's disgusting...'

Okeke turned to see Warren holding a Pot Noodle. He showed her the skin of fungus growing inside.

Liam's bedroom was exactly what she'd been expecting: dirty, messy and smelly. The floor was an obstacle course of balled-up socks, noxious pants and crisp packets. His clothes spilled from drawers like passengers frantically escaping the *Titanic.*

'I want phones, tablets, games consoles, laptops and memory sticks,' she reminded him.

'I know, I know,' replied Warren. 'The problem is, looking for them requires actually moving things... touching stuff.'

'Don't be such a girl,' Okeke retorted.

She glanced around the room, making a mental map of it, while Yates took pictures of it with his phone for their evidence dump. The posters tacked on the walls suggested that Liam's taste leaned towards the macabre and dark. They were mostly of horror movies – 'video nasties', the tabloids of another time would have called them: *Saw X, Chucky, Five Nights at Freddy's.*

She wondered what kind of grisly shit they were going to find stashed away on his bedroom tech. If he'd been bold enough to store rape and torture-fantasy images on the PC downstairs, God knows what delights he'd kept for his personal pleasure up in his room.

The images she'd glimpsed back at the station were the stuff of nightmares. Even though she knew they were computer-generated images, photo-realistic depictions of events that had never happened, they had still taken her breath away. The boy would have had to tell the AI exactly what he'd wanted... in great detail. Over and over, refining what he was after. Liam clearly not only harboured a fantasy about his stepmother but also doing some pretty awful things with her body too.

∼

BOYD HAD Andrew Hincher sitting at the table in the kitchen and a uniformed officer standing guard beside the back door, just in case – like father, like son – he decided to bolt out of it.

'So, come on, Andrew... where's your boy likely to be heading?' Boyd asked.

Andrew shook his head. 'I dunno.'

'Does he have any friends locally? Is there any other family he'd go to?'

'No,' Andrew replied. 'Not family anyway. He certainly wouldn't go to Becca.'

'What about mates?' Boyd persisted.

'I... I don't really know of any. If he has any, they're probably online friends... He was always gaming and shit-chatting with people, but I've never actually seen him with any actual friends.' He scowled. 'Why the fuck have you lot come looking for my boy anyway? Did you find something? What exactly has he done?'

'That's what we want to find out,' Boyd answered. 'What about girlfriends? Does he have one?'

Andrew made a *pffft* noise. 'I don't think he's ever had one. Not one he's brought home for me to meet, at least.' He looked at Boyd. 'I always thought he might be gay.'

Boyd shook his head. Definitely not if Liam's fantasy portfolio was anything to go by.

'You told us earlier that Liam and Audrey didn't get on,' Boyd said.

Andrew nodded. 'They hardly ever spoke, to be honest.' He gave Boyd a you-know-how-it-is smile. 'You know what kids his age are like. It's almost impossible to get a coherent sentence out of the little brats, eh?'

'He's not a little brat, though, is he?' Boyd pointed out. 'He's twenty-three.'

'Yeah. So?' Andrew shrugged. 'He's not all there.'

Now there was an understatement if ever Boyd had heard one.

'He's got a car,' said Boyd. 'How can he afford a car if he doesn't work?'

'We helped him out with a cheap one. I thought it might make it easier for him to go find a job. Look...' Andrew paused. 'What's going on? What do you know? Just tell me what's he gone and done!'

Boyd looked at him. 'I think he may well be the reason Audrey's missing.'

26

Okeke opened the bottle of cheap prosecco that she'd found in the fridge. Frankly, though, she could have done with something a bit harder than 9.5%. Today had been a long day and coming home to an empty house to stare at her phone, waiting through another night, hoping to hear from Jay, wasn't something she was prepared to do sober.

The phone buzzed in her hand and the tiny tickle of hope that flared inside her was quickly squashed when she saw it was Karl. She answered anyway – he might have heard something from Jay.

'Heard anything?' was her greeting to him.

'No, sorry, Sam. Still nothing,' Karl said.

'Fuck.'

'Yeah.' He sighed. 'I've been trawling through various websites to see if his name has turned up anywhere.'

'Trawling? You mean hacking?' Okeke said.

'Call it *fishing*... ' he replied. 'The back doors are there to be pushed open for a quick look around.'

'And there's nothing at all?' she said.

'Nuh. Doesn't mean to say he's not on some cop's database, though,' Karl said. 'They're not as centralised over there as we are.'

'Jesus... I know he's in trouble, Karl. He'd have called me if he could, I'm sure,' Okeke said. 'I mean, I know he was pissed off with me and was on some mission to prove something, but even so –'

'Yeah, he'd have called you. Or me, if he needed help,' Karl agreed.

She chugged a mouthful of the cheap fizz. 'So what the hell am I supposed to think that means? That he's –'

'Busy, Sam. He's busy,' Karl cut in. 'Like I said last time, he made a big thing of telling me his job was meant to be totally off the radar. He didn't give me any details. He was pretty serious about the whole confidentiality thing.'

'He didn't give me much either,' she said.

Some rich Brit with an American trophy wife who he suspected was cheating on him. That's all Jay had volunteered. That and some puffed-up BS that he intended to be 'proper professional' about the job. No names. No details. Get the job done and return home with a shit ton of cash, a smug smile and a huge 'I told you so' for her.

'Look, Sam. He's a big boy. He can take care of himself,' Karl said.

'No, Karl, he's not,' she countered. 'He's a big gullible idiot who's perfectly capable of walking himself into a mess that he can't get out of.'

'Give him some credit, Sam.'

'Really?' she snapped. 'And how long am I supposed to wait before I'm allowed to do something?'

'If you start ringing around... you'll probably *get* him into trouble,' Karl pointed out. 'You do realise that, right?'

She sighed. The one person she most wanted to call was

this Ronni character – the woman who'd set him up for the job. But that first name was all she had.

'I could try the British Embassy,' she ventured.

'No, that's a bad, bad idea,' replied Karl. 'Because then *they'd* make some calls and get him into trouble. Listen... he said this job was three months, yeah? So, he's already well into it.'

She set her glass down. 'And I'm supposed to just sit tight and wait?'

'Yes,' said Karl. 'Unless you want to be the one who gets him arrested for working when he shouldn't be. For entering the US under false pretences. The authorities don't take well to that, you know.'

'He'd get what? A travel ban and a fine?' she said.

'No, no, no. Come on. You said yourself he's on a frigging watch list. As are you. They're really bloody twitchy about that kind of thing over there. If you start making calls, it's going to land you both in hot water. To be honest, I'm surprised that his entering the US didn't trigger a visit from your spooks.'

Okeke had been too. In fact, she'd been surprised he'd managed to even leave the UK in the first place.

'Look, Sam... it's down to you. If you're really that worried about his welfare, then make some calls... but, I promise you, all you'll be doing is drawing attention to him.'

'Christ...' She sighed. 'He's an idiot.'

She heard Karl huff along with that. 'He has his moments.'

27

Boyd watched them both being carried out, to a song by Take That. Noah's coffin on top of Julia's so that they could be close to each other. As the six pallbearers – five of his colleagues from work and Paul, his friend from school, best man at his wedding and, in recent years, an increasingly distant friend – slowly walked them towards the drapes and out of view, Boyd found himself wondering how heavy the load must be for them, two coffins instead of one.

He could feel Emma shuddering in the seat beside him. He put an arm around her shoulders and pulled her close, relieved that she was sobbing, letting the pain out. He so wished he was able to do the same, but he felt numb, detached from the whole thing, like he was viewing it as a video call from another continent.

Beyond Emma sat Mum and Dad, smartly dressed and rigid in their seats, their sun-leathered faces composed and still, eyes on the coffins with barely a twitch or quiver of emotion. That was their generation, he supposed – stiff upper lip and all that. But it pissed him off mightily. Not a single tear for their daughter-in-law or grandson.

The rest of the seats behind him were filled with a mixture of his colleagues from work, Julia's friends and some mums from Noah's primary school. The room was filled, at least. Which was gratifying. There was nothing sadder than a sparsely attended funeral service.

He watched as the two leading bearers slowly stepped into the darkness beyond the drapes as Take That sang a song that no one but Julia seemed to have ever heard of – 'Wooden Boat'. The words of the final verse suddenly seemed to be infused with prescience and meaning. Julia had loved that song. Their best, she'd said... *If I ever die before you, Bill, you'd better play that one for me, okay?*

And it *was* the perfect choice. As the song played out and the coffins disappeared into the darkness, he managed to smile at the perfect timing of the moment. Then his fucking phone began to buzz insistently and loudly, filling the hall with the noise.

He fumbled in his pockets, trying to find the bloody thing to kill the sound.

He tried every damned pocket in his jacket, his trousers, his waistcoat...

Buzz... Buzz... Buzz...

The loud pulses obliterated the final fading cadence of the song.

Ruining everything...

Destroying his very last moment with his wife and son...

Buzz... Buzz... Buzz...

∾

The Vanishing

BOYD FELT Ozzie's wet tongue rubbing across his nose, probing his lips and nostrils. He opened his eyes and realised it was ridiculously early, still dark. The phone on his side table was buzzing and Ozzie, bless his little cotton socks, was doing his best to wake him up to take the call.

'Easy, mate, easy... I'm awake. I'm awake,' he muttered softly, gently pushing Ozzie away from his face.

He reached out, fumbling for the phone in the gloom, careful not to knock his glass of water and trigger a crisis that would necessitate switching his bedside light. He really didn't want to wake Charlotte up. His fingers found the buzzing phone. He picked it up and swiped to answer it.

'Boyd,' he announced with a whisper.

'Sorry, Boyd, were you asleep?' It was DI Abbott.

He wiped gunk from his eyes and glanced at the time on the screen. 'Of course I was. It's five seventeen in the morning.' He sighed. He was pissed off to be woken so early, but also relieved that it had pulled him out of that dream. 'What's the call for?' he asked.

'They've got him. Liam Hincher's in custody,' Abbot said.

'Right, good news... Thanks for letting me know,' Boyd said, and ended the call. He set the phone down on his bare chest, not sure whether he should try to get back to sleep for another couple of hours or get up.

He opted for the latter, quietly extracting himself from the bed. He slid his feet into a pair of slippers and grabbed his dressing gown. As quietly as possible, he led Ozzie downstairs by the pale light of his phone screen, along the hall, through the dining room and into the kitchen. He snapped the light on, filled the kettle and flicked it on.

As it gently began to gurgle and hiss, he looked out of the kitchen window and up at the sky. It was just light enough that he could see the swooping silhouettes of gulls heading towards the dash of sea visible between the rooftops on the far side of Ashburnham Road.

That dream was a brand-new one – his sleeping mind usually gravitated towards the crash and his final few words with Julia as she slowly slipped away in the driver's seat of her mangled car. His unconscious loved playing that memory again and again for him. But now it seemed it had found another one to dust off and play on the dream jukebox. The funeral.

The kettle clicked off, and Boyd made himself a strong black coffee to blow the cobwebs and the memories away.

'Early start it is then, mate,' he muttered to Ozzie.

Ozzie seemed to be perfectly okay with that. An early start meant an early breakfast.

'Thanks a bunch, Abbott,' Boyd added under his breath.

28

Boyd arrived at the station just before 8 a.m. He read up on Liam's arrest report, which had been apparently typed by a police sergeant wearing boxing gloves and who possessed a limited vocabulary and had been in a hurry to finish their shift.

Liam's car had triggered an ANPR camera along the A259, heading towards Kent. Boyd wondered why Liam had fled Hastings in that direction: did he have a friend over that way? Another thought occurred to him. The Romney Marshes and Jury's Gap beach were that way. Might Liam have been heading there? To check Audrey's body was properly concealed, perhaps? Boyd jotted that thought down on his pad, one of many others that he was intending to discuss with the lad this morning, once Liam had had his mandatory rest period and been served his breakfast, of course.

The police officers who'd booked him had been returning from a call out to Winchelsea. They'd been driving the other way when their patrol car's on-board recognition system had flagged the Mini Cooper as *wanted*. The lights had gone on, they'd done a U-turn and pulled

Liam over within minutes. The reporting sergeant had noted that the young man had not tried to escape and had pulled over. He'd also noted that Liam had, however, been 'very agitated' as they'd cautioned and cuffed him, and had repeatedly claimed that he 'wasn't the one who done in his stepmum'.

Next, Boyd reviewed Okeke's notes on Liam's bedroom search and the pictures that Yates had taken of it.

'Christ,' muttered Boyd as he skipped through the images. He'd seen enough messy lads' rooms over the course of his career, and this one ranked right up there with the worst of them. Among other things, Yates had photographed the posters and a small bedside bin that was almost overflowing with scrunched-up tissues, empty Red Bull cans and crisp packets – though more seemed to be on the floor than in the bin.

The evidence that had been bagged, tagged and entered in the evidence log by Okeke included the contents of the bin, a pair of trainers that appeared to have streaks of blood on them, Liam's phone, a laptop, a games console and some other items of clothing that had dark unidentifiable stains on them. Possible blood markers?

He was just starting on the CSI update submitted by Sully when Sutherland's chirpy voice echoed across the floor. 'Morning, Boyd. You're in early!'

'Morning,' he replied. 'Liam Hincher was arrested last night. I'm just reviewing the notes.'

'Ah, good.' Sutherland headed towards Boyd's desk. 'Is this about the missing woman?'

Boyd nodded.

'What did the house search give us on the lad?' Sutherland asked.

'More of that AI porn,' Boyd said.

'Featuring his stepmother?' Sutherland ventured.

Boyd nodded again.

Sutherland grimaced. 'Oh, the god-awful things these kids can produce with their computers these days, eh? And what about Andrew Hincher? Have you ruled him out now?'

'No. He's still got an alibi that doesn't stack up. But it's Liam who we're focusing on for the moment.'

Sutherland adjusted his glasses. 'If it turns out the lad did it, the press will –'

'Have a field day, I know.' Boyd could well imagine – the story would be exactly the sort of thing the tabloid trolls would be looking for: *Son's Porn Addiction Leads to Murder of Stepmother! Monster Plans Murder in his Bedroom! AI Video Nasties Turns Hoodie to Horror!*

'Are you interviewing him later?' said Sutherland.

'With Minter,' replied Boyd. 'I'm aiming for about ten.'

'And will you have an update for the press?'

'If there's enough in the interview to charge him,' Boyd said. 'Or if Sully et al find anything compelling on his phone, then, yup, I suppose we'll have to put something out there later on today. Before they start coming up with their own stories.'

The double doors of CID clattered open and a dishevelled and tired-looking Okeke wandered in. She had the appearance of a woman who'd slept in a wheelie bin.

'You look rough, Sam,' said Boyd.

'Thanks,' she replied limply as she dumped her jacket and bag on her desk. 'I didn't get much in the way of sleep last night.'

'Jay?' Boyd asked.

'Yes, Jay,' she replied.

'Is that your big strapping fellow?' asked Sutherland.

She nodded.

'What's up with him, then?' said Sutherland.

'It's... uh, it's a bit complicated, sir,' she replied.

Sutherland took the none-of-his-business hint and nodded. 'Well, I'll... I'm off to the canteen, Boyd. I'll catch up with you later.'

'Right you are,' said Boyd.

He and Okeke watched Sutherland go to his office, dump his things and return to the double doors and the stairwell.

'Still radio silence from Jay?' Boyd asked.

She nodded. 'I'm past thinking he's just being an arsehole and now I'm starting to get worried.'

'He's a big boy,' said Boyd. 'He can take care of himself.'

'I'm glad you think so. I'm not so sure,' she said.

Boyd decided to change the subject. 'Do you know if Sully or Mags are on those trainers and the other bits and piece of forensic you picked up last night?'

'I've just got in. I guess so,' Okeke said.

'Can I get you to hold Sully's feet to the fire on those? We've got Liam for a couple of days at most. If Ellessey can do a quick turnaround while we still have him in custody...'

She nodded. 'I'll see what I can do.'

29

The custody officer led Liam into the interview room, sat him down and placed a paper cup of coffee and a Twix on the table in front of him, before leaving the room. Liam stared at the floor the whole time.

Boyd nodded to Minter, who placed his notepad on the table and reached for the interview recorder.

'Just a sec,' said Boyd. 'Liam...'

The young man's eyes remained cast down.

'Liam,' said Boyd again, more gently this time. 'Son... this is going to be a recorded interview and we're going to be talking about some very difficult things. I want you to know before we start that the more honest you are with us, the better it will be for you in the long run, do you understand?'

Liam nodded silently. Despite being in his early twenties, he looked like a small boy who'd been dragged into an after-school meeting with his headmaster.

Boyd nodded once more at Minter to proceed. Minter hit the record button. 'The date is Wednesday the twenty-fourth of April and the time is 10.03 a.m. Present in the room are interviewing officers DI Steven Minter and DCI William Boyd, and interviewee Liam Hincher.'

Boyd looked down at his notepad. 'I've got a simple question to start with, Liam... Why did you run from us yesterday?'

The young man's eyes slowly lifted from the floor to meet Boyd's. 'I was scared, all right?'

'And why were you scared?' Boyd asked.

'Because... you lot came charging in for me,' said Liam.

'We didn't exactly charge in, sunshine,' said Minter.

Boyd nudged him beneath the table. 'We knocked with a warrant, Liam. That's how it's done. But you were off and running before we'd even stepped through the front door.'

'I was scared,' Liam repeated.

'You were scared because...' Boyd prompted.

Liam's eyes dropped down.

'Because you guessed we'd found those images on the PC... Is that it? Boyd said.

Liam remained silent.

Boyd kept his eyes on him. 'Liam?'

He nodded. 'They're illegal, aren't they?'

On that particular point, Boyd wasn't entirely sure. The images were horrific, that was for certain, but he'd been assured by Sully and his technical whizz Julian that they were definitely artificial. Boyd would have missed the small details that screamed 'AI' if he'd viewed the images alone. They'd looked so authentic. He would have sworn that he was staring at the trophy pics of some vile sadist. Not only had he clearly recognised Audrey's face but it had been contorted in agony. Perhaps the only giveaway was that each image had been perfectly lit and perfectly in focus, revealing every grisly detail.

'I'll be honest with you, lad, I don't know,' Boyd said. 'I'm not sure the law has caught up with AI-generated images yet, but I could be wrong. If you'd shared them, then yes... I think you'd be in a lot of trouble.'

'How did you get your mum's face into those images?' asked Minter.

'She's not my mum,' replied Liam.

'Audrey's face, then,' said Minter.

Liam shrugged. 'From family snaps, all right?'

Boyd wasn't convinced by that. One thing there seemed to be a paucity of in the Hincher household were 'family snaps'. There were, however, on Liam's iPhone plenty of images of Audrey's face that seemed as though they had been taken without her knowledge: pictures of her watching the telly with a mug of tea in her hand, photos of her in the kitchen preparing dinner, washing dishes. She wasn't smiling for the camera in any of them.

'And what?' continued Minter. 'You cut and paste them into your snuff porn, eh?'

Liam stared at him as though he was an idiot. 'No. You load them in as visual prompts. You, have to *train* the AI to be able to recreate a face.'

Minter nodded. 'Ah, I see.'

Boyd wondered if Minter actually did see. Technical nerdery really wasn't his thing.

'Can I ask you why you created all those images, Liam?' asked Boyd.

Liam's eyes shot down again – his version of a 'No comment'.

'Liam?' prodded Boyd. 'It's really important that we understand why you did this. We know those images aren't real. We know that what happened in the images hasn't necessarily happened to Audrey in real life, but we need to know... *why?* Why did you make them?'

Liam shook his head.

'Are you sexually attracted to her?' asked Minter.

'Fuck off,' Liam muttered.

'Was it a hate thing?' said Minter. 'A revenge thing?'

Liam glared at him. 'It was for jokes, right? Just... just for a laugh, okay?'

'She's naked or partially naked in most of those images, matey,' pressed Minter. 'I'd say you were making those to add to your little wank bank, eh?'

Boyd glanced noticeably at the recording machine to remind Minter that any or all this could end up being replayed in a courtroom.

'There's a clear sexual element to them,' said Boyd. 'And we've recovered the text prompts you used to generate them. Shall I read one or two out?'

Liam stared at him, eyes wide, clearly horrified that his descriptions and requests had somehow been baked into the under-the-hood data of his slideshow.

'*The woman is tied down to a kitchen table, stripped completely naked, legs stretched wide apart and a –*'

'Stop! Please stop!' snapped Liam.

Boyd paused. 'All right. But you recognise those words, don't you? That's something that you entered into the prompt box, isn't it?'

Liam's cheeks were colouring.

'Let's take that as a yes,' said Boyd. He leant forward. 'I think it's safe to say, Liam, that there's an... interest in her there, right?'

'You wanted to see her naked,' added Minter, 'and violated.'

'I don't want to talk about this. I was just...' Liam began.

'Just what?' Boyd said.

'I was just playing around with the software,' Liam finished.

Minter huffed. 'I'd imagine most lads your age would be hoping to see Taylor Swift or Miley –'

Boyd nudged his foot under the table again. 'Let's move on. We've also found some interesting search phrases that have been recently typed on that same computer. "How to hide a body", "how to dispose of a human body"... Stuff like that. Do you want to explain to us why you were looking these things up?'

'It wasn't me,' Liam replied.

'Really? Well, judging by what we found on the computer, it would seem that you are the main user...'

'No.' He shook his head. 'Dad does his accounts on there too. And Audrey sometimes used... *uses* it.'

'So you're suggesting one of them might have tapped in those searches?' Boyd said.

Liam nodded. 'Well, they must have, because it wasn't me!'

Boyd smiled. 'Okay, okay... Well, that's something we can probably check.' He looked at Minter.

'Liam,' Minter began, 'where were you heading in your car last night? You were caught speeding straight out of Hastings and on your way to Kent. What was that all about, eh?'

'I told you... I was scared,' Liam said.

'Is there someone you know over there?' Minter went on. 'A friend? A buddy?'

Liam reached for his coffee and took a sip.

'Or was there something you were going to check on?' Minter asked.

'What do you mean?' Liam said warily.

Minter puffed his cheeks and sighed. 'Well, you tell me,

sunshine. It looked like someplace you were very keen to get to.'

The young man's face suddenly froze. Boyd could see that he'd finally started to put the pieces together in his head.

'Oh my God,' he blurted out. 'You... you... think I *killed* her?'

~

SULLY AND MAGNUSSON finished pulling on their overalls and gloves, then stood, hands on hips, to appraise Liam Hincher's battered Mini Cooper.

'Well, he's clearly not a proud owner,' said Sully, circling the car and taking in the mud-spattered wheel arches and sides, a collection of scrapes and dints on the front and the grime of many years encrusted on its rear.

'I believe the technical term is a shed on wheels,' Magnusson told him. 'So, who's doing what, Kevin?'

'I want eyeballs and fingers inside and out, then swabs from the handles, steering wheel, gear stick and handbrake for starters,' Sully said.

She looked at him. 'Swabs? Really, Kevin?'

He met her stare, surprised by the question. 'Of course, Karen. Why wouldn't we?'

She frowned. 'What's the point? We know we'll get Liam, and we know we'll get Audrey, since he's supposedly given her lifts to work, and finding Andrew won't be a big surprise either.'

'Thoroughness is the point,' Sully replied archly.

'And it's an unnecessary expense. That's going to be about six thousand pounds just to tell us what we already know,' she pointed out.

'That's Sutherland's problem, not ours,' Sully replied. 'I'd rather demonstrate that we did our jobs thoroughly than find myself in a courtroom telling some defence barrister that we skipped an important step because we wanted to save a bob or two.'

Magnusson sucked in air. 'Well, rather you than me submitting the expenses to Sutherland, then.'

'He can have his embolism, but I'd rather not be branded a half-a-job.' Sully clapped his gloved hands together. 'Come on then, Karen my lovely, shall we get this party started?'

She nodded. 'I'll work the inside. You can do the boot.'

∽

'WHY THE FUCK would I *murder* her?'

Minter shrugged. 'I dunno... Let me see... Maybe she stumbled across your torture porn when she used the computer to buy something on Amazon? Maybe you got careless? Left a search tab or a folder open?'

'*What?*' Liam exclaimed.

'Maybe she confronted you about it, eh?' continued Minter, 'and said she was going to tell your dad or even take it to the police? How's that for a theory? Am I getting warm?'

'What? No. No... that's...' Liam trailed off.

'Or perhaps you just got bored of whacking off over images of what you'd like to do to her and decided you wanted to do it for real?' Minter said.

Boyd let Minter run with these theories. Liam Hincher was looking increasingly like a deer caught in the headlights of a truck and – given that the lad had yet to realise he could be 'no commenting' his way through Minter's assertions, plus the fact that it was all being recorded, post caution – there could be some useful stuff here to use down the line.'

'Well, anyway, that's what I think has happened, Liam. I think she found your stash, confronted you about it and said she was going to tell your dad when he got home, and the police. So what did you do? You decided to go and find her the next day. You picked her up at lunchtime... Maybe with some offer to drive her back to work? Or maybe you asked if she could jump into your car so you could talk about what she'd found on the computer?'

'No,' replied Liam, shaking his head vigorously. 'No, that didn't happen!'

'And then you drove her somewhere out of the way...' Minter went on. 'Perhaps the conversation got out of hand and you threatened her? Or hit her?'

'Or maybe you planned to kill her all along,' added Boyd. 'Which explains those searches on how to dispose of a body?'

'No! NO! That's not –' Liam wailed.

'Is that where you were off to last night?' asked Minter. 'To make sure, wherever you'd dumped her, she was properly hidden and wouldn't be found?'

'No! I told you! I was scared... I was –' Liam suddenly stopped mid-sentence. 'I'm not saying anything else. I want to go home now.'

Boyd shook his head slowly. 'I'm sorry, Liam – that's not how this works.'

'I want a lawyer then!' he snapped. 'I get one if I ask for one, right? For free?'

'You're officially asking for legal representation, are you?' Boyd asked.

'Yeah! I am. I want a lawyer right now!' Liam said.

Boyd nodded. 'All right then. The interview is suspended...'

Minter leant across to the recording machine. 'Interview with Liam Hincher suspended at 10.37 a.m.'

∽

'Hello, hello, hello,' chimed Sully softly.

Magnusson's head emerged from the driver's side of the Mini Cooper. 'Have you found something?'

Sully came round the side of the car and held something up for her to see. 'One pair of coral-pink, size-fourteen knickers from Marks and Spencer's,' he said.

Magnusson climbed out and stared at them, dangling from Sully's fingers like a limp flag. 'Oh, my.'

'It's not looking good for young Liam, I'd say.' Sully pulled out a forensics bag and gently dropped the item of underwear inside before sealing it up.

'It doesn't mean he took them right off her,' Magnusson replied. 'He might have pinched them from the laundry basket or something.'

'Well now, if there's a speck of her blood or his semen on them, I'd say that young man's going down,' Sully said.

'If it's just semen...' Magnusson looked at him cautiously. 'He could argue he nicked them and, let's say... masturbated over them?'

Sully clucked his tongue. 'Again, it's not a good look for him, though, is it?'

'*Blood*, Sully... We need her blood on them, or somewhere in the car – only *then*, Mr Sullivan, can we crack open a bottle of bubbly.'

She could see his eyes crinkling above his mask. He was

smiling. 'Oh, I think the odds of us finding a blood deposit somewhere in there have just increased tenfold.'

'Don't count your chickens, Kevin...' she cautioned him.

Magnusson ducked back inside the car, bumping her head on the frame as she did so. 'Ow!' she muttered, rubbing her scalp. Minis, she decided, must have been specifically designed for hobbits and not for normal-sized folk wearing bulky overalls.

She resumed picking her way through the rubbish around the seats. It appeared that Liam Hincher was a big fan of McDonald's drive-through service: the rear seat and foot well were both cluttered with brown paper bags and empty cardboard cartons. She carefully picked them all out and stuffed them into a large forensics bag. They could be checked later and swabbed if necessary. With the back clear of clutter, she scanned for any marks or stains that might warrant a closer look, but there was nothing that seemed unusual.

She then focused her attention on the front seats. There was a small amount of rubbish in the passenger-side foot well, which she bagged up too. She'd just started examining the rubbish in the door pocket when she spotted a small cluster of dark dots.

'Oooh, hello there,' she muttered.

Magnusson reached into her kit bag, pulled out her spray bottle of luminol and gave the area a couple of squirts. Then she reached for her UV light.

She trained the light on the tiny cluster of dots and her smile broadened.

'Bingo.'

30

'Everyone got their chips, packed lunches and coffees?' said Boyd.

The team gathered around the table nodded. The atmosphere in the Incident Room was bullish. They had their suspect, after just six days of Audrey's disappearance, and they'd managed to do it before the case could blow up into some kind of Nicola Bulley public relations nightmare.

'Right then,' he said. 'Let's begin, shall we? So, myself and Minter had a very interesting coffee morning with young Liam Hincher, charming young man that he is.'

Minter huffed. 'I'd like to punch a hole right through his ruddy face.'

'He *is* our prime suspect, then, isn't he?' said Warren.

'It looks very much like it,' replied Boyd.

'What's the saying?' chipped in Sully. 'If it looks like a duck and quacks like a duck... then it's time to get out the plum sauce.'

Magnusson huffed. 'Well, that's not *really* a saying now, is it?'

'It certainly should be,' retorted Sully.

'Anyway,' Boyd pressed on, 'we're resuming the interview after lunch, once his defence bod has arrived and read up.'

'He's going to be all "no comments" this afternoon, boss, isn't he?' said Minter.

Boyd shrugged. 'I think we got a lot of damning stuff down already. The clincher of course –' his eyes settled on Sully and Magnusson – 'will be whatever you two have managed to find for me to present to the CPS.'

Sully beamed. 'It's your lucky day, Boydy... We have for you one pair of size-fourteen knickers found in the boot of his Mini. I very much suspect they're the kind a woman of Audrey's age would wear. You know – sensible, roomy, not frilly.'

Okeke eye-rolled at him. 'What would you know about that?'

Sully ignored her. 'We've had them sent over to Ellessey. They've promised to process them asap. And –' he looked sideways at Magnusson – 'would you like to deliver the coup de grâce?'

Magnusson nodded. 'I found several groups of small blood spots on the passenger-side door and on the glove compartment,' she said. 'They appear to be cast-off patterns, which would suggest an act of violence taking place in the car.'

Boyd nodded. 'Okay. That's good. Very good.'

'*If* it comes back as Audrey's,' Okeke pointed out.

'What about his tech?' continued Boyd. 'His phone, laptop, games console, et cetera, et cetera.'

Sully shook his head. 'Apart from the usual smut and grubby stuff you'd expect on a young man's phone, there's nothing that looks incriminating. It seems he kept all the really damning stuff on the family PC.'

'Which is a bit careless, isn't it?' said Minter.

Boyd shrugged. 'Or smart. He's got some degree of deniability. He could claim it was his dad's.'

Sully nodded. 'He was exceedingly careful to tuck everything away in folders that no one without a decent level of computer knowledge would find.'

'Did Ellessey say whether they can process the underwear and blood before end of play today?' asked Boyd.

Sully nodded again. 'They said they can have a report emailed back to us by about five. It'll cost extra, though.'

Boyd rolled his eyes. 'Of course it will.'

'So what's the sequence of events, then?' asked Okeke.

'Our working theory is that either Audrey discovered something and threatened to go to the police,' replied Boyd, 'or Liam's morbid interest in her escalated to the point where he set out to act on it. So he went into town, maybe he offered her a lift back to work...'

'She wasn't that far that she needed a lift,' said Yates. 'I mean it's literally five minutes away.'

'I don't know,' said Boyd, shrugging. 'Maybe she accepted the lift, because it seemed like a surprisingly kind gesture from him? Maybe she saw it as a chance to talk to him? Maybe he begged her to get in? Like I say, if she'd stumbled across his pictures somehow, I imagine he'd have been desperate to explain himself.'

'I'm telling you,' Okeke said, 'if she'd found the pictures, there's absolutely no way she'd have got into any car with him.'

'Perhaps he suggested a coffee and a chat. Somewhere they could talk it through. A McDonald's or something?' Minter offered.

'She'd still have been wary.' said Okeke.

'Right. Well, maybe Audrey wanted to deal with this

without Andrew finding out and getting involved. We know he has a temper,' Boyd said.

'God, poor, poor woman,' sighed Okeke. 'What a shit situation to be stuck in.'

'Anyway,' Boyd went on, 'somehow she ends up in the car and he drives her out of Hastings...'

'She'd have been worried about getting back to work, though, wouldn't she?' said Magnusson.

'Maybe she saw this as more important,' suggested Boyd.

Okeke shook her head. 'If she really knew what he'd been up to, she'd have run for the hills. Christ, I know I would.'

'Look, we're going in circles here,' said Boyd decisively. 'Let's go with this for now. She's in his car. He's driving her out to, let's say, a McDonald's...'

'And perhaps they were heading towards the Romney Marshes,' said Warren. 'At some point she's going to say, *Where are we going? What's going on? Take me back.*'

Boyd nodded. 'And maybe that's when Liam lashes out.' He glanced at Magnusson. 'Potentially the source of your blood spots. He hits her. And there we are... He's now crossed the line. There's no turning back. If he was unsure what his plans were, it's kind of decided now, isn't it?'

'So she's knocked out,' said Minter. 'He takes her somewhere quiet, out of the way...'

Boyd nodded again. 'And did whatever he did to her.'

'What about her phone?' asked Warren. 'That was dumped in the next street to where they lived?'

'He dumped it on the way back home,' said Minter. 'What did your homeless guy say? A chap wearing a hoodie tossed it?'

Warren nodded. 'That's right.'

Boyd looked at Sully. 'Can we get a geolocation on Liam's phone for that time?'

'Already done that, Boydy,' Sully said, flipping through the notes he'd brought with him. 'Ah, now, here we are...' He slid the printout across the table. 'Though, you won't love it.'

'Why?' Boyd picked it up and started scanning the unintelligible splurge of hexadecimal numbers at the top. At the bottom, for techno idiots, was a map with a red pin marker.

'He was at home the whole time,' replied Sully.

'You mean his *phone* was at home,' said Minter.

'Yeah,' said Boyd with a nod. 'That cuts both ways. Either he's innocent or he's savvy enough to have known to have left his phone on and at home.'

'Is he that smart?' asked Okeke.

'It's not exactly rocket science,' said Sully. 'I think anyone who's watched a true-crime show knows that a phone is a liability.'

'Was there anything else on his phone that might be helpful?' asked Boyd.

Sully shook his head. 'Not unless you want to count the oh-so-many visits to Pornhub and YouPorn.' He sighed. 'Honestly, I think he must have worn his little pecker right out.'

'What about socials?' said Boyd.

'He has TikTok, Insta, Discord... the usual stuff for lads his age. But nothing that's worth flagging up. He's obviously smart enough to know his phone, his laptop and his games console need to be kept clean.'

The discussion about Liam hit a pause.

Boyd cast a glance around the table. 'I think this is what we'll present to him after lunch. To see how he reacts.'

'What about Andrew Hincher?' asked Okeke. 'And Carol

Docherty? Is it worth me doing any more digging around that?'

Boyd pursed his lips thoughtfully. 'Yes, that's something we really do need to follow up. Fine... Okeke, you do that. Meanwhile –' he glanced at Minter – 'we'll see how Liam goes this afternoon. He turned to Sully. 'If you can keep pestering Ellessey this afternoon for the DNA tests...'

'Maybe you should aim to interview as late in the afternoon as you can?' suggested Sully. 'Ellessey said late afternoon at the very earliest.'

31

'Interview two: the date is Wednesday the twenty-fourth of April; the time is 4.15 p.m.,' announced Minter. 'Present in the room are interviewing officers DCI William Boyd, DI Steven Minter, interviewee Liam Hincher and his solicitor...' He turned to her.

'Ms Saleena Vikram,' she said.

'Right then,' began Boyd. 'Have you had sufficient time to read the notes and consult with your client, Ms Vikram?'

'I have, yes,' she replied.

'Good. So, Liam...' Boyd said, his eyes settling on the young man. 'Let's crack on, shall we?' He checked his notes. 'All right. Since we last spoke, Liam, your Mini has been forensically searched and we found a couple of things that might interest you. Do you want to know what they are?'

Liam looked at his solicitor. She shrugged.

'No comment,' he said.

'We found a pair of women's knickers. In a size fourteen,' Boyd told him.

'I'm presuming they're not yours, Liam,' added Minter.

'No comment,' Liam replied.

'Were they Audrey's?' asked Boyd.

'No comment.'

'Did you remove them from her? Did you keep them... as some sort of a trophy?' Boyd asked.

'No comment,' Liam said again.

'It's quite possible,' his solicitor cut in, 'that they ended up in his car perfectly innocently. Especially if he was regularly giving Audrey lifts to work.'

'Really?' asked Minter sceptically.

'Or he could have purchased them himself?' she offered.

Liam shot a glance her way. '*What? No!*'

'Well, since they're currently being tested for her DNA, we'll know soon enough,' said Boyd.

'My client could easily have obtained them from anywhere in the house. From the laundry basket?'

Boyd looked at him. 'Hmm. Is that something you do, Liam? Go digging around for Audrey's dirty underwear?'

'No!' Liam exclaimed.

Ms Vikram nudged him gently.

'No comment!' he muttered.

'All right then, moving swiftly along,' Boyd said. 'The other thing of interest that we found in your car was what appears to be splatters of blood on the inside of the passenger-side door. There were several, in fact. Can you explain why those might have been there?'

Liam shook his head.

'For the recording, Liam Hincher indicated a negative,' said Minter.

'That blood is also being tested as we speak, Liam. If it turns out to belong to Audrey, you will certainly have some explaining to do.'

'She had a nose bleed,' said Liam quickly. 'That's it... I

remember. Yeah, she had a nose bleed. She sneezed, like, a dozen times and it made her –'

'She sneezed?' Minter said.

Liam nodded eagerly. 'In my car.'

'Really?' Minter raised an eyebrow.

'I'm not fucking lying!' Liam protested. 'She's got hay fever. So on a bad day... she's sneezing all over the place! It's gross.'

Ms Vikram gently nudged his arm in a bid to get him to shut up.

'So when was that?' said Boyd. 'Was it recently?'

'Yeah,' Liam said.

'Okay, so how recently? Are we talking last month? Last week?' Boyd asked.

'I can't remember. Maybe –' Liam began.

Ms Vikram nudged him again.

'No comment,' he said with a glare at her.

Boyd smiled. 'All right. Well, we'll find out soon enough.' He checked his notes again. 'So, we had a jolly good look at your phone, your laptop and your games console. On your phone, I notice you're quire a frequent visitor to a number of porn sites.'

Liam dropped his gaze to his hands on the table.

'That's not abnormal, Liam. I suspect most men on the planet have a somewhat cheeky search history tucked away somewhere,' Boyd said.

'Do *you*?' Liam snapped. He looked at Minter. 'Or *you*?'

'The thing is Liam,' Boyd continued, 'we have a record of the search phrases you've been using on your phone. "Gilfs", "cougars", "mature women".' He glanced at Liam's solicitor. 'You're going to have to excuse us; we're going to get quite explicit.'

Ms Vikram shook her head. 'Oh, don't mind me, detective. I've heard it all before.'

'There were also some pretty concerning search terms, Liam,' Boyd continued. '"Rape scene", "tied up", "bound and gagged", "drugged up".'

Liam looked up. 'They don't show that kind of stuff! It's not legal! They'd get done!'

'Of course, you'd know that, wouldn't you?' huffed Minter, 'because those are the words you typed in, right? Looking for something a little more suited to your personal tastes, were you?' He leant forward on his elbows. 'And because they couldn't deliver what you wanted, off you go downstairs to the other computer when Mummy and Daddy are out... to play in some grubby corner of the web and make your own pictures.'

'Look, I know what you're doing,' said Ms Vikram. 'You're trying to provoke him. That's really not acceptable –'

Minter persisted. 'Using snaps you took on your phone of Audrey, without her knowledge, to make something realistic you could whack off too...'

Boyd could see Liam's face paling.

'And your dad... Liam. I wonder what your dad's going to make of this when he finds out what you've been up to on his computer.' Minter sat back in his chair.

Liam shot a glance at him. 'Please... don't tell him about the stuff on there! Please!'

'That's enough,' snapped Ms Vikram. She nodded at Liam. 'Let's keep it to "no comment", please, Liam. They're just trying to manipulate you.'

Boyd realised that he'd struck a nerve. 'What's he going to say, Liam? To torture porn on his computer. To pictures of his wife bound, gagged, abused...'

'PLEASE! Don't tell him!!' Liam pleaded.

Boyd nodded. 'That's why you ran, isn't it? You were worried we'd find them and tell your dad, weren't you?'

'No comment,' Liam whispered.

Boyd checked his phone, hoping that maybe something had pinged through from Sully. There was nothing yet.

'Look, Liam...' He moderated his voice to sound a bit friendlier, 'if we get confirmation that the blood in your car is Audrey's, and the underwear is hers too, we'll have enough to charge you. That means you don't get to go home, and that the ball gets passed to the Crown Prosecution Service. I'm pretty sure they'll be happy enough with what we have to move forward... even if we don't find her body.' He leant forward on the table. 'Liam, you're stepping into a small window of opportunity where you can help yourself. Have some degree of influence on what happens next. Cooperating with us now *will* make a difference down the line.'

Boyd sipped his coffee, hoping the pause would prompt the lad to pipe up. He looked again at his phone, which was face up on the table.

'If my phone buzzes – and it will do any moment now – it means we've got the forensics results and are good to go. We will charge you, you will go to court, and you will go down for murder. But if you can help us now, before it buzzes... if you can tell us what happened and where she is... well, it will definitely be taken into consideration.'

Liam's eyes flickered down to the phone.

'That's right,' said Boyd. 'What's going to happen first? It's your choice.'

Liam glanced at his solicitor.

'You're not obliged to say anything, Liam,' she reminded him.

Liam turned back to Boyd and opened his mouth to speak...

The phone buzzed loudly on the table.

32

'So what's your next step, Boyd?' asked Sutherland. The DSI looked at his watch. 'Lesley Lloyd will be packing up for the day and heading home soon. Are you calling her for charge advice or not?'

'I'm going to authorise another twelve hours in custody,' said Boyd. 'Let him sweat on it overnight and we can hit him with what we've got in the morning.'

'Why wait? You've got her blood and her knickers in his car,' Sutherland pointed out.

Boyd had found it difficult keeping a neutral face in the interview room once he'd taken Sully's call to say that Ellessey had delivered the goods and had a positive match on both blood and underwear.

'Because I don't think that's going to be enough for CPS once they review the case,' replied Boyd. 'The pants could have been lifted from the laundry basket. The blood, well, Liam claims she sneezed blood in his car. Plausible answers for both items of evidence.'

'But there's all that grotesque porn he made, starring the poor woman,' Sutherland said.

'And a defence barrister might argue that's the first thing young lads do with new technology: they make porn.' Boyd shook his head. 'Plus, we've got no body. There's no point calling Lesley... She's not going to green-light a murder charge just yet.'

Sutherland sighed. 'All right, Boyd. It's your call.'

'We've got a witness who says he saw someone dump Audrey's phone,' Boyd said. 'I'm going to get him in tomorrow. If he can pick out Liam's face and we put that to the lad, I think we might get a confession.'

'Really?' Sutherland's head bobbed on his shoulders.

Boyd nodded. 'To be honest with you, I think he's a little frightened of his dad. A lot frightened, actually. I suspect he's more worried about his dad finding out than anything else. Another night downstairs... and I think he'll crumble.'

'Fair enough,' said Sutherland, checking his watch again. 'So you *don't* need me?'

'No,' Boyd said.

'Good. I've got to get a wiggle on if I don't want to be late.'

Boyd got up out of his seat. 'Are you going out tonight?'

'I'm off to the theatre,' Sutherland replied.

'Oh, to see what?' Boyd asked.

Sutherland stood up and pulled his jacket from the back of the chair. 'I'm *in* a play.'

'You're *what*?' Boyd said, not sure that he'd heard correctly.

'A play, Boyd – I'm in a play. I'm a member of Hastings Dramatic Society. Rehearsals start tonight. And don't look so ruddy surprised, man,' he added indignantly. 'The director said I've got a commanding stage presence. I believe *charisma* is what she actually said.'

33

'How's your missing-lady case going?' asked Charlotte.

Boyd threw the tennis ball again for Ozzie and Mia. It was the first time they'd been down to the beach for an evening walk in months. The evenings were getting a little lighter, but it was still bloody freezing.

'It's a bit hard to work out what we've actually got,' Boyd said.

'What do you mean?' Charlotte asked.

He explained what they'd found on the family computer.

Charlotte's face blanched. 'Oh my God.'

'I mean, it's really horrific stuff. But... it *is* fake. It's all fake,' Boyd assured her.

'Are you sure?' she asked.

He nodded. 'The more you look at it, the more you notice... The weird number of fingers, limbs bending wrongly. Sometimes Audrey's likeness is off.' He glanced at Charlotte. 'It's definitely fake,' he said, shaking his head. 'Even so, it makes the boy look very guilty. But the internet is awash with shock images being produced by sad little prats using software. It doesn't make them murderers.'

'But... of his stepmum?' Charlotte pointed out.

Boyd sighed. 'Right. It's twisted and very weird.'

'And illegal, surely?' she said.

'I actually don't know if it is.' He shook his head again. 'I mean... if he shared them or posted them online, then I think maybe. But for personal use?' Boyd glanced at Charlotte and shrugged. 'However, if we end up finding Audrey's body, it does give us intent and motive.'

'Oh gosh. I hope that's not what happens,' Charlotte said, and tutted sadly. 'Things like this always seem to turn out that way in the end, don't they? We rarely get a happy ending.'

Boyd hadn't mentioned the forensics in Liam's car. Nor was he going to. That was being kept under wraps for now. He sighed. 'I was beginning to hope she'd just walked out on Hincher and his son. Left them to it, you know?' he admitted. 'But there are just too many red flags. And honestly... I still think either of them could have done it.'

Ozzie returned from the sea with a dripping wet ball and dumped it at Boyd's feet. He bent down to pick it up. 'Or there's one thing we haven't really explored yet...'

'What's that?' Charlotte asked.

Ozzie harrumphed in a bid to get Boyd to stop the layman psychoanalysis and throw the ball. Boyd tossed it towards the rolling waves.

'We could find her body at the bottom of a cliff,' he said. 'Given how utterly shit her life at home sounds.'

'You mean suicide?'

He nodded.

Ozzie was back with his ball already. Mia was nipping at his muzzle to get him to drop it so that she could grab it.

Charlotte silently raised her index finger at Ozzie and he dropped it obediently.

'I really hope it isn't that last one, Bill,' she said as she picked up the ball. 'That's an awful thought... to think that she couldn't see any other way out of her situation.'

34

DC Rajan finished the last of his breakfast roll, booted up his terminal and opened his email. There were messages from both Minter and Okeke. He doubled-clicked on Okeke's first, to find she'd sent him a to-do list to start on as soon as he got in this morning. Among the various requests was a deep dive into Andrew Hincher's former partner, the missing Carol Docherty.

Clearly DS Okeke wasn't about to let that investigative branch wither and die. She wanted him to run the DNA taken from the Hinchers' floor against the NDNAD again, but this time with all the filters taken off. Not just unknowns, not just mispers, not within any time period, but against every single entry on the entire database. She also wanted him to track down Docherty's relatives and set up interviews with them.

He clicked on Minter's. He also had a to-do list for Rajan. At the top of *his* list was a review of the hotline calls that had come in on Audrey Hincher in the last twenty-four hours. Now that they had a prime suspect, Minter was obviously –

and desperately – hoping for some supporting eyewitness evidence to pop up out of the blue.

Rajan navigated to the folder where the audio for the hotline calls was stored and looked at a depressingly long list of .wav files.

He pulled his headphones on and settled into his seat for a morning of listening to a succession of hoaxers, pranksters, the bewildered and the bored, in the vain hope of stumbling across something vaguely useful.

∼

'So what's this acting role you're going for, then?' asked Boyd, spooning coffee into a couple of mugs.

'Well, I'm glad you asked, Boyd,' Sutherland replied. 'Truth be told, I'm not too sure yet. The director can't decide if she wants me to play the alcoholic father-in-law or... the creepy uncle with a penchant for younger ladies.'

'What's the play?' Boyd stirred the coffee and handed a mug to Sutherland.

Sutherland frowned. 'Do you know, I can't remember the title! It's not a famous one. By a local writer, I think the director said. It's a play about the grubby goings-on in a seaside bedsit.'

Boyd cast around for a reply, and settled on: 'Nice...'

Sutherland nodded. 'It was Mrs Sutherland who suggested I do it. She says I need to start thinking about developing hobbies as retirement looms. She thinks I have a talent for role-playing.'

Boyd spluttered as his coffee went down the wrong way.

'Goodness, are you all right?' Sutherland asked.

'Fine. I'm fine,' Boyd croaked. He took a deep breath.

'You've got a few more years to go before you retire, haven't you?'

'Four,' said Sutherland. He smiled. 'But she's very keen to make sure I've got something to do with my time once I hang up my hat. She's very thoughtful like that.'

'Guv?'

Boyd turned to see Rajan's face in the kitchenette doorway. 'Do you want a brew as well?' he asked.

'Uh, no, sir. I've been listening to calls from the tipline...' Rajan began.

Boyd smiled. 'Okeke's got you listening to the cranks, has she?'

'It was Minter, actually.' Rajan grinned. 'There was one called Hector. He must've called about a dozen –'

'Ah yes, Hector the Hoaxer,' sighed Boyd. 'We really should give him his very own number to call. Was there anything useful?'

'I've got a possible sighting of Audrey on Queens Road. The morning she went missing,' Rajan said.

'On Queens Road?' Boyd repeated.

'In the CCTV blind spot,' said Rajan. 'The bloke who called said he saw her getting into a taxi.'

~

MINTER PARKED the pool car on the double yellows right outside Alfred's Antiques on Queens Road and left his lanyard on the dashboard to prevent them from getting a ticket.

'Odd place for a junkshop,' said Boyd as he unclipped his seatbelt and climbed out. Most of the bric-a-brac businesses were over in the old town, clustered along George Street, perfectly placed amid the Diagon Alley ambience to cajole visiting DFLs to step in and buy crusty old tat that would seem out of place the moment they got it back to their bijou, Ikea-decked London apartments.

The modern part of Hastings was all vape stores, phone shops and estate agents. Alfred's Antiques looked as though it had missed the memo.

Minter stood before the store's entrance. 'This *is* the right address, boss.' He pushed the dusty glass door inwards and, of course, a bell jingled.

They stepped into a dimly lit labyrinth of dark oak furniture and absurd curios. To their right was a vast oil painting of Pelham Arcade and the boating lake on a lovely sunny day. A masterpiece of paint on canvas, except that every person in the beautifully rendered painting had a seagull's head instead of a human's.

Well, it is Hastings... thought Boyd, *of course they do.*

'Are you gentlemen from the police?' a voice echoed from somewhere beyond a shelving unit, which was lined with pith helmets and Second World War gas masks. A portly man emerged into view, sporting a neatly trimmed silver beard and waxed moustache.

'Are you Alfred?' Boyd asked.

'Alfred Parsons!' The man extended a hand for Boyd to shake. 'None other.'

Boyd lifted his lanyard. 'I'm DCI Boyd and thi–'

'Ahhh! No need to introduce yourself, sir.' Alfred beamed. 'I know who you are. I recognise your face from the YouTube. My nephew showed me it a while ago. You know, the one where you're wearing a bra over your ear and you drop an almighty F-bomb in front of the TV cameras.'

'Right.' Boyd sighed. He would have thought that little gem would have dropped off everyone's radar by now.

'You called the hotline?' Boyd asked.

'Indeed I did. I saw your piece on the evening news the other day.' Alfred frowned. 'Actually, I'm a little perturbed it's taken you lot so long to get around to calling me back.'

Boyd could have replied that they were short-staffed right now, or that they'd had a more compelling angle of investigation to follow over these last few days, but the truth was, he should have had one of his DCs trawl through the voice messages earlier. 'Can you tell me what you saw, Mr Parsons?' he asked.

'I certainly can,' Alfred said, stepping up towards the dusty window of his store and looking out onto Queens Road. 'I was standing right here, you see, eating my lunch and watching the world go by. I do that at the same time every day, when it's a bit quiet. Just after midday. Anyway, I was right here when I saw the woman you're after...'

Boyd waited for a moment before he realised that Parsons was the kind of person who *projected* rather than talked, and liked a little feedback from his audience in return.

'And?' Boyd asked obligingly.

'She was over there, across the road,' Alfred said, pointing theatrically. 'The woman, you see? She was trying to flag down a taxi.'

'And did she managed to flag one down?' prompted Boyd.

'Oh yes. It took her a little while. She was strutting up and down the street, flapping her hands at various taxi cabs going past until one eventually stopped.'

'This isn't New York,' said Minter. 'You have to call one of the local taxi companies and book one if you want a cab, surely?'

'Well, quite,' replied Parsons. 'I was of a mind to go over

and give her the number of the firm round the corner, you know?'

'Anyway...?' Boyd said, in a bid to get him back on track.

'Well, she got in, of course,' Alfred replied. 'And off it went.'

'Which way did it go?' asked Minter.

Parsons pointed left, towards the far end of Queens Road. Minter looked at Boyd. 'She wasn't intending to head back to work, then, boss.'

Boyd nodded. He looked at Parsons. 'And you're certain it was her?'

'Absolutely. She was quite frantic, you see? Pacing back and forth like a lion in a cage.' Parsons acted that bit out for them. 'I think I watched her trying to get someone's attention for a good five minutes.' He turned to look back out onto the street as if he could still see her there. 'She must have been in a jolly big hurry to go somewhere.'

'And you're sure it was a taxi?' asked Boyd. 'Not a friend, say, picking her up?'

'Oh, yes,' Alfred said. 'It had a phone number on its side.'

'Any chance you can remember the number?' Boyd said.

Alfred's face crinkled with a sulphurous smile. 'It's the devil and his son,' he replied.

'Excuse me?' Boyd said, confused.

'Ahhh...' muttered Minter. Apparently it made sense to him.

Boyd looked at him and shrugged.

'It's Goblin Taxis, boss. They're just round the corner – phone number's 666333. The devil and his son,' he repeated. 'That's how they get you to remember their number.' He smiled. 'Pretty clever, eh?'

35

Boyd stepped into Goblin Taxis' tiny waiting room. The walls were plastered with crudely printed flyers and handwritten adverts on index cards. The place stank of something that took Boyd a moment to identify: Cornish pasty. It made his empty tummy gurgle with hope. The two chairs were plastic relics that needed replacing – one had a crack across the seat that he was certain was a death trap for any unwary bollocks headed its way.

'Can I help you, gents?'

Behind a counter, also covered in hand-scrawled ads, was a man in his sixties. He wore a scuffed black leather jacket and a Black Sabbath tour T-shirt, his thinning grey hair pulled back into a flimsy rat's tail.

Boyd flashed his card. 'DCI Boyd and DI Minter, Hastings CID.' He folded his arms, then leant on the top of the counter. 'I wonder if I can ask you a few questions, mate?'

The smell of Cornish pasty intensified and Boyd had an overwhelming desire to nip out and buy himself one, until he realised the smell was, in fact, coming from the taxi controller. Boyd's urge for a pasty vanished instantly.

'Sure, man,' the controller replied.

'We're investigating Audrey Hincher, the woman who went missing last week,' he said.

'Oh right, yeah.' The controller nodded. 'That's been all over the news.'

'Yeah,' Boyd said. 'Well, we've just been speaking to a bloke round the corner on Queens Road. He said he saw Audrey climb into one of your cabs the morning she went missing.'

The controller's eyes rounded. 'He did?'

'I'm presuming you have a record of jobs done? Fares taken...?' Boyd said.

The controller grinned, revealing a mouthful of brown gappy teeth. 'I've got my log book, man, if you wanna take a butcher's?' he said, easing himself up onto his feet.

'Sorry, what's your name?' Boyd asked him.

'Gary,' the controller replied. 'When exactly was it that you're interested in?'

'Last week,' replied Boyd. 'Thursday, eighteenth of April.'

'Right, gimme a sec. That's not gonna be in my current notebook.' He got up from his seat, pushed his way through a door behind him and disappeared.

'If it *is* Audrey Hincher,' said Minter, 'you know that changes everything, boss?'

Boyd nodded. If there was anything at all to confirm this sighting: a card payment, a dashcam video, then that, alongside the taxi driver's positive ID, it would mean that Audrey was alive and they would have to let Liam Hincher go.

Through the open door, they could hear Gary shuffling

around and moving things. 'Won't be a minute, gents,' he called. 'It's a bit of a mess back 'ere.'

Minter took a step back, sat down on one of the plastic chairs and let out a yelp.

Boyd turned round to see his colleague back on his feet and rubbing his behind. 'That bloody chair pinched my bum,' he complained.

The idiot had picked the cracked seat. Boyd smiled. 'It could've been worse, mate.'

'Ahh!' They heard Gary shuffling his way from the back room and a moment later he emerged with an A4 notebook. He slapped it down on the counter and took his seat. 'Now what date and time were we looking at again, man?'

'Eighteenth of April. Between twelve and half twelve,' Boyd told him.

Gary flipped through the pages. 'Twelve to twelve thirty, eh?'

Boyd nodded.

'Tony and Bill were on,' he muttered to himself as he scanned the log. 'Bill had a job over in Bexhill at that time...' He looked up. 'I see Tony had a quick run to St Leonards. But after that he was free. He'd have been on his way back here.'

'Then could it be this Tony?' Boyd said, glancing at Minter.

'There's no record of a fare taken, man,' Gary said.

'When was his next fare, after the St Leonard's trip?' Boyd asked.

Gary looked back down at his log book. 'The next job he had was picking someone up from the Tesco in Ore at half one.'

'So there's a blank hour?' Boyd said.

'That's not unusual, ,' replied Gary. 'It can be slow

during the day, right?'

'Right. So do you know where Tony was between the St Leonards fare and the Tesco one?' Boyd asked.

Gary shrugged. 'It's up to my drivers what they do between jobs. Tony tends to park up in Pelham car park when he's got a break. Grab himself a coffee and doughnuts.'

'We need to speak to him,' said Boyd. 'Can you get a hold of him?'

'Yeah...one sec. Lemme call his number.' Gary pulled an old phone out of his leather jacket, pecked at the keyboard, then held it to his ear.

'Tony? It's Gazza. Yeah... not bad, not bad. Listen, man, I've got some coppers just come in who want to have a quick word with you. You got a minute?' He listened for a few seconds and then nodded. He handed his phone over the counter to Boyd. 'He's good.'

Boyd took the phone. 'Tony?'

'Yeah?' the voice on the other end replied.

'This is DCI Boyd, Hastings CID. I'm investigating the disappearance of Audrey Hincher.'

There was silence from the other end.

'She's a local lady,' Boyd continued. 'Maybe you've seen the story on the local news?'

'Nah. Sorry. I don't really do news. So how can I help?' Tony replied.

'An eyewitness spotted her climbing into a Goblins Taxis cab about the same time she went missing,' Boyd explained. 'And after talking with your boss here... it looks as if it might have been your cab?'

'When was this?' Tony asked.

Boyd gave him the date and the time. There was a long pause from the other end. It was long enough that Boyd wondered whether the other man was weighing up what to say next.

'Tony?' he prompted.

'Look...' Tony replied. 'Uh... is Gazza right there with you?'

Boyd took the hint. He wandered over to the doorway and stepped out into the street. 'Okay, he's not now. I'm outside.'

'I took a *cash* fare, okay,' Tony admitted. '*Off the books.* Gazza would have my guts for garters if he knew. Please don't tell him.'

'I won't,' Boyd assured him. 'But look, Tony, this is important. Who did you pick up?'

'A woman,' Tony said.

'Middle-aged? Late fifties?' Boyd asked.

Another pause. 'Yeah... yeah, that sounds like her,' said Tony.

'Where did you take her?' Boyd said.

'To the train station,' Tony said. 'Well, actually, I took her back to her home first. She had me wait outside for a bit and *then* we went to the station. She paid in cash. About ninety quid I charged her. But, see, as it's not on the books, I–'

'You get to keep it all,' Boyd finished.

'Yeah. Right. Which is why Gazza's gonna have my balls if he finds out. The usual deal is thirty per cent to him,' Tony said.

'Okay,' Boyd said. 'Don't worry about Gazza for the moment. So, you took this woman to her house. I'll need to know where that was and if there was anything at all about her behaviour that struck you as, I dunno... out of sorts?'

'Sure.' He heard Tony give a wheezy laugh down the line. 'I can tell you this, she was as mad as a box of bleedin' frogs.'

36

'She was *frantic*,' said Boyd. 'That's what the cabbie said.'

'Tony,' explained Minter for the others' benefit.

Boyd resumed his briefing. 'He said she was someone who seemed to be in a desperate hurry to get home.'

'Like a cat with a fire alarm tied to its tail,' added Minter. He looked around at the others. 'Tony's phrase, not mine.'

'The cabbie took the fare because she said she'd pay him cash,' Boyd continued. 'Off the books. Which is why he was being so skittish with me initially. Anyway... he took her back to her house and she said she'd be ten minutes inside, then wanted him to take her somewhere else.'

'Where?' asked Okeke.

'I'll get to that. Because it gets weird before we get to the station,' Boyd said.

'Ah, the station, okay.' She nodded.

'Audrey came out of the house a little while later, carrying the same shoulder bag she'd gone in with, but it was stuffed to the gills. He said she was wearing a hoodie, and that she actually pulled the hood up over her head.'

'A hoodie?' Rajan asked.

'Uh-huh. Probably one of Liam's,' Boyd replied. 'She obviously wanted to disguise herself. Anyway, then she asked Tony to take her to the station. He drove her down her street and then he turned up the neighbouring road.' He looked at Warren. 'Harold Street. The one where your homeless guy lives. Halfway up, she tells him to stop. He did as she asked... and apparently she got out, pulled something from her bag and tossed it into the bushes.'

'Her phone,' said Warren.

Boyd nodded. 'Right. Then he took her to the station. She paid him in cash, then he asked her if everything was okay... and she replied, "*It will be. Soon.*" Then he watched her hurry into the station.'

Boyd let his team process that information.

Sully was the first to break the silence. 'Our lady, then, appears to have done a runner.'

Boyd nodded. 'That's what it looks like. Hopefully that means we're *not* going to find her body bobbing around in some remote bit of marshland after all.'

'But what about her blood in Liam's car?' asked Rajan. 'And her knickers in the boot.'

Boyd shrugged. 'Maybe Liam's story about the nose bleed was true.' He sighed. 'And Audrey's knickers in the boot? Well, we know he's a kinky little pervert. But not a murderer.' He glanced around the room. 'So, the question is: *why?* Why did she suddenly get it into her head that she needed to hurry home during her lunch break, pack a bag and run like a bat out of hell?'

'Her colleague...' Yates flipped through his notepad. 'Tracey Robbins said she seemed perfectly normal when she left to go and get her lunch. There was nothing weird about her behaviour.'

Okeke nodded. 'Audrey even offered to pick something up for her. Which clearly suggests she was expecting to return to work.' She clucked her tongue absently. 'So something happened to her between leaving work and jumping into that cab.'

'Right,' said Boyd. 'In the space of ten, fifteen minutes something happened. In public. In full sight of anyone who was on Queens Road at that time.'

'Perhaps she'd received a message? A call from someone?' suggested Minter.

Sully shook his head. 'There's nothing that came through to her phone during that time.'

'No searches on the internet?' pressed Minter. 'Nothing she might have stumbled upon?'

Sully shook his head again.

'So maybe she bumped into someone she knew?' said Okeke. 'Maybe someone she didn't want to see?'

'Could be,' replied Boyd. 'But clearly whatever or whoever she encountered, it spooked her massively. The cabbie said she was frantic, remember. Yates?' he said, turning to the detective constable.

'Sir?'

'You reviewed the CCTV footage, didn't you? Was there anything more there?'

'No, nothing,' Yates said. 'I mean, the stuff I assembled for the press conference was all that I managed to scrape together. She's doing what we'd expected her to do and doing it normally, calmly – she nips into the Tesco Extra, and Costa for a coffee, then turns into Queens Road and we lose her halfway down the road.'

'So, whatever made her suddenly decide to flee... must have happened in that blind spot.' Boyd looked at Rajan, Yates and Warren. 'You three need to head down there, and do a door-to-door on whatever shops and businesses are along that street beyond the CCTV blind spot. Check to see if they've got internal cams that look out onto the road. Or cams showing her entering their premises. Interview the staff there, see if anyone can recall her coming in or acting weird.'

'Boyd,' cut in Sutherland.

'Sir?'

'Uh... this is looking a lot less like a murder investigation now.'

'And thank God for that,' Boyd replied.

'Yes, yes, of course, *thankfully*. But it does mean I can probably have a few live bodies back on my main floor again.' His face pulled into a pug-like pleading grimace. 'It's like a ruddy ghost town out there. There's plenty of bits and pieces that need attending to. The lovable scrotes and rogues of Hastings haven't been taking a holiday, you know.'

Boyd glanced around the Incident Room. At the moment, the only person not in there with them was DI Abbott.

'In fact, Boyd,' Sutherland continued, 'we'll leave one or two on this, but honestly the in-tray's building up out there. It might not be wildly exciting stuff, but it's still *crime*.'

'Right,' Boyd conceded. He looked around the table, wondering who to cut loose from the team. Sully and Magnusson were obvious choices and could head on back to their side of the floor and get on with whatever tasks were sitting in their in-trays. 'Thanks for your help,' he said to them.

'Ah... it seems we're now surplus to requirements,' Sully replied tartly. 'Come along, Karen.'

They pushed their chairs back, got up and left the room.

Boyd looked at the rest of the team. He didn't need both

a DI and a DS on what was now just a misper case. And he paused his gaze on the DCs – he didn't need Huey, Dewey *and* Louie.

'Okeke, Warren, Yates, I release you from your bond of servitude.'

None of them seemed to find that at all amusing. Okeke glared at him. Their chair legs scraped as they got up, gathered their notes and followed Sully and Magnusson out of the door.

Sutherland got to his feet and scrunched up the wrapper from his cheese sandwich. 'And I might as well get back to scratching around for bodies to restock our empty floor.'

Sutherland closed the door, leaving Boyd, Minter and Rajan sitting at the table.

'Boss,' Minter said, 'What about Liam Hincher?'

Boyd sighed. 'I suppose we'd better release him back into the wild. Minter, could you...?'

Minter pulled a face. 'Me?'

'And try to be civil to him,' added Boyd. 'He's a creep, not a killer. Drop him back home and then you can join the others on the floor.' He looked at Rajan. 'You go to the station. Scrape whatever CCTV footage they have inside. See if we can find out which train Audrey got on. Then can you pick up those door-to-doors on Queens Road?'

'Yes, sir,' Rajan replied.

'And I guess I'd better put together another announcement for the press,' Boyd muttered.

'What're you going to say?' asked Minter.

Boyd sighed. Almost certainly some arsehole was going to raise the fact that he'd brought in two different suspects and that both had come to nothing.

37

The custody sergeant signed Liam Hincher out of the system and handed him a plastic bag containing the personal items that had been taken off him thirty-six hours before.

'There you go, sunshine,' the sergeant said. 'It's all in there.'

'I can go now?' Liam grunted, turning to Minter.

'Yep,' said Minter. 'They'll send the accommodation bill on later.'

'The *bill*?' Liam looked horrified.

'I'm joking, lad,' Minter said. 'Come on... I'm here to give you a lift home.'

Minter led him up the stairs from the custody floor, past the front desk and outside.

'I told you cockwombles I didn't do nothing to her,' Liam said.

'And we listened, Liam. Which is why we're out in this lovely sunshine and I'm giving you a free ride home. How about that, eh?' Minter replied, a congenial smile welded onto his face. He led him over to the three CID pool cars and blipped the fob.

'Hop in. You can even have the front seat if you like.'

Liam climbed in, Minter rounded the back of the car and joined him inside.

'Enjoy your stay with us, did you?' he asked casually. He couldn't help himself.

'Yeah, you think you're so very fuckin' funny,' Liam said. 'I might sue you all.'

Minter started the engine, pulled out of the parking space and paused at the car park's exit, waiting for a gap in the traffic on Bohemia Road.

Liam fumbled in his bag for his phone. 'So when do I get my PlayStation, my laptop and the computer back?'

'Don't worry, lad. Somebody will drop those things back later,' Minter replied. 'Properly cleaned up, of course. And minus all the granny horror-porn.'

Liam turned his head to look out of the window.

Minter let the silence sit for a minute, then asked. 'So, Liam... why?'

'Why what?' he asked.

'Why Audrey? You know... why all that granny-porn?'

'I don't want to talk about it,' Liam muttered.

'Well, you don't have to... but... I'm curious. It's not exactly usual for a lad your age. Right?'

Liam continued to stare out of the window and Minter suspected he wasn't going to get another word out of him all the way home, but then, unexpectedly, he replied.

'Audrey was all right to me, you know. Nicer than Dad. I wouldn't have hurt her.'

'She was all right to you?' Minter glanced his way. 'So you thought you'd make torture-porn images of her?'

Liam shrugged. 'It wasn't real, was it?' he said.

Minter stopped at the lights, waiting for them to turn

green so that he could turn left. 'So... Liam? Maybe this is a good point to reset your life, eh? Get your shit together?'

Liam turned to stare at him. Irritated. 'Piss off. You're not my dad.'

Minter rounded the bend at the bottom of the road and pulled up at the traffic lights with the sea and pier ahead of them. 'I'm just saying. You're what... twenty-three? Most lads your age are out and about doing something. You know, instead of moping around at home and watching porn. Maybe you should get out and find a job...'

Liam snorted. 'Like what? There's nuffin' out there. I got no qualifications. No experience. I've tried,' he mumbled. 'There's just... nothing. No one wants me and everything's shit.'

Minter was somewhat surprised to find that he was actually starting to feel sorry for him. There didn't seem to be a lot going for the lad. He wondered how much of Liam's behaviour was down to having that vile twat Andrew Hincher as his only role model.

'You know, Liam, anyone's life can be turned round with a bit of a kick up the arse to get them started.' The lights went green; Minter pulled right and headed towards Silverhill. 'Even if you start with just getting out for a little jog or something. Start working on your fitness, eh?' Minter glanced at Liam, and this time his smile was genuine. 'It gives you a bit of lift. A more positive outlook on life.'

Liam snorted. 'Right. Sure.'

Minter shook his head. He was wasting oxygen on him. Some folks were born to stumble, to spiral downhill from birth and end up in prison. Or an early grave.

'So you found her, then?' said Liam after a while. 'That's why I'm free now, right?'

There was no point lying to him. The boss was going to

brief the press today anyway. 'We haven't found her,' Minter replied, 'but it looks like she took off by herself. Maybe she'd had enough of your dad.' *And you*, he was tempted to add.

Liam said nothing as he watched the shingle beach roll by, the tourists and DFLs making use of the sunny outbreak. 'I'm not surprised,' he said eventually.

'Do you have any idea where she might have gone, Liam?' Minter asked. 'Do you think it's possible she might have had a friend? Maybe a boyfriend?'

Liam snorted. 'No.' He was silent for a moment, then: 'She might have gone on holiday.'

'You mean abroad?'

Liam hunched his shoulders. 'She was always watching those pathetic "new life in the sun" shows. She fuckin' loves that stupid *Mamma Mia* film. She's always watching and rewatching that one. Maybe she's just decided to book herself a break and didn't bother to tell Dad.'

'Because he'd have been annoyed?'

Liam nodded. 'Yeah.'

'Would that have led to a fight?' Minter looked his way. 'Would he have had a go at her?'

'Yeah. He'd be *really* pissed off at her spending money without asking him,' Liam said.

Five minutes later, Minter pulled up outside the Hinchers' house. There were still a couple of paps lingering outside, like wasps around a half-full Coke can.

Liam sighed and pulled up his hoodie. 'They really think I done it, don't they? They think I murdered her.'

'Not for much longer,' Minter replied, unclipping his seat belt. 'There'll be a press announcement later to say that you're no longer a person of interest. Come on... let's get you inside, sunshine, eh?' He nudged Liam. '"No comment" – that's all you need to give them, right?'

'I thought "no comment" really pissed you off?' Liam said.

Minter laughed. 'Not when you say it to those scumbags.' He climbed out of the car first and walked over towards them. 'Nothing to see here, gents. Why don't you move along?'

Liam hurried up behind him and dashed up the path to his front door.

'That's the Hincher kid,' one of them stated, pulling his camera up. His lens shutter clicked rapidly as he fired off several shots.

'You're wasting your time, mate,' muttered Minter, shaking his head. He turned round and followed Liam up the path. He stepped through the front door and closed it quickly behind him.

Andrew Hincher was waiting just inside. 'Finally done harassing my boy, have you?' he said.

'Relax, he's no longer a person of interest,' replied Minter.

'What does that mean? Do you think you're bloody well going to haul me back in again?'

Minter shook his head. 'Neither of you are persons of interest. It looks like Audrey took herself off.'

Andrew's eyes widened. '*What?*'

'She's cleared off, mate. Pegged it.' Minter couldn't help the smile spreading across his lips. 'I think she's had enough of you, Andrew.'

'So you've found her? Where the hell is she? I want to know right now!' Andrew barked. 'I've got the whole bloody world out there accusing me and my son of all sorts of –'

Minter raised his hands to calm him down. 'There'll be a briefing from Hastings station later this afternoon, but we think she took a train,' replied Minter. 'We don't know where to... We're looking into it right now. Your son was saying he thought she might have decided to go abroad.'

'*What?*' Andrew said again. '*Audrey?*' He shook his head in disbelief. 'She hasn't got the gumption to catch a bus by herself, let alone go and get a plane!'

'Has she got a passport?' Minter asked.

Andrew nodded. 'We took a holiday abroad a few years ago. I had to organise her passport for her since she didn't have one.' He went into the lounge and headed for the filing cabinet in the corner. 'It should be still valid,' he added. He jerked the top drawer open and thumbed through the folders. 'Here we are...' And stopped.

'What is it?' asked Minter.

Andrew turned to look at him. 'Fuckin' hell. *It's gone!*'

38

DC Ravindra Rajan counted a total of fourteen cameras around the station's entrance and inside and along the four platforms.

'Erm... can I help you?'

He turned to be faced with an incredibly short woman wearing a high-vis jacket, a name tag – Jenny First – and a stern look on her freckled face.

'I've been watching you for the last ten minutes. Can I ask what you're up to?' she asked in a squeaky voice.

Rajan knew he probably looked as though he was up to no good, casing the joint as he was. Plus he was brown-skinned, thickly bearded and had a rucksack slung over one shoulder.

He fished inside his puffa jacket and pulled out his lanyard. 'DC Rajan, Hastings CID, love,' he said.

She blushed, confirming his suspicions. 'Ah,' she said.

'I'm just checking your cameras,' he added. 'You got fourteen?'

'Eighteen,' she replied, then managed a smile. 'They're like Pokémon. You've got to find them all, right?'

'Right.' He laughed. 'Is it possible I could speak to your supervisor?'

'You mean the station manager?'

'Yeah. If he's around, like.'

'You're speaking to her,' she replied.

Rajan smiled and nodded, silently conceding that he'd also made an assumption. They were even. 'I'm working on a missing persons case,' he said, 'and we have reason to believe she came here and took a train.'

'Oh.' Jenny First nodded. 'That local woman who went missing in the high street?'

'That's her,' he confirmed.

'Ooh, that's good news, then,' she said. 'I was beginning to think you lot might end up finding a body.'

'So were we,' he admitted.

'You think she came to the station? Do you want to review our CCTV footage?' she asked him.

'If that's okay?'

She pulled out a set of jangling keys. 'Come with me, then DC...'

'Rajan. Or just call me Raj,' he said, inwardly wincing.

'I'm Jenny,' she replied, pointing at her name tag and then looking up at him as though she was admiring a New York skyscraper. 'Come this way.'

She led him across the concourse to a door marked 'Station Manager', unlocked it and waved him in. 'My office is like me,' she said, 'small but well organised. Take a seat.'

She stepped behind her desk and clicked the mouse to bring her computer back to life. 'What date are we looking at?'

'Last Thursday. That would be eighteenth of April.'

'And what time?'

'Let's say between twelve thirty and two,' Rajan said.

Jenny clicked away with her mouse a dozen or so times, then finally spun her monitor round for him to see. She had all eighteen cameras up on the screen as grid of thumbnails. 'You can click on any of them to maximise them,' she told him. 'Use the control bar at the bottom to scroll through the time.'

'Thanks, that's great,' he replied.

'Here, you can have my seat.'

They both got up at the same time and rounded the same end of the desk, blocking each other's path. Rajan stepped aside to let her pass and bumped the back of his head against a shelf with a loud thunk.

'Ow!' he yelped.

'Oh God. Are you all right?' Jenny asked.

He winced, rubbing his head. 'Yeah, I'm good.'

'I need a stool to reach those. Until now, I thought they were safely high.' She suppressed a little smile. 'You look like Gandalf stumbling around Bilbo Baggins' burrow.'

'The lads at my old station used to call me Buddy,' he said.

She frowned. 'Huh?'

'Buddy the elf'? From the Will Farrell film?'

She laughed. He sat down in her seat, still rubbing his head.

'Do you want a coffee?' she asked.

'Nice – that'd be sound,' he said with a smile. 'Something frothy and sugary, if that's possible.'

She nodded. 'I'll see what I can do. I might even let you have one of my home-made chocolate cookies.'

He grinned at her. 'Perfect.'

∼

'Guv?'

DCI Boyd stopped pecking away at his keyboard and looked up at DC Rajan. 'What've you got for me?'

'I've got Audrey on the station's cameras,' he said excitedly. 'Do you want to come and take a look?'

Boyd nodded, pushed back his chair and got up.

Rajan led him over to his desk, sat down and tapped the screen to maximise one of the video files he'd brought back on a memory stick. He'd also brought back a certain station manager's phone number, but Boyd didn't need to know that.

'That's her,' he said, 'coming into the station. 'See?'

The video had captured Audrey Hincher rushing into the station, her bag swinging from her shoulder. The quality of the station's CCTV footage was better than average. It was a decent resolution and smooth sequence that clearly showed Audrey wearing flat shoes, a tartan skirt and the kind of pale-grey hoodie that teen lads tended to spend most of their time slouching around in.

'Now that's a person in a big hurry,' said Boyd.

'Aye.' Rajan nodded. 'And she's twitchy as hell. See how she keeps looking around all the time.'

'Hmmm. It's as though she's just stuffed the Crown jewels into her bag,' Boyd agreed.

Rajan opened another file that showed Audrey at the ticket office. 'This is her buying a ticket fifteen minutes later. She's paying with cash.'

Boyd nodded. 'She really, *really* doesn't want to leave any sort of trail behind her, does she?'

Rajan clicked on a third video. 'And *this* is her getting the 2.25 p.m. train to London Victoria.'

Audrey walked up the platform, checking windows and

regularly checking behind her as if she suspected someone was shadowing her.

Minter joined them. 'You've managed to pick her up at the station, then, Raj?'

He nodded. 'She got on a train to London.'

Okeke appeared next to Minter. 'Did I hear that right? You've got Audrey?'

Rajan nodded again.

'Off to London,' added Minter. 'That makes sense.' They all looked at him. 'Her passport's missing from their house,' he explained. 'That's obviously what she went home for.'

'And to ditch her phone,' said Boyd. He shook his head. 'You don't think she's some Soviet-era sleeper agent who's just been recalled home by Putin, do you?'

Minter and Rajan stared at him in shock.

'I'm joking,' said Boyd. 'Obviously. But... sheeesh, she looks flustered as hell, doesn't she?'

'Do you think she's worrying that her husband's after her?' asked Minter.

'He was in London,' said Boyd. 'As far as she knows, right? And nothing's come through on her phone. No calls, texts or even emails. So what the hell's spooking her?'

Minter shrugged. 'You got me, boss.'

'Okay,' said Boyd finally. 'Good work, Rajan. Can you drop that lot into the log folder for me?'

'Will do,' Rajan replied.

Boyd checked his watch. It was gone two o'clock. 'I've got the press room booked for five,' he said. 'We'd better get a move on and piece this all together.'

Minter drew in air. 'Maybe you're right, though, boss. Stranger things have happened, eh?'

'Right about what?' Boyd asked.

'Her being... you know, some super-secret spy?'

Boyd and Okeke glanced at each other.

'Oh, behave, Minter,' said Okeke quickly. 'This is Hastings. The answer'll be weirder than that.'

39

Boyd tapped the PowerPoint clicker and the screen behind him displayed the montage of CCTV images from the train station that Rajan had stitched together, with a red circle highlighting Audrey as she moved from one shot into another across the concourse.

'As you can see,' he said, 'she's clearly agitated. In this shot you can clearly see her buying a ticket.. and... *here* she's boarding the 14:25 train to London Victoria.'

Boyd stopped the video and turned to the journalists. 'So there it is. What we have is a pretty unambiguous indication that her disappearance was voluntary. We are, of course, still keen to make contact with Audrey. I'll take any questions,' he said, expecting a poor showing of hands.

Pretty much everyone in the four rows of seats before him raised theirs.

He pointed at the chap from the *Argus*. Jack something. After two years in Hastings, Boyd was starting to recognise the regulars.

'Jack Flynn, *Argus*,' the journalist said. 'So... does that mean both Liam and Andrew Hincher are no longer suspects?'

Boyd nodded. 'We released Liam this morning and we have no reason to suspect either he or his father have anything to do with Audrey's disappearance. From the evidence you've just seen, this is evidently a decision she herself made.'

He pointed at another vaguely familiar face in the first row.

'Michael Hodge, *BBC South East*. Is there any suggestion that she may have been *coerced* in some way? Could she have been contacted by a third party? Perhaps someone trying to blackmail her or leverage her into going somewhere?'

Boyd shook his head. 'We've found nothing so far to suggest that.'

'Could she be running from someone then?' pressed Hodge. 'Or maybe debt? Or a scandal?'

Boyd shook his head again. 'I really don't think so. There's no evidence to indicate that she was living a double life or had anything going on, certainly financially, that would have compelled her to suddenly pack her bags and run.'

He directed his eyes at another journalist.

'Suzanne Hart, *Global News*,' she said, introducing herself. 'Was she fleeing an abusive relationship?'

Boyd would have loved to say 'yes', because frankly in his mind Audrey had definitely been in one for the last ten years. But, without an accusation from Audrey herself, he'd be stepping into actionable territory. He paused a fraction too long, though.

'She looks very scared in that CCTV camera footage,' Suzanne prompted.

Boyd nodded, because she had indeed looked afraid.

'She appears agitated, yes –which is a concern. We think that she may have been in a fragile state of mind at the time of her disappearance, which is why we're still determined to ascertain her whereabouts or to hear from her.'

'Do you believe she's a suicide risk?' asked Suzanne.

How the hell was he supposed to answer that? 'We're concerned for her,' he said firmly, 'as we would be for anyone who was acting out of character and hadn't been in contact with their loved ones for a period of time.' He turned his gaze to direct his answer towards one of the TV cameras that were positioned on tripods at the back of the press room. 'Audrey, if you're watching this... I implore you to reach out and contact the police. You're in no trouble whatsoever. We just want to know that you are safe and well. Your mother, your stepdaughter, your work colleagues... all want to know that you're all right. Please... just pick up a phone and reach out to us.'

∽

BOYD WAS PRETTY SURE the press mob had cleared off by the time he powered his computer down. He grabbed his jacket and checked out of the plastic-wrapped station for the day.

'DCI Boyd?'

He turned to see Suzanne Hart, waiting outside. She hurried over to him.

'I'm off the clock,' he said as he strode towards his car.

'You didn't really say no to my question about Audrey's relationship being abusive,' she said.

'I didn't say yes either,' he replied. He reached his Captur and dug in his jacket pocket for his keys.

'But it's a yes, isn't it?'

He paused to look at her. 'Off the record?'

She nodded.

'Then yes – I have my suspicions. But, as I'm sure you're aware, there's not much we can do unless a report is filed.'

'And that's where the system falls down,' Suzanne pointed out.

'I couldn't agree more,' he said, tapping his key fob to unlock the car. 'But what do you want me to do about it?'

'So there were no callouts? Or cautions against Mr Hincher?' she probed.

Again, tempting. Andrew Hincher had a caution on his file, but nothing that Boyd could share with a journo.

'Nothing we can use,' he replied, letting her infer from that what she wanted to.

'So maybe this was her parachute jump?' she said.

'Sorry?'

She smiled. 'If you've ever been in an abusive relationship, you'd understand. A grab-bag of essentials, a jam jar of squirrelled-away money and a friend who'll take you in, no questions asked – all on standby, just in case.'

'You think that's what this is? Audrey's parachute jump? According to her family, she doesn't have any friends,' Boyd said.

'More often than not, they're *old* friends. Not ones you go out with for a drink after work but someone from the distant past. Someone you might touch base with only once every now and then.' Suzanne smiled again. 'It's got to be worth a shot, DCI Boyd. Right?'

'I'll give that a go. Thanks,' he said, getting into the car.

Suzanne Hart nodded. 'Contrary to popular belief, we're not all hacks after an "*if it bleeds, it leads*" story. Sometimes we're actually here to help.'

40

Charlotte smiled as she twirled her fork in her tagliatelle. 'I think that's wonderful news!'

Boyd nodded. 'Well, it's a shedload better than the alternative.' He poured some more wine into her glass. 'Ems?'

Emma shook her head. 'I think Maggie's going to keep me up tonight. She's got a bug.'

Boyd topped himself up. 'I've gotta admit, I really thought we were going to end up finding her body somewhere.'

'You may still,' said Emma. 'If she's, you know, mentally unstable.'

'I don't think she's unstable,' said Charlotte. 'Quite the opposite, in fact.'

Boyd looked at her. 'What makes you think that?'

'She's taken matters into her own hands. She's plotted her exit strategy and taken it. And good for her,' Charlotte said matter-of-factly.

'You saw the footage in the station,' said Boyd. 'She looked as twitchy as hell.'

Emma shrugged. 'Who wouldn't be?'

'And... her departure *wasn't* planned,' said Boyd. 'She took a taxi back to her house to pack a bag. Surely, she'd have gone to work that morning with everything she needed if she knew she was going to run?' He grabbed a piece of the garlic bread. 'No... I still think something unexpected happened. Something triggering. This wasn't planned; it was a reaction to something.'

'I think that journalist was right,' Charlotte said. 'It was her "parachute jump".'

Emma looked confused. Boyd filled her in on the conversation he'd had with Suzanne Hart.

'Good phrase, that,' Emma said, smiling.

'It is, isn't it?' Charlotte replied. 'I called mine my *running kit*.'

'Not to be confused with Lycra joggers and nipple cream?' chuckled Boyd.

Charlotte frowned, as did Emma. 'Dad!' she exclaimed.

He nodded. That was thoughtless. 'Sorry, Char.'

Charlotte shrugged it away. 'It's all right – it's ancient history now. Ewan was another time, another life. And I did the right thing and left him as soon as he started getting violent.' She looked up from her dinner. 'Audrey and I are the lucky ones. There are so many women who suffer in silence until the bitter end, without saying a word.' She sighed. 'And for some, the bitter end is...'

Dead. It so nearly had been for Charlotte.

Boyd changed the subject. 'Any news from Danny Boy and his merry minstrels?' he asked Emma.

'They're back from Europe,' Emma replied. 'He said the gigs were bloody awful. The ones they headlined were virtually deserted and at the support slots they had they were heckled.'

'Oh...' Boyd began.

Emma waved her fork. 'He said it was just bad bookings by the agent. They put them in front of the wrong kind of crowds.'

'Ah...' He nodded. 'That would do it. Is he coming by to see his daughter at any point?'

'About that...' Emma looked at him. 'Is it okay if he stays with us for a while?'

'Of course!' Boyd reached for his wine. 'It would be good to catch up with him.'

'Not just overnight, Dad...' Emma said. 'I mean for *a while*. He's lost his flat. The landlord wants him out so she can refurb it and sell it on.'

'Can't he just look for another flat?' Boyd asked, dismayed.

'That's just it – there aren't that many places going spare in Hastings, and those that are, are becoming ridiculously expensive,' Emma explained.

'I thought he was doing well,' Boyd said. 'What's the phrase you used... *minted*?'

'Yeah, Dad, he's doing well for a musician,' Emma said. 'That sort of money can't compete with some city twat from London who wants a weekend shag pad.'

'There's room for him here,' said Charlotte. 'We've still got two rooms upstairs that are doing nothing particularly useful.'

'That would be really helpful,' Emma replied. 'He'd need one to store his stuff.' She turned to Boyd. 'If that's okay, Dad?'

Boyd pondered on that for a moment. Maybe it wouldn't be so bad. It might be nice to have Danny around. Another male in the house, and a pleasant one at that. And if he was living here, Boyd would be able to keep an eye on him. He'd be able to see for himself that Danny put Emma and Maggie first. Truth be told, Boyd was sympathetic to Danny trying his luck with his band. You only ever got one bite at that cherry, and you either went for it or spent your life wishing you had.

'All right,' he said at last. Then smiled. 'Do you think he'd let me noodle around on one of his guitars?'

Emma grinned. 'He'd love that. You could jam.'

Charlotte looked at him wryly. 'You can still play the guitar, can you, Bill?'

He shrugged. 'It's been a while,' he admitted. 'I expect it'll be horribly embarrassing.'

41

Andrew Hincher sat in his deckchair beside the brick barbecue and pulled open his second can of Carling. He heaved a deep sigh of relief. The previous week had been unbearably stressful. Not only because both he *and* Liam had been hauled in and held overnight by the pigs but because of that baying crowd of parasites that had been lingering outside his front door, mobbing him every time he stepped out and hammering on the windows to get him to show his angry face through the net curtains. And, only minutes later, there it was in the *Mail Online* or some other clickbait news page.

Anyway, they were gone now.

Wankers.

He took a slug of his beer.

Now that Audrey had been spotted getting a train to London, the whole bloody clown show had moved on to find another poor bastard to hound to death. He looked at the garden in the waning light. That was a mess too. Despite the huge trenches that they'd dug along the bottom, the only thing those idiots in white romper suits had managed to find was a dead cat.

Andrew lit a cigarette and puffed out a cloud of smoke, along with another huge sigh of relief. He glanced up at the house. Liam's bedroom light was on; he could see light flickering away against the curtain. Either he was gunning someone down on his bloody PlayStation or the dirty little bastard was whacking off over something or other again.

He'd have invited his son down for a beer to celebrate, but the lad was probably on the weed already.

Christ alive. What a week. What. A. Fucking. Week.

But it was over, finally, and he couldn't help but think he'd dodged a huge bloody bullet.

The cops had been all over him like a rash *and* all over the house like an invasion of ants... and they'd only managed to find that decades-old stain of Carol's blood on the lounge floor.

He was pretty sure there were poor bastards like him who'd been sent down for life for less evidence than that.

Yes, it was Carol's blood, and yes it had been a sizeable stain... and, sure, he'd been the one to cause it. He'd punched her. But no – he hadn't murdered the stupid drug-addled bitch. He'd slapped her – admittedly hard – and she'd cracked her head on the way down. She'd cut her scalp, and, boy, had it bled like buggery. He'd had to drag her to one side to clean up the mess. Which was what Becca must have seen. He shook his head at the thought that his ungrateful, treacherous bitch of a daughter had been more than happy to see her dad banged up for murder, when in fact she owed him for all those years of looking after her, providing a roof over her head. He'd been a single dad, doing his best for her...with no help, no support and no money.

'Bitch,' he muttered, taking another slug of beer.

He was the Good Guy here. He'd stuck around to raise her and Liam. It was Carol who deserved to be demonised. She was the one who'd packed her bags, pissed off and left them all to rot. If that haggard old cow was still alive, somewhere out there, the least she could have done was come forward and let the police know that he, Andrew Hincher, wasn't a murderer. Mind you, he wouldn't at all be surprised to hear that she was long dead, unless she'd miraculously managed to kick the booze and the drug habit.

He'd dodged a bullet with Audrey too. That muddle-headed, miserable old sow had been driving him nuts recently. It was lucky for him that he hadn't smacked her more recently and left traces of forensic evidence – bloody tissues in a waste bin, for example – that the pigs could have used to support their theory that he'd done away with her.

She had surprised him, though, taking off like that. She had no one else in her life, apart from that old shrew of a mother. He couldn't imagine any other man would be interested in a frump like her … Her face looked as though she was permanently sucking a lemon. Plus she had a figure like a sack of potatoes and all the personality of a damp dishcloth. The only thing she had ever brought to their relationship was a steady income and a piggy bank full of money that had been left to her by her dad. She'd been dumb enough, even during their honeymoon period, to believe that he felt a damned thing for her. That she'd caught his eye and won him over with her wit and sexual charm.

Stupid cow. Stupid *cash* cow...

So it was something of revelation to him, watching the news earlier, when that big muppet of a DCI had shown Audrey making a run for it in Hastings station.

He chuckled as he took another chug of his beer. 'Well, well, well, Audrey... you're a dark horse, aren't you, love?'

She'd taken her passport, for Christ's sake! Where the hell did she think she was heading? Deepest, darkest Peru? He smirked. Maybe she was. Maybe there was some shithole corner of the world where some desperate short-sighted rice farmer might think she was a catch.

He finished his beer and climbed out of the deckchair to retrieve another from the fridge.

Andrew stepped inside the kitchen, beginning to feel the buzz from the first can cutting through some of the stress and anxiety of the last week. There hadn't just been the looming threat that he'd go down for something he hadn't done; there was also the reputational damage. His small roster of customers – mostly female – were undoubtedly having second thoughts about hiring him again, and, more concerning, Berkley Security might be worrying about their public image and there was every chance they'd be pondering dropping him out of their franchise. Just when, for the first time in his life, he was starting to make some decent money.

'Fucking bitch,' he muttered as he paused in front of the fridge.

A thought occurred to him. The beers could wait a moment. He hurried to the lounge, to his filing cabinet. On the last job he'd had, the woman had kindly paid him in cash as he'd asked, so that he could keep Berkley from taking their hefty share. He'd been flirting with the old tart all week to get that.

Oh, she'd better not have... She'd better not have...

He opened the top drawer and pulled the files forward so that he could grope at the very back for the brown envelope. He had fifteen hundred in there.

His fingers patted the back of the cabinet and found nothing.

'Fuck!' he hissed. '*Fuuuuuck!*'

42

Audrey Hincher peered out of the window of her Travelodge room at the cars parked outside. The *thunk* of a closing car door had startled her into taking a peek. She spotted a bald man in a suit, looking tired and beaten, grabbing an overnight bag and briefcase from the rear of his Hyundai. She heaved a sigh of relief and went back to bed.

She unmuted the TV and returned to watching-but-not-really-watching Paul Hollywood and Pru Leith evaluate a row of choux buns. She dipped her hand into a box of Celebrations, unwrapped a mini Twix and dumped the wrapper among the many others on the bed.

She was on her second box of the day.

All this waiting around was killing her. Shredding her nerves. Her anxiety level was through the roof, not helped at all by what she'd seen on the TV earlier this evening. Not for one moment, not one darned moment, had she thought that her hasty departure from Hastings would make the local news, let alone the *national* news. She'd made the mistake of vanishing during a week in which the only big news story was the impending wet summer. The country was bored witless with politics and tittle-tattle. Bored to the point that one woman had packed her bags and fled a violent bully and *that* had become *news* for goodness' sake!

There she'd been, on the telly – images of her shuffling anxiously through Hastings station – and an avalanche of questions for the police officer as to what she was up to and where she was going. And, anyway, why were the police involved? It wasn't as if she'd broken any laws!

The money that Andy thought he'd managed to hide away was rightfully *hers*. God knows she'd had no option but to let him drain her bank account over the years to fund his various get-rich-quick schemes, to pay his debts, to buy his work van, to fix up his house, to feed and clothe his kids... The list went on. She'd paid for everything while he pratted around and did whatever he wanted.

She glanced at herself in the mirror. The photograph of her that the police had used was eight years old, taken from Andy's Facebook page. It was a picture taken during their family holiday to Ibiza when Rebecca was only nineteen and Liam fifteen. She'd been slimmer back then and she'd worn make-up too. Back then, she'd still been making an effort for him.

All the same, the passing years withstanding, it was recognisably her.

She was going to have to disguise herself somehow, especially if she was stepping out to meet with *those people* tomorrow.

She'd need hair dye. Something dark. And different clothes. Some glasses perhaps? Would that be enough? Or would they see through her disguise and figure out who she was the moment they caught sight of her? Would they recognise her name?

No, she assured herself. It wasn't an uncommon name. And there'd be no need for them to do any checks on her. She'd brought everything they said they wanted to see. So long as she could calm down a bit and stop herself from twitching and fidgeting when she finally sat down with them.

'It's going to go all right,' she told her reflection in the mirror. 'It's going to be fine. You'll show them what they asked to see... they'll click a button... and it'll be done.'

And this interminable waiting would be over.

And she'd be free.

Audrey took another chocolate out of the box and unwrapped it, tossing the paper on the bed to join the others. It was nearly ten o'clock. She reached for the remote control and turned over to ITV. The news would be on in a minute.

Hopefully her disappearance from Hastings would have dropped off the radar. *They surely had bigger, more serious news by now, right?*

43

'Morning, mate,' said Rajan. 'Do you mind if I ask a few questions?'

The balding man inside the corner shop had a clipboard in one hand and was shuffling stock around on the shelf with the other. Rajan smiled. The old boy reminded him of his uncle – he wore a long cardigan and was busy rotating all the nearly-out-of-date stock to the very front of the shelf. Rajan's uncle had always had a calculator in one pocket and an open packet of crisps in the other.

'I'm police,' Rajan added, noticing the man's suspicious expression, and he lifted his lanyard to show his ID. 'DC Ravindra Rajan. And you are...'

'Mr Hassim,' the shopkeeper replied cautiously. 'The owner.' He frowned. 'This is about the vapes, yeah? Because if it is... we don't sell them kiddie ones no more.'

'Nah, it's not about the vapes,' Rajan said lightly. 'It's about that missing local woman.'

The blank look on Hassim's face suggested he didn't spend much time sitting in front of the TV. Which didn't surprise Rajan. He approached the old man and held out his own clipboard. There was a picture of Audrey Hincher on top.

'*This* lady,' he continued. 'She went missing somewhere along this street a week ago.'

Hassim leant forward to peer more closely at the printed image. There were two images, in fact: the one from Facebook and one from the train station's CCTV – the clearest screenshot they'd managed to grab. 'I just wondered if you might have –'

'Yes,' the shopkeeper replied quickly.

'*What?*' said Rajan, taken aback.

'Have I seen her?' Hassim nodded. 'Yes, she's a regular. This lady, she comes most days. For milk, bread, beans... sometimes post office,' he said, tilting his head towards the other counter at the back of the small shop. 'My wife deals.'

'So you're saying she was in here last Thursday?'

He nodded. 'Lunchtime.'

'You're sure about that?' Rajan asked.

Hassim's eyes widened slightly as he nodded again. 'Very.'

'How come you're so sure? Rajan said.

'Very odd,' he replied. 'Very, very odd behaviour.'

'How do you mean?'

'She come in, pick up a couple of things, then waits in line, all normal, yes? When it's her turn, I scan her things, she pays... then she suddenly goes all what-the-bloody crazy.'

'How so?' Rajan asked.

'She gives me lottery tickets, yes? To scan for win, then suddenly she snatches them back. I ask her, "What is the problem?" She says nothing. Just starts this...' Hassim comically mimicked heavy breathing, his nostrils flaring, his chest heaving. 'Then she runs out of my shop! Leaves her stamps and what-not on my counter!'

'Why did she do that do you think?'

Hassim raised his narrow shoulders and dropped them again. 'Like she had a big scare. I go to the door with her things. She is outside... walking backwards, forwards.' Hassim acted that out for him too, pacing a couple of steps left, then back again. 'I shout, "Your things missus, your things!" She totally ignores me. I'm like, *What the bloody!* Very rude. Then...'

He grabbed Rajan's arm and led him to the front door, pulled it open and led him outside onto Queens Road. Hassim pointed down the street. 'I see her go to that and use it.'

Hassim was pointing at an old phone box. Not an old-old red one, but one of those half-arsed scuffed Perspex three-sided ones.

Rajan looked up and down the street. They were two thirds of the way down – the CCTV blind spot.

'Could you hear what she said on the phone?'

Hassim shook his head. 'Lunchtime. Very busy. Very noisy.'

'How long was the call?' Rajan asked.

'Not long. Only a few minutes. I am waiting outside. I still have her things she paid for, yes?'

Rajan nodded.

'She finishes call, so I shout out again: "Missus, your things!" She doesn't even hear me. She just walks off in a big, big hurry!' Hassim shook his head and tutted. 'Crazy, crazy lady.'

∼

BOYD SET down his breakfast wrap and looked at the smudged printout that Rajan had just dropped on his desk. 'What's that?' he asked.

'It's the call log from the phone box on Queens Road, guv.'

'Sorry, Rajan. Can I have some context, mate? I'm looking at this because...?'

'Because of the door-to-doors on Queens Road?' Rajan offered.

Boyd checked his watch; it was ten past nine. 'Christ, Rajan, you've done that already?' The door-knocking along Queens was a task Boyd had parcelled out to him yesterday, and had, in truth, completely forgotten about in the aftermath of finding out that Audrey was alive and well.

'The very first shop I went into,' Rajan replied. 'It was a grocer's and post office.' He relayed what Mr Hassim had told him.

'And this old boy's certain it was her?' Boyd said.

Rajan nodded. 'He said she suddenly started acting batshit crazy.' He tapped the piece of paper. 'No one uses phone boxes any more, right? Look at the call log. Days go by between calls. Sometimes even weeks. But see – there it is...' He tapped his finger beside a log entry. 'Thursday, 12.24 p.m. Duration four minutes, fifty-six seconds.'

Boyd squinted at the very small, smudged print. 'Blimey. You're right.' And there was a phone number beside it. 'Have you check–'

'Already did a number search. You're not going to believe it,' Rajan said.

'To be honest, I'll believe pretty much anything at this point,' Boyd said. 'Try me.'

'It was for Carnivale Lotto,' Rajan said, grinning. 'I think our Audrey suddenly learned she'd won a ton on the lottery.'

~

'THE LOTTERY?' exclaimed Sutherland.

'Not *the* lottery, the Camelot one... It's another one, run by a company called Carnivale,' Boyd said.

'Never ruddy heard of it,' Sutherland said.

'Me neither. But apparently they're big in Europe. She rang the number printed on the ticket – the one you call if you've got a substantial win.'

Sutherland's eyes boggled behind his glasses. 'How much did she win?'

'I don't know,' Boyd said. 'But I'm guessing it was a sizeable chunk.'

'Are you going to call them, then?' Sutherland asked.

Boyd glanced out at the barely populated CID floor. 'Well, that's the question. It's not really any of our business now, is it?'

Sutherland shook his head. 'With all her cloak-and-dagger shenanigans? Failing to get in contact when the police have launched a ruddy murder enquiry? I'd say it *is* our business. At the very least she's wasted a load of police time. At the very worst... she could be acting fraudulently. All that sneaking off, dumping her phone, taking her passport, lying low?' He wagged his pen like a finger. 'Has she made a claim using someone else's ticket? Perhaps that's Andrew Hincher's winning ticket. Or Liam's...'

Sutherland had a valid point, and this had crossed Boyd's mind already. However, he had been on the cusp of downgrading the case to a 'No Further Action'. Audrey Hincher had done what so many women do, or dream of doing – she'd escaped an abusive partner. And good luck to her.

'The very minimum we're required to do, Boyd, is ask Andrew and Liam Hincher if the ticket might be either of theirs,' Sutherland said.

44

Audrey looked into the bathroom mirror at the stranger staring back at her. The hair dye had promised a subtle hazel brown. Instead her hair had become almost mahogany. It looked like a wig and didn't even remotely match her brows.

'Oh God,' she gasped. 'Too much.'

She'd wanted to look a little different to the picture the police had shown, not like some FBI Most Wanted on the run. Well, it was too late to do anything about it now.

She checked her watch. It was 10.15 a.m. The woman who'd taken her call at Carnivale had arranged their validation appointment for 2 p.m.

Audrey needed to be cool and composed, not flustered and fidgety and checking over her shoulder all the time. Andrew wasn't going to be coming for her. He rarely checked the numbers.

'Be calm,' she whispered to her reflection. 'You *are* the winner, Audrey. This is your ticket.'

Except it wasn't. It was Andrew's. And in a few hours' time she was going to walk into the Carnivale office and claim that the name 'Andy' untidily scrawled on the winning ticket was in fact 'Audrey' – and written in *her* handwriting. That's what he did with the five tickets he bought every few weeks, put his name on each and every one. She wondered if they'd request a copy of the signature or ask her to sign her name then and there on a scrap of paper.

Did they do that?

Just in case, she'd practised writing his name dozens of times and had got, she thought, close enough that it could pass as his hand. Thank God for their similar names. The building society paying-in book had only his initial on it, and the bank statements and utility bills she'd brought along were the same. Just plain A. Hincher.

What she had no idea about at this stage – and the very reason she'd been biding her time all week, tucked away in her Travelodge room watching *Bake-Off* and eating chocolates to take her mind off the looming showdown – was whether Andrew *had* spotted that his numbers had finally come up. Was she about to walk into a situation where the adjudicator would announce that someone else had made a claim against the same numbers on a ticket purchased in Hastings. Or worse: was he going to be there, along with the police... ready to arrest her?

If so... then she was going to look one hundred per cent guilty with her disguise and his paperwork. The other thing she'd done this week – while waiting for the days to pass until a *new* batch of lottery numbers appeared on the screen above every point-of-sale machine – was set up a brand-new bank account. She was hoping the Carnivale people would take those new details without asking any questions as to why it was so recently opened and would happily pay the money straight into that account... and off she'd go. But God help her if Andrew had caught on and was waiting there for her...

What she was about to do was fraud.

I could end up in prison.

'Be calm,' she uttered again to the stranger in the mirror. 'Be calm.'

~

BOYD WASN'T QUITE ready to speak to Andrew Hincher again. Instead, he called the number that Rajan had pointed to on the phone-box list.

'Enquiries, how can I help you?' a cheerful young woman answered after a couple of rings.

'Is this the line that deals with winning numbers?' Boyd asked.

'Uh-huh, and let me say first of all – congratulations on purchasing a winning Carnivale Lottery tic–' she began.

'I'm not a winner,' Boyd replied. 'I'm just after some information.'

'Oh.' Her chirpy tone fell away instantly. 'We don't share information with anyone. Particularly not with journalists.'

'Wait! I'm police,' he said quickly. 'Not a hack.' He could hear the faint sounds of a busy open-plan office in the background.

'How do I know you're a real copper?' she asked.

'Search this phone number I'm calling you from,' he said. 'It'll give you Hastings police station. My name is DCI William Boyd. I can wait.'

He heard the clatter of a keyboard. Then: 'What's this concerning, please?' she asked in a friendlier tone.

'I'm calling to see if there have been any claims made against last week's lottery numbers?' he said.

'Okay,' she replied. 'But I can't reveal specific details. You know that, right? That particular information is strictly confidential.'

'It's all right,' he said. 'I just need to know if the prize money has been claimed or not.'

'It's not one big prize, you understand?' she told him. 'It's a pool of money divided between verified winners. Well, actually, it's three pools. We have six-number, five-number and four-number winners. There's a one-week claim window for the six-number fund, two for the five-number and a month for the four-number fund. Which category are you enquiring about?'

'The five-number one,' replied Boyd.

'I can tell you that we've had five claims settled and paid, and two are outstanding.'

'Outstanding? What does that mean?' he asked.

'It means that people have called to say they won, but they haven't yet verified the winning ticket and provided the required documents as proof in order for us to pay them.'

'And you can't give me any names?' he said.

'I can tell you the five names of the settled claims if you want. They've all signed waivers.' Without him asking, she happily rattled them off. None of them were Audrey, Andrew or Liam Hincher.

'And what about the two unclaimed ones?' he tried again.

'Sorry,' she replied. 'I can't tell you anything about those. Not until they've been verified and have signed the waiver.'

'Could you at least tell me where they're from?' he asked. 'Do you know where they bought their tickets? A town, a region, anything?'

She paused. 'Can I ask what this is to do with?'

'It's a missing-persons case I'm investigating,' he told her.

'Oh, that happens,' she replied. 'Sometimes the winners like to almost go off-grid for a bit to avoid being badgered to death by people with begging bowls in hand.' 'It's someone from Hastings, I'm presuming?' she asked.

He smiled. 'Ah... that's something, I'm afraid, *I* can't tell *you*.'

She laughed. 'Well, we're even, then.'

'I don't need a particular town or shop,' he pressed. 'The two unclaimed ones. Are they from England, Wales... north, south?'

She sighed. 'One claimant is from Greater Manchester and one from Sussex.'

Boyd smiled. *Bingo.*

'Is the Sussex winner male or female?' he asked.

'I'm sorry.' She sighed again. 'That's all you're getting today until they've been in with their details. You can try calling again tomorrow, if you like.'

'So they're coming to *your office today*?' he said.

'I didn't say that,' she said.

'All right,' Boyd replied, pretty sure she was smiling. 'Thanks very much for your help.' He hung up.

Today. He looked at his watch. It was approaching eleven. He realised too late that there were other questions he should have asked. How long did the verification process take? Did they pay out then and there? How much money was at stake? He mentally eye-rolled.

So one of the winners was from Sussex. Given Audrey's sudden and unplanned disappearance and the call she'd made outside the corner shop, it was almost certainly her.

But, as Sutherland had brought up her cloak-and-dagger act, he did need to check it was actually her ticket and not Andrew Hincher's. Boyd really didn't want to call him... If Andrew was the rightful owner of the ticket and the winner, the last thing Boyd wanted to do was give that bastard a heads-up that he might be in for a sizeable windfall if he hurried up.

Nonetheless...

He dialled Andrew's number and waited for an answer. It rang a dozen times and he was about to hang up when it flipped over to voicemail. Perfect. Boyd left a bland message for Andrew to call back. Then he hung up.

45

Andrew Hincher's head was still pounding, despite the fact that he'd stayed in bed and let the morning pass him by. His four cans of Carling last night had been supplemented by some cans of strong cider that he'd found lurking at the back of the fridge.

Discovering that the bitch had stolen the cash payment from his last job had been tempered by the fact that he was no longer a murder suspect, plus the realisation that he wouldn't have to roll over in bed and look at her ugly fat face on the pillow beside him in the morning.

Good riddance to her.

As he lay in bed, with only the throbbing pain in his head for company, he considered the pros and cons of the road ahead. She was gone, fine. She'd walked out on him, fine. That meant then he could file for divorce. She'd left him ... and that was called abandonment, right? And given that he'd endured over ten years of her, she'd have to give him something in a settlement. It worked both ways as far as he was aware. If she went after his house, he'd go after her money.

He checked his watch and was surprised to see it had gone eleven o'clock. Wow. He really had slept the whole morning away. Over the steady tapping of rain on his window, he could hear Liam's music thumping from his room across the hallway. The lazy arse hadn't even offered him a brew this morning.

He sat up, still dressed in yesterday's clothes. He barely remembered drinking that last can of cider and he certainly couldn't remember making his way up to bed.

Time to get your shit together, mate. He had customers to call in a bid to reassure them that he wasn't a murderer and had been cleared of any wrongdoing by the police. Berkley Security needed a call too, to assure them that the police were done with him and he wasn't a liability to their company's brand. And, of course, there were leads to chase. Life went on, right?

He reached for his phone and saw that he had a missed call and a voice message. He tapped his phone and listened.

It was that bloody copper again.

'What now?' he grumbled as he dialled the number that have been left.

The phone rang for ages before it was finally answered. 'DCI Boyd.'

'It's Andrew Hincher,' he said. 'You asked me to call you back.'

'Right,' Boyd said. 'We're not hauling you or Liam back in, but I do have a quick question to ask, if that's all right?'

'Christ... all right. What is it?' Andrew asked.

'Um, are you heading out anywhere today?'

'What the...' Andrew frowned. 'What's it to you what I decide to do today?' He shook his head.

Boyd paused. 'Fair enough. I do have another question.'

Andrew sighed. His head was hurting far too much to face this bloody joker. 'Go on.'

'Do you do the lottery?' Boyd asked.

That threw him. 'Er... yeah. Every now and then. If I can be arsed. Why the hell are you asking me that?'

'Do you pick regular numbers?'

'My birth date. Not that that's ever won me anything. What the hell is this, Boyd? Is there anything else you want to know? What my inside leg measurement is?'

'No, that's it,' Boyd said. 'I'm all done.'

'Are you sure you don't want to haul me and Liam in to ask us what our favourite colours are? What football teams we supp–'

Boyd hung up.

Andrew lowered his phone and stared at it. 'Jesus... what the fucking hell was *that* all about?'

A thought occurred to him.

'Shit... Surely not...' He tapped his browser and pulled up the lottery results page. He hadn't bothered checking it for ages, given that for all his diligence over the years he'd won the princely sum of a tenner. And that was just the once.

Last night's numbers sat at the top. They weren't his.

But beneath those were the ones from the week before.

'Oh... fuck me!' he whispered.

~

BOYD HAD MADE the decision to get off his arse and act. He had his jacket on and had just grabbed his car keys when his phone vibrated in his trouser pocket. He pulled it out as he made his way towards the double doors and the stairwell beyond.

It was Andrew Hincher. Boyd answered. 'Yeah?'

'She's stealing my fucking lottery money!' Andrew roared down the phone. 'She's took my ticket and she's gone to claim my money, hasn't she?'

'We don't know,' Boyd replied. 'Possibly. If she has, can you prove the ticket is yours?'

'Of course it's my bloody ticket! I bought it. Those numbers are *my* numbers!' he yelled.

'There's no law against someone using your numbers,' said Boyd, taking the stairs to the ground floor.

'There *is* a fucking law against stealing someone else's ticket!' Andrew stormed.

'And you've got proof it's yours, have you?' Boyd asked again.

'Yeah! Too right I have! I always sign my name on them. I'm not stupid.'

'Sorry, what was that?' Boyd asked. 'Andrew, you're fading in and out. The signal's bad...' He hung up, took the rest of the stairs in twos and threes, then and barrelled through the lobby and outside to the car park.

He needed to stop Audrey Hincher before she got herself into more of a mess than she was already in.

46

Audrey checked her watch again. It was 1.26 p.m. The person she was due to meet at 2 p.m. had a rather grand-sounding job title: the Adjudicator. She'd looked that up on the Carnivale website. She knew that the Adjudicator was a man, because the young chap on the helpline had revealed that 'he' was busy with another claimant this morning.

The job title sounded somewhat ominous – as though he was some kind of magistrate or, worse, some sixteenth-century Witchfinder General with piercing eyes beneath thunderous brows and a dunking chair ready to drown her in if any of her paperwork failed to meet his precise standards.

She'd been standing in the rain, on the other side of Carnivale's car park, for over an hour now, having checked out of the Travelodge. She was sheltering at a covered bus stop, pondering how the meeting was going to go. She gazed across the packed car park at the large glass-and-breezeblock building, the cars and tarmac glistening in the rain, and feared that the moment she presented herself at the doors some security men or policemen were going to descend upon her like a pack of dogs.

She shuddered at the thought of the cuffs coming out, the mandatory caution, being escorted to a waiting police car, the shame, the embarrassment and the headlines tomorrow. And those wouldn't be kind to her, would they?

Vanished Woman is Lottery Thief
Police Time-waster and Scammer
Audrey Hincher the Money-Pincher

A low-flying commercial aeroplane roared overhead, no doubt heading off to some sunny and far-away place. Audrey desperately wanted to get this over with. To receive the money, head straight to Heathrow, board a plane to Europe and start her new life on some sun-dappled Mediterranean island.

Not for the first time, she wondered whether she should just turn up early. Perhaps the Adjudicator would be fine to see her now, rather than waiting for the scheduled appointment.

She had decided to go for it, and had stepped out from the bus shelter, when suddenly a crowd of people spilled out from the Carnivale building and into the rain, umbrellas popping open here and there like blossoming daffodils. There were dozens, no hundreds of them. The whole building was emptying out, or so it seemed.

As she approached, she could hear the insistent trilling of an alarm. For a moment, a silly moment, she imagined it was for her – an alert triggered by the presence of some wicked person seeking to steal what wasn't theirs.

Audrey stopped dead in her tracks as the office workers spilled out among the cars, many of them taking the opportunity to light up cigarettes or pull out their vapes. She caught overlapping threads of conversation.

'Come on. Another drill? In this bloody weather?'

'Not a drill. I heard some moron triggered the fire alarm in the gents.'

'That'll be Steve, secret-smoking again. Idiot.'

A fire alarm. Just a fire alarm. Audrey heaved a sigh of relief as she watched several staff members in high-vis jackets count the people assembled in the car park.

∼

BOYD CLEARED the outskirts of Hastings and was on a long straight and mercifully clear section of the A21, heading up to the M25, before he tried calling Carnivale again.

'Hey, Siri... call the last number,' he instructed.

Siri called Hincher's number.

'No, stop!' Boyd yelled at the phone. His phone had been buzzing almost constantly for the last ten minutes with unanswered calls from Andrew. Like an idiot, in his haste he'd forgotten to hook it up to his in-car system.

Boyd fumbled for his phone and quickly thumbed to his 'recents' – one eye on the road, the other on the screen – and picked the number before Hincher's. He was put through to a switchboard and automated instructions, which explained that all operators were currently busy and began to take him through an exhaustive menu of options.

He ended the call. 'Bollocks.'

The satnav advised him he'd arrive at Carnivale's head office in Hounslow in ninety-four minutes' time. He could only hope that he got there before Audrey turned up. Boyd was still undecided what he was actually going to do if he *did* manage to intercept her, because technically she wouldn't have committed a crime *yet*. A gentle word of advice, perhaps? Just enough to put the idea out of her mind and send her on her way.

His phone suddenly buzzed in his lap. He glanced down. It was Charlotte. He tapped the screen. 'Hey there.'

'Hello, Mr Boyd,' she replied cordially. 'Sounds like you're out and about.'

'Driving to Hounslow, as it happens,' he replied.

'Oh? Was it something I said?'

He laughed. 'I'm on my way to stop someone making a mistake,' he told her.

'Anyone I know?'

'Actually, kind of. It's that missing woman. Audrey Hincher. We've found her – sort of.' He relayed this morning's manic sequence of events.

'Hmm,' Charlotte replied after a few moments. 'Well, I for one wouldn't hold it against her if she pocketed his winnings.'

'Nor me. But if Andrew's right and his name's on the ticket, and she tries to make out that it's *her* name, then she *will* be in trouble.'

'I guess if he's just written A. Hincher or Andy Hincher, she has a shot at getting away with it,' Charlotte said. 'Good for her, I say.'

'She'll have committed an act of fraud,' Boyd said.

'What will you do?' Charlotte asked. 'Will you arrest the poor woman?'

'That's a good question,' Boyd said. 'If I'm too late, then I'm going to have to. I'll have no choice in the matter. But, to be honest, I'd really rather not.'

'Does that awful hubby of hers know what she's up to?'

'Yeah.' He sighed. 'Oh, he knows all right… and he's been spitting blood about it. I've got a string of missed calls from him. I'm guessing he may have also been trying to call the lottery company.'

'In which case, they'll be forewarned,' she replied.

'Right. And the moment she goes in and says it's her money...'

'She'll be in big trouble,' Charlotte finished.

'Uh-huh. Hence my haste to get up there and stop her going in.'

'Does anyone else know what you're up to?'

He hadn't had time to tell anyone else where he was off to. 'No.'

'Is this going to get you into any trouble, Bill?' she asked.

Boyd thought Sutherland might have a thing or two to say about it. He chuckled, though, and said, 'Nope. It's what I like to call preventative policing.'

'You're not really going to arrest her, Bill... are you?' Charlotte said.

'Hopefully not,' he replied. That is, if he managed to catch her before she went in.

47

Audrey watched as the last of the Carnivale staff entered the building. She looked at the screen of her brand-new pay-as-you-go phone. It was 1.56 p.m.

She hadn't wanted to cut it this fine and actually end up late for her appointment, but, given that everyone had been kept outside until just now, she presumed that being a minute or two late wouldn't be held against her. In any case, the unexpected disruption to the day had probably put everyone behind.

She stepped inside and approached the reception desk, where a young woman was busy shaking the raindrops off her jacket and getting ready to resume her working day.

'Excuse me?' Audrey said.

The young woman looked up and smiled. 'How can I help you?'

'I... I have a two o'clock appointment,' Audrey told her.

'With whom?'

'With the person who verifies if someone has won some money.' Audrey said.

'Ah, the Adjudicator,' the receptionist said, and her smile widened. 'Ah, congratulations. Can I take your name?'

'A. Hincher,' Audrey replied.

'And what's your first name?' the receptionist asked.

Audrey could feel her cheeks beginning to colour. 'Audrey. My name's Audrey,' she said, her heart nearly beating out of her chest.

'Please take a seat over there, Audrey,' the receptionist said, pointing at a leather couch by a coffee table. 'I'll let them know you're here.'

'Them?' Audrey had only been expecting to see one person.

'The verification team,' the receptionist replied. 'We have an investment advisor, a counsellor and a solicitor who also sit in on the process,' she explained. 'A big win can be a bit of a shock to the system... so we make sure to help you take the first steps.' She nodded at the couch. 'Go and take a seat and I'll let them know you're here.'

Audrey wandered over to the couch and took a seat, feeling very much like there was a blinking sign hovering above her head, stating she was a fraud.

It's going to be fine, she told herself. *They'll just want to see my winning ticket, my passport and my ID details.* She'd brought six months' worth of bills and statements, in case they asked for them. She presumed there'd be some security questions: how long she'd lived in the UK, whether she was a British national, her NI number and so on. Then, all being well, she hoped that it would be as easy as someone tapping a key on a keyboard with a 'Ta-da!' and the money would be transferred to her and Andy's account.

And the instant it appeared... it would be off again. Taking another journey to her newly opened account.

Hopefully before Andy had time to realise what had happened.

~

BOYD WAS NOW on the M25, speeding – for once – along an empty road. His satnav indicated that he had another thirty-seven minutes to go until he arrived at Carnivale's head office. It was, he'd noticed, a stone's throw away from Heathrow. He wondered if that might be Audrey's next stop, once she'd secured her money. That's what he would do in her place. He'd buy the first ticket to anywhere and then, once he'd landed, he'd move his money to some local bank that really couldn't care less about UK financial regulations, so that if anybody back home had an issue with his winnings it would be tough titties for them.

The whole scenario felt vaguely absurd. From the mental picture he'd drawn of her, from Andrew's description and her work colleague's account, she really didn't seem like the kind of person who would try to pull off something so brazen. And something so cleverly contrived. This, he reminded himself, had been organised at very short notice. It was just over a week ago that she'd discovered there was a significant win to be had and she'd reacted entirely on impulse. She'd been cool-headed enough to leave barely a trail, ditching her phone at the first opportunity and effectively vanishing for a week. There were plenty of seasoned criminals he'd come across in his time who'd have been dumb enough to leave a credit card, CCTV, ANPR *and* phone trail that almost any idiot could follow.

They'd found Audrey's trail quite by chance – through Rajan's door-to-doors. Which, Boyd reminded himself, he'd have told the DC not to bother with if he'd realised that was still on his to-do list. He'd been on the verge of flagging the case as a NFA, and would have done if it hadn't been for the call made from that public phone booth.

Clever Audrey. Even in the state she must have been in – excited, paranoid, agitated even terrified – from the moment she stepped out of that corner shop she knew exactly what she had to do.

∼

'Sorry for the delay, Ms Hincher.'

Audrey glanced up from her phone. She'd been playing Puzzley Words in an attempt to distract herself, and had somehow managed to get sucked into the game. She jumped to her feet, almost dropping her phone as she reached out to grab the proffered hand.

'My name's Damian Porter. I'm Carnivale's official Father Christmas,' he said. beaming at her. The man was tall and whippet thin, with thinning short dark hair on top and a well-clipped dark goatee, framing his tiny, tidy teeth.

'I'm sorry?' she said, startled.

'I'm the Adjudicator,' he clarified.

'Oh, right.' She smiled and let go of his hand.

He looked at his watch. 'We're twenty-five minutes late. I'm sorry we've kept you waiting for so long. We had a wretched fire alarm here earlier. Some idiot decided to have a crafty smoke in one of the toilets,' he said with a sigh. 'Everyone's soaked through from the rain and mightily annoyed.'

'Oh,' was all she could think of to reply to that. 'Right.'

'Well, come on then,' he said, his smile widening to show even more tiny teeth. 'Let's go and make you a little bit richer, shall we?'

BOYD LEFT the clear run of the motorway and hit the dead crawl of the Hounslow traffic. Apparently he was four miles from Alexandra Business Park. What should have been a journey of a few minutes could take him the best part of an hour at this rate.

Up ahead, the road was clogged with white vans and cabbies honking angrily at each other while Just Eat scooters and motorcycles blithely whistled past them. A timely reminder to him that if he thought rush hour in Hastings was bad, it was never going to compete with regular Greater London traffic.

His phone started to buzz. As he was stationary and going nowhere fast, he checked to see if it was Hincher calling him yet again. It wasn't – it was Sutherland. He answered.

'Sir?'

'Where the hell are you, Boyd?' Sutherland sounded decidedly pissed off.

'Hounslow, sir,' he replied blithely.

'What are you doing up there in *Hounslow*?' Sutherland demanded.

Deciding that honesty probably was the best policy in this instance, he said, 'I'm chasing down Audrey Hincher.'

'Right – well, that bloody man Andrew Hincher has turned up here at the station!' replied Sutherland. 'He's raising hell about her stealing millions of pounds of his money!'

'I doubt it's millions, sir,' Boyd said.

'I don't care. He's giving me a ruddy headache! He said he's been trying to get through to you and the lottery people... and if he doesn't have any answers soon, the next thing he's planning to do is ring the bloody papers!'

'Tell him I'm very nearly at the lottery place and I'll arrest Audrey as soon as I see her,' Boyd said.

He heard Sutherland mutter to himself, then: 'Well, keep me updated, will you? Honestly, he's at the point where I may have to take him down with a ruddy tranquilizer dart!'

'Will do,' Boyd said, and hung up. The *last* thing he wanted to do was arrest the poor woman. He just needed to intercept her.

48

'So once again,' said Damian Porter as he led her into a small glass-walled conference room, 'I'd like to apologise for the delay and the chaos this afternoon, Ms Hincher.'

Audrey stepped into the room to find a conference table with three other people sitting patiently round it. Damian ushered her to an empty seat.

'This is Colin Ronson, a solicitor retained by Carnivale for legal advice,' he said, indicating the only other man in the room. 'And this is Sandra Weiss, financial advice, and this is Claire Barratt, our counsellor.'

Audrey sat down and nodded politely at them all.

Sitting opposite her, Damian opened a folder. 'Right then, I'm sure the very first thing you want to know is how much money you've won, yes?'

Audrey nodded. That was most definitely the first thing she wanted to know.

'So, I believe, when you called, you said your ticket was a match against five of the numbers that came up last week,' Damian said.

'Five of them, yes,' Audrey replied.

'Well...' He smiled again. 'I'm very pleased to inform you that, because, the number of claims against the five-number fund was relatively low... you've won quite a sizeable sum.'

'How much is it?' asked Audrey.

Damian took in a deep, somewhat theatrical breath. 'It's seven hundred and sixty-seven thousand pounds.' He grinned. 'And change.'

Audrey had done her homework last week, looking at the publicity releases from previous weeks. She'd been expecting somewhere in the region of half a million as a thumb-in-the-air average. 'Gosh,' she whispered.

'There'll be no tax for you to pay on that, of course,' said Sandra Weiss, offering her the same brand of PR smile that seemed to have been welded onto all their faces. 'Carnivale pay for that, so the sum Damian mentioned *is* the exact amount you will receive in your bank account.'

Damian Porter tapped on an iPad in front of him. 'Okay then, we should start working our way through the formalities. Audrey... can I call you Audrey?'

She nodded.

'Can we take a look at your lottery ticket?'

She unzipped the inner pocket of her shoulder bag, where it had been safely tucked away all week and carefully pulled it out. She slid it across the table to him. He picked it up reverentially, and checked the ticket against his iPad screen.

'Yes indeed, I can confirm five matches,' he said. He looked up at her. 'Congratulations, Audrey.'

She nodded. 'Thank you.'

He turned the ticket over and nodded approvingly. 'Good, I see you signed the back too. That's something we do encourage players to do. So... I have to ask, is this your signature?'

Audrey felt as though she was taking her first blind step onto a rickety walkway across an abyss. The moment she planted her foot down on it, there'd be no turning back.

'Yes,' she replied. 'That's my signature.'

He tapped the iPad screen, presumably to tick a box, then leant forward to examine the ticket more closely. Audrey could feel her heart pounding in her chest like some wild animal trying to break out of a cage. He entered some numbers on the tablet, then something flashed up.

It took every ounce of Audrey's self-control for her not to jump out of her seat and run for the door.

'The ticket vendor was Hassim's General Store, Queens Road, Hastings,' he said. 'Is that where you bought the ticket?'

She suppressed a sigh of relief. 'Yes. Yes... that's where I bought it. Yes.'

'Lovely,' he replied. 'And can I ask... was it a purchase for yourself, on behalf of someone else, or bought as a gift?'

'Me,' she blurted out. 'I bought it for me... for myself.'

'Good, good,' he said, tapping another box. 'Right then. Can you give me the time and date when you purchased it?'

'What?'

'It doesn't have to be precise, Audrey. The date, if you can. Morning or afternoon will do.'

She had no idea when exactly Andy had purchased it. 'Ummm... it's... Gosh. I... I...' She could feel her face turning beetroot.

'Relax,' said Damian. 'It's not a question you need to get exactly right. This is just a safeguard in case there's more than one person claiming ownership of the ticket. Could you give me a day?'

'It... it was... was...'

'Sometimes,' said the counsellor Claire, 'if there's a disagreement between two people claiming ownership of the ticket, we have to check the vendor's CCTV to see if we can spot them making the purchase.' She tilted her head. 'It's nothing to worry about, Audrey. It's just a safeguard for you in case someone else tries to claim your win as theirs.'

'Right. I see,' Audrey said.

Think! THINK! she told herself. Andy, she was sure, tended to buy his ticket on the same day that he went into town to get his work bits and pieces from Jewson's. 'Friday... I think,' she said at last.

'So that would be the Friday before Wednesday, the seventeenth of April?'

Audrey nodded quickly. 'Yes. Yes. That's it.'

Damian nodded, then entered the date on his iPad. 'Lovely.' He sat back in his seat and clasped his hands together. 'That, you'll be relieved to hear, is all we need to do to confirm that this ticket is a winner. Now then... we just have to confirm you are who you say you are. You've brought some form of photo ID and bank account details along with you, I presume?'

'Yes.' She dug into her bag again and pulled out her passport and the wad of statements she'd grabbed from Andy's filing cabinet.

Damian's eyes widened. 'We only need the last three months,' he said with a reassuring smile.

'Oh, right.' She picked them out and handed them over. He quickly scanned the papers. 'Wonderful,' he said, and slid them back across the table to her. 'And another A. Hincher, eh?'

'Sorry?' she said, momentarily flummoxed.

'A. Hincher and A. Hincher. On your bank statement,' he said.

'Andy,' she said quickly. 'My husband is Andy.'

'He must be thrilled to bits,' Damian said. 'Is he waiting outside? You should have brought him in.'

'No,' she replied. 'No. He's down in Hastings, working.' She managed a smile. 'Waiting to uh... to hear from me how much money we've won.'

'Do you have any plans tonight?' asked Claire. 'A party perhaps?'

Audrey glanced her way. 'Yes... Yes, right. We'll have a party, maybe. I hadn't thought about it, actually.'

'Not everyone does,' Claire replied. 'Some winners just want to keep things low-key and normal and not go crazy.' She suddenly paused and frowned for a moment. 'You look vaguely familiar, Audrey. Have we met somewhere before?'

'What?' Audrey felt her stomach flop over queasily.

'I'm pretty good with faces,' Claire said. 'I could swear...'

'No!' Audrey replied quickly. 'No... I'm pretty sure we haven't met.'

'A friend of a friend, maybe? On Facebook?' Claire mused.

Audrey shook her head. 'I never did Facebook.' An unnecessary lie. She did have a page, but just hadn't put anything on it in years.

'Well now, Audrey,' Damian resumed, sliding her passport back across the table. 'That's most of the formalities dealt with... There's just one more tiny thing I need to look into,' he said, getting up from the table.

She twisted in her seat. 'What? What thing...?'

But he'd already stepped out of the room.

Boyd cursed the bus in front of him, blocking the street like some gigantic metal turd. He found himself drumming his fists on the steering wheel as he watched some old dear shouting something up to the bus driver from the bus stop. Then she cupped her ear as the driver yelled a reply.

'Oh, for Christ's sake,' Boyd muttered. Obviously, she couldn't hear the driver. She slowly took a step onto the bus to ask her question again.

The afternoon was ticking away. It was nearly three, and he was pretty sure his race to Hounslow to prevent Audrey Hincher from getting herself into trouble had been a fool's errand.

And a mistake in more ways than one. Having taken the action to intercede, he would now be obliged to log his journey. LEDS would ask for a reason and a case number. Which meant – unless she'd chickened out of getting the winnings – putting Audrey onto the system as a wanted person.

It was very unlikely that Sussex Police would want to waste manpower tracking her down, but it would mean she might trigger some action further down the line. If she re-entered the country after going abroad, for example. Border Force's system tapped into LEDS and did a very efficient job of flagging up any crims trying to come home.

The old woman had finally finished having her conversation with the bus driver and was now stepping – slowly – back down onto the pavement.

Finally, finally... the bus's pneumatic brakes hissed, the door slid shut and it began crawling forward once again.

∼

'So, Audrey,' said the solicitor Colin, breaking the silence while they awaited their colleague's return. 'Have you a will set up? Not a lot of our winners do. And having a sum like this suddenly arrive on the doorstep can lead to some awkward –'

'Yes. There's a will,' Audrey replied quickly. 'That's all sorted. But thank you.' She turned back to look at Sandra, the financial adviser. 'Are we nearly done now? How do I, you know, receive the money?'

Sandra smiled. 'Damian has the money transfer all ready to go,' she said, nodding at his iPad. 'It's just one tap, now that he's got your bank details... and over it goes.'

'How long will it take?' Audrey asked.

'A couple of minutes,' Sandra replied, 'and then you'll see your bank account looking very different indeed!'

'Good. Yes.' Audrey managed a smile, a genuine one this time. 'Wonderful.'

The door clicked open and Audrey spun in her chair to find Damian Porter standing in the doorway, looking very serious and with somebody else standing behind him.

Oh God.

'Audrey Hincher,' Damian said sternly. 'There's one last question I forgot to ask you...'

Oh God. Here it was, the thing that was going to snag her. The one little detail she hadn't thought about. God help her.

'How did you get here?' he asked. 'Did you *drive* up here from Hastings this morning?'

'What? No...' she whispered. 'I... I...' *Oh God, they know I've been missing!* Damian must have recognised her name, if not her face. And the man lingering, out of sight behind the Adjudicator – was he a policeman? Was she about to be arrested?

Damian's straight face suddenly folded into a gleeful

smile. 'Then a little celebratory champagne won't do any harm, then!' He stepped into the room and held the door open as a young man wheeled in a catering trolley loaded with a bottle of champagne, five tinkling champagne flutes and several foil-covered plates of canapés.

Audrey felt ready to collapse with relief as the trolley rolled up beside her and the man set the plates out on the table and removed the foil.

Damian sat back down. 'Just a little thing we like to do here,' he explained, 'as I press the magic button. A toast and some nibbles to celebrate!'

The last thing Audrey wanted to do right now was eat anything: even a slice of cake that had been decorated to look like money. She just wanted the wretched man to press that button on his iPad and then she could get away from here as quickly as possible.

There was a pop and a gentle fizz as the young man uncorked the champagne and began to pour a little into each glass. Damian handed her a flute, then grabbed one for himself. 'On behalf of Carnivale I'd like to congratulate you on your win, Audrey, and wish you the very best.' He set his glass down and, unable to restrain himself from a little theatrical flourish, he let his finger descend slowly to the screen. He tapped the button. 'And, there it is, Audrey... Your money is on its way.'

She let out a rush of air. The others laughed and shouted congratulations.

Claire leant forward to pick up her glass. 'I'm honestly thrilled for you!' she said, and took a gulp of the champagne.

Sandra Weiss reached for hers. 'Now, I know it's probably something you haven't thought about just yet, and maybe you won't want to think about it for a few days,' she said, 'but it might be worth discussing the best investment options for your windfall? May I sugg–'

'Could I just have a cab?' Audrey found herself blurting. The entire room fell silent.

'I just... I just want to get back home to Andy with the news,' she said. 'I... I want to be with him.'

'That's fine,' said the young man who'd wheeled in the trolley. 'I can call you one. There's a firm just round the corner.'

'Thank you!' she gushed at him. 'Thank you!'

'Where do you want to go to?' he asked.

'Uh... the... uh...' she stuttered.

'Hounslow station? For the train?' he asked her.

'Yes!' She nodded quickly. 'That's it. Yes, the train. I need to get a train from London, you see. Back down to Hastings.'

He nodded. 'I'll get one to come right over.'

49

Boyd finally arrived at Alexandra Business Park, cursing and muttering to himself as he located Carnivale House at the far end of the car park and found a solitary visitor's slot to squeeze his Captur into.

'Bloody hell,' he muttered. That frustratingly slow crawl from the motorway through the clogged high streets of Hounslow. He climbed out and slammed the door shut, still grumbling to himself as he hurried through the spitting rain, across the drenched tarmac to the shelter of the overhang that ran along the front of the building. He was heading to the plate-glass-fronted lobby and the double doors of the entrance, just a dozen yards away, when he noticed a taxi pulling up outside.

Shit. He stopped dead. *Is that her?*

As he watched, Boyd suddenly realised that he looked very much like the copper he was, about to go knocking on someone's door. There was no alcove for him to discreetly slip in, so he pulled out his phone and tapped at something random on the screen, while he waited for whoever was in the back of the taxi to climb out.

Nearly a minute passed before he realised it wasn't dropping anyone off but waiting to pick someone up. He shook his head, tucked his phone back into his pocket and headed inside, to wait in the lobby. If Audrey was there already, he could arrest her on the way out. If she'd yet to arrive, he could catch her on the way in, to save her from making a big mistake.

As he reached to pull the door open, a dark-haired woman was pushing it from the other side. He held it open for her and nodded politely as she bustled past him.

'Don't mention it,' he muttered as he stepped inside the lobby and looked around at the leather couches and the handful of people sitting on them. There were several men, a couple of women – all smartly dressed, young and nervous. Job interviewees he...

Wait.

He spun round on his heels and peered back outside at the woman who'd just passed him. She was climbing into the back of the taxi. She glanced over her shoulder and he caught a second glimpse of her face just as the rear door slammed shut.

That woman, goddammit... that was Audrey Hincher!

~

'HOUNSLOW TRAIN STATION, RIGHT?'

'Uh, no,' replied Audrey. 'I mean, this taxi is meant for me, but I'm not going there any more.'

The cabbie sighed. 'All right – where are we off to, then?'

'Heathrow, please,' she replied. 'The airport.'

'Which terminal?' he asked.

'Excuse me?'

'Which *terminal*?' He twisted in his seat to look at her.

'Where are you going?'

She stared at him blankly for a few seconds. Suddenly this whole experience, from everything that had happened last week to walking into the building and claiming her money suddenly felt like some bizarre, protracted lucid dream. Now, here she was, sitting in the back of a black cab and that question she'd dreamed about was finally being asked of her... *Where are you going, Audrey?*

'Greece,' she replied. 'I'm going to Greece.'

He considered that for a moment, then nodded. 'Nice. Bet they've got better weather going on right now than we do.' He flipped the charge meter on and pulled away from the main entrance to Carnivale House. 'So you'll need terminals two and three. They're where your euro flights are, mainly.'

'Okay.' She smiled at him, meeting his eyes in the mirror. 'Take me there.'

He frowned. Confused. 'No big case?'

She shook her head. 'Just me.' She lifted her shoulder bag. 'And this.'

'You off on a lastminute.com are you, eh?' He chuckled. 'Don't blame you!'

She turned to look at Carnivale House, still half expecting a fast-forwarded Benny Hill trail of people chasing after her, as though she was a mutt scampering away from a butcher's shop with a string of sausages in her mouth. But all she could see was a man striding across the car park, hurrying, no doubt, to get out of the rain and into his car.

'No, I'm not off on holiday,' she replied. 'I'm going away for good.'

'For good?' he repeated.

'I'm emigrating,' she added with a broad smile. 'I've always wanted to live on a Greek island.'

'Like that *Mamma Mia* film, eh?' He began to sing a few very out-of-tune lines from the song.

'Yes,' she said, chuckling, 'just like that film.'

∼

BOYD JUMPED INTO HIS CAR, reciting the licence number of the black cab out loud, over and over. He found a Bic biro in the coin tray and quickly scribbled the number on the back of his hand before starting the engine.

'She's done it... She's flipping well gone and done it!' he muttered to himself. Now he really did have no option but to arrest the silly woman.

He threw his car in reverse and backed out of the narrow parking bay, swinging around in a tight arc that nearly had him pranging the neighbouring Land Rover. He fished his phone out of his pocket and dropped it on the passenger's seat, as he switched to first gear and lurched forward. He would have to verify that she'd made the claim, obviously. He should call Okeke, or Rajan maybe, and get one of them to call the lottery to make sure he wasn't chasing Audrey without cause.

Through his rain-spattered windscreen, he followed the road markers that pointed him towards the car park's exit and then, as he rounded one final row of parked cars, he caught sight of the black cab's rear as it turned onto the busy road ahead.

∼

AUDREY PULLED her new phone out of her bag and swiped it on. It was so new that the screen still had its protective film of plastic. She swiped to the banking app she'd installed a couple of days ago: Revolvo. Setting up her own online account had been remarkably easy. It had to be over fifteen years since she'd last walked into a bricks-and-mortar bank with ID and a utility bill to set up an account. It was so very different these days; there was no waiting in a queue for someone at a window to give you a pile of forms to fill in and several glossy leaflets to take away. Nowadays it was just a couple of taps and a few boxes to fill in and, voila, she had a new bank account.

She switched to her building society app, logged in and checked the balance. The money hadn't arrived just yet. It still showed £237. 32, the tail end of her wage from last month. Andy's money from his fledgling franchise business, when it very occasionally came in, barely added a thousand to that after Berkley's fee had been subtracted... and then it went straight back out again on whatever it was he spent all his money on.

Some of it, she knew, went on his booze and fags. But a lot more of it went out of the cash machine when he was away on a job. She had a pretty good idea of what he spent it on, though. Sixty here, eighty there – what was the going rate for a bit of nookie down a backstreet?

She wondered if he'd figured out yet that his numbers had come up, and that he was going to be rather rich man very shortly.

But for only a few brief moments.

She smiled to herself. She almost hoped he'd see it there. That he'd glimpse all those lovely noughts sitting in a tidy row, that he'd start dancing around the living room with joy, only to watch them vanish minutes later.

Was that mean? Yes, a little. But, in truth, she wished him only the worst. She'd spent too many years being his Hausfrau, his money bank, his punch bag and his occasional whore when he returned home from the pub drunk and literally anyone would do.

∽

BOYD HAD MANAGED to hook his phone up to his Captur's system now, so that he wasn't fumbling for it like an idiot any more. But that meant the screen kept flashing up distracting call notifications. The damned thing was buzzing almost constantly, with a steady procession of missed calls and texts from Andrew, Sutherland and now Charlotte.

He reached out and tapped the screen. 'Hey,' he said.

'How's it going?' she asked. 'Did you find her?'

'I'm following her,' he replied.

'You're driving?'

The *thwup-thwup-thwup* of his windscreen wipers had given him away. 'Yup.'

'Has she claimed the winnings?'

'I think so. She's in a cab heading for Heathrow. So, uh-huh, I think she's gone and done the deed.'

'Oh no...' Charlotte sighed. 'I guess you have to arrest her.'

The cab was just about in sight, a dozen cars ahead, creeping along as the traffic inched its way forward in limp spurts. 'As soon as her cab drops her off. Yeah.'

'Is it possible...' She paused, long enough that he guessed what she was thinking.

'That I let her go? Not really,' he replied. Part of him, a large part of him, was sorely tempted. The world seemed to be full of people who got off scot-free for doing far worse. Billionaires who routed their money through financial black holes to safe havens, politicians who allowed friends to skim tens of millions out of the public purse via uncontested contracts and hidden backroom deals. These were hardly victimless crimes when every hospital, school and care home in the country seemed to be failing or falling down around.

If Audrey had taken the money, the only victim would be Andrew Hincher. And if one could pick a victim of petty crime, then he'd do very nicely.

Boyd sighed. 'I can't just let her walk, Char... Not when I've got eyes on her and I know she's just committed a crime. Can I?'

'No... I suppose not,' Charlotte said uncertainly.

~

'WE'RE NEARLY THERE,' announced the cabbie. They were half a mile from the turn-off for the various Heathrow terminals. He flicked his indicator, then nipped out of the middle lane and onto the exit lane, provoking a honk from the white van that had been scooting up to fill the gap they'd just taken.

'Go on – piss off, mate,' the cabbie barked pointlessly.

His eyes met Audrey's briefly in the rear-view mirror, then lingered for a moment. 'Have I had you in my cab before?'

She stirred from her thoughts – nice ones, of turquoise water and silver beaches. 'Sorry?'

'I'm good with faces, me,' he said. 'I never forget a face. I've seen yours before, I'm certain.'

'No, I don't think so,' she replied. 'I think I must have one of those everyday faces.' She glanced out of the side window. 'Someone once told me I looked a little bit like Felicity Kendell.'

That someone had been Andy. That, in fact, had been his chat-up line. She'd been in a wine bar with some colleagues for an after-work, TFI Friday drink. It had been the kind of evening that wrapped up pretty quickly with everyone having excuses to go early, trains to catch, kids to feed, dogs to walk. She'd worked as an accountant back then, not the admin dogsbody that she'd become in recent years.

Andy had broken the ice with that particular line about her looking like Felicity Kendell as they'd both waited to be served at the bar. She'd not heard that from anyone before and she'd thought, at first, that he'd been making fun of her. But, as they continued to talk, she realised he was actually *chatting her up*.

After she'd delivered her round of drinks to her colleagues, she'd gone back to Andy. They'd continued to talk and by the end of the evening she had his number. She recalled sharing a taxi with him as they were both heading in roughly the same direction. He'd paid, and he'd been a perfect gent, dropping her off and kissing her goodnight on the cheek.

And she remembered thinking that she was punching way above her weight; he was gorgeous. He was tall, slim, well dressed... although, to be fair, she'd not looked so bad herself. She'd worn make-up, kept herself trim, dressed reasonably fashionably and had worn her hair longer. More to the point, she thought sadly, she'd been a far more confident and capable person all those years ago.

A far cry from the wretched creature she was nowadays.

God help her – she'd made the dreadful mistake of dialling his number the very next day.

And... she'd discovered he had two kids and that, admirably, he was raising them on his own. She would find out, much later, that he was no doting father and had little patience for either of them. He had his own house with, impressively, no mortgage. It would be a number of years before she learned that the lack of mortgage wasn't down to his hard work and financial prudence but that he'd inherited the house from his late parents. He had been gregarious, self-confident, witty and charming – but that had simply been his A game, deployed to get what he wanted. The harsh truth, revealed too late, was that Andrew Hincher was a violent bully with a short fuse. During those first few months together, he told Audrey that her being a few years older was what attracted him to her, that he wanted something long-term with her, to get married and for them to grow old together. She'd learned, much later, that he had his eyes on her money *and* that he had a preference for ladies a good deal younger.

She'd endured ten years with him. She supposed it was no wonder she looked and felt a good deal older than she was. Her self-confidence had been beaten out of her. The desire to look nice had been eroded like the well-worn heels of an old pair of shoes. He'd turned her into a victim, a role she'd resisted at first but finally come to terms with, and eventually embraced as her lot in life.

'Bloody hell, *finally!*' the cabbie exclaimed, once again jerking her from her wool-gathering. He pulled out of the stop–start traffic and onto the slip road. By the look of it, they had a relatively clear run ahead to the airport.

50

Boyd spotted the black cab signalling to take the exit lane, and then, as the traffic slowly shrugged forward, it slipped out of the jam and sped up the sloping road towards the roundabout at the top.

'Sod it,' he muttered. Instead of waiting for the cars ahead to inch forward, he spun his wheel and repeatedly honked his horn until the car in front of him inched forward enough for him to squeeze out onto the hard shoulder. As Boyd passed by, he was greeted with an angry face glaring his way, and an index finger.

'Yeah, well, same to you with knobs on!' he snapped as he sped along the hard shoulder, then onto the slip road to catch up with the black cab.

Miraculously, no other traffic had gone up the slip road and he was now right behind the cab. Through the rear window, he could see the outline of Audrey Hincher's head. Beyond it was the cabbie, twisted round in his seat to talk to her as he waited his turn to enter the roundabout.

Boyd wondered what they were talking about. Had she told him her good news? More likely, he thought, just like every other London cabbie, he was giving her his view on the world and telling her exactly how he'd put things right again.

∼

'*Dancin*' *qu-e-e-e-n!!! Feel the be-e-e-at on that tambor-i-i-ine!*' the cabbie bellowed tunelessly along with the music. Audrey shook her head and laughed at his courageous effort. He was just as awful and tuneless as Piers Brosnan had been in the film.

'Love that tune! It's a right belter!' he called back over his shoulder as he pulled onto the roundabout. 'Always makes my missus smile, that one!'

'Gosh, surely she's laughing not smiling at you, murdering it like *that*?'

The cabbie guffawed. 'We've got one of them old Sing-Star things at home. You know the PlayStation karaoke game with those little plastic mics? We get a bottle of the merlot for her, some beers for me and we spend a whole evening knocking out Abba classics... That's how we roll round our gaff on a Friday night!'

Audrey smiled. A little sadly. How lovely it would have been for her to be able to say, 'Me too...'

They sped along the connector road towards the next roundabout.

∼

Boyd had Carnivale on the line. 'Yes please, and quickly please. It's important.'

He was put on hold and the speakers in his car distorted unpleasantly as patchy, loud muzak began to play. Boyd turned onto the roundabout and took the first left. He could still see the cab ahead of him.

The muzak suddenly, mercifully, ceased with a loud click. 'Damian Porter. Who is this?'

'DCI Bill Boyd, Hastings CID,' Boyd said.

'Police?'

'Yeah, police. You just processed a ticket winner this afternoon, right?' he said.

'Well, Mr Boyd... I can't share confidential inf–' Damian began.

'I'm after Audrey Hincher,' Boyd cut in. 'She's a five-number winner from Hastings, correct?' He slowed to a stop at another roundabout, right behind the cab.

'Ah... no disclosure waiver has been signed, so I'm afraid I can't confirm –'

'I'm a bloody police officer!'

'Well now, you say that... you could just as easily be a reporter.'

Boyd sighed, gave the man the number for CID's floor. 'Call them.'

A keyboard clattered. 'All right,' said Damian, 'it does appear to be a police line.'

'Get someone to call them if you want... but do it quickly! Because you've just been scammed.'

'What?'

'Did you pay out any money?'

Damian Porter sounded rattled. 'Um... yes. We... we... uh... verified and approved the payment about twenty minutes ago.'

'It was a fraudulent claim,' Boyd said.

'*What?*' Damian exclaimed.

'The ticket wasn't hers. It was her husband's.'

'It had her name signed on it. "A. Hincher" and –' The

rest of whatever Damian was about to say suddenly died in his mouth. 'Ah. I see.'

'Yeah, they're both "A. Hincher". She's gone in with *his* ticket and passed it off as hers. It looks very much like she's heading off into the sunset with his money. Unless you can put a stop on it...'

'I'm afraid not,' Damian said. 'The money's already been transferred out of our accounts.'

'Well, the money's going to the wrong person!' Boyd said. 'Is there nothing you can do?'

'Look, Mr –'

'*DCI* Boyd.'

'DCI Boyd, as far as Carnivale's concerned, it *was* the right person,' Damian said. 'She satisfied all our verification checks and was, as the holder of the ticket, quite correctly deemed the owner and winner.'

'Christ, you must have situations where this sort of thing is contested, right?' Boyd asked him.

'We do, from time to time, yes. But that's something that will need to come from her husband if he has an issue with it. He'll need to prove that he purchased it.'

Boyd ended the call. He entered the roundabout, suddenly realising that he'd lost sight of the cab. 'Bollocks!' The first exit was signposted for Terminals 2 and 3 and the next was for Terminals 4 and 5. From what he could remember, Terminals 2 and 3 were for the smaller airlines with mostly local routes. Terminal 4 was the British Airways hub and 5 was for all the other big international names... *wasn't it?* If she was off to somewhere further afield, then she'd be heading to Terminals 4 or 5...

He did a long, lazy loop of the roundabout as he pondered where she might be going. Was Audrey the kind of person who'd take herself off to Costa Rica or Costa Del

Sol? As he came to where he'd entered the roundabout, he opted for the latter and took the exit for Terminals 2 and 3.

He sped along the interconnecting road between the roundabout and the next one and realised that he'd probably lost his chance to catch her.

51

Andrew Hincher, who hadn't taken his eyes off his phone, saw an incoming call from DCI Boyd flash up on the screen. He answered it immediately. 'You got her?'

'No,' replied Boyd. 'But I have an update for you. She was at the lottery HQ less than an hour ago and has staked her claim.'

'Bitch!' Andrew spat.

'Where are you now?' Boyd asked.

'Just parked outside my house,' said Andrew. 'Your bloody boss told me I had to go home and wait.'

'That's just as well. You should probably check your joint bank account. In fact, you should probably contact them immediately and tell them to freeze it.'

'Shit. The money's in there?' Andrew said.

'The people at Carnivale said they've done their bit. So, yup, it's probably there right now,' Boyd told him.

'How much is it?' Hincher asked.

'I've no idea, mate,' Boyd said. 'But I'd suggest you get a move on.'

'Right.'

'Wait... one more thing, Andrew...'

'What?'

'If Audrey was flying abroad, where would she go? Has she got any family abroad? Is there anywhere she's, I dunno... familiar with?'

'Greece,' Andrew replied. 'We went on a package holiday to Greece. She never bloody stopped going on about it.'

'Right. Okay. Thanks.' With that, Boyd hung up.

Andrew climbed out of his van and hurried up the path to his front door, jangling his keys in his hands. He opened the door, ran through the hallway and into the lounge to find Liam was on the downstairs computer.

'Get off that *now*!' Andrew shouted.

'Huh? What's up?' Liam asked.

'I said get the fuck off the computer, right now!' Andrew yelled.

'But I'm in the middle of –'

Andrew grabbed his son's hoodie and yanked him away from the computer. He closed down the weird-looking browser that Liam had been fiddling around with.

'Dad! For fuck's sake!' Liam moaned.

Andrew opened up Chrome and clicked 'banking' in his bookmarked favourites. The building society's log-in page popped up and he frantically typed his details.

'Jesus. What's going on?' asked Liam.

'SHIT!!!' Andrew all but screamed. The password wasn't working. He tried again and got the same unhelpful 'Forgotten your password?' on the screen. The stinking, thieving little bitch must have changed it.

'Dad?' Liam whined.

Andrew ignored him and scanned the page for an emergency support number to call.

~

'AND HERE WE ARE,' announced the cabbie as he pulled into the drop-off lane for Terminal 2. He paused the Abba playlist and turned in his seat. 'That's going to be twenty-seven pounds and fifty pence.'

Audrey opened her shoulder bag and delved inside for the diminished wad of Andy's cash. She pulled out two twenties and handed them to him. 'You can keep the change.'

His eyes rounded. 'You sure?'

She smiled at him. 'I had fun.' Their impromptu, noisy sing-along had taken them through all the big hits – carpool karaoke at its most tuneless and hilarious. She dug into her bag again and pulled out another twenty and handed that to him too. 'If someone comes asking you where you dropped me off, could you tell them it was the other terminal?'

'Who's goin' to ask me that?' he said.

She shrugged. 'Maybe my husband.'

He stared at her. 'You on the run, love?'

She considered that for a moment, then nodded. 'Yes, I suppose you could say that.'

'With his cash, is it?' he asked, looking at the notes in his hand.

She shrugged again. 'I suppose you could say that too.'

'That's why you're running away to Greece, huh?'

She nodded.

He smiled and winked. 'Well, good luck to you, missus.'

~

Andrew Hincher was on hold. James bloody Blunt was making his ear bleed with that shrill emotive whining of his about someone being *beautiful*. He checked his watch; it was approaching five. He presumed, given it was option seven he'd selected from the menu – "stolen or lost card, or suspicious activity on your account" – that somebody was on duty twenty-four hours a day or what was the bloody point of having that option in the first place?

Could those lazy morons at Hastings police station be any more incompetent? Audrey, hardly a criminal mastermind, had managed to fool the lot of them into accusing him *and* his son of her murder and now – with evidence handed to them on a plate and a clear idea of where she must be heading with his stolen money – they still didn't seem to be able get their shit together and collar her.

Christ. If she got away... if she *escaped* with his winnings, he was going to raise merry hell. He would go straight to the *Mail*, *The Sun*... whoever, and he'd fucking well make sure that every one of those hopeless bastards got the sack.

∽

Boyd pulled up in the taxi rank for departures at Terminal 2, climbed out of his Captur, slammed the door and headed for the glass doors.

'Hey! *Excuse me!*' a voice barked from behind. He turned to find a security guard with an ID tag and high-vis vest striding towards him. 'You can't leave your car unattended!' He pointed at Boyd's car. 'You're not even a taxi.'

Boyd dug his lanyard out and held it up. 'It's police business, mate.'

'I don't care, *mate*.' The security guard nodded at the

multi-storey car park opposite the terminal building. 'You can park over there.'

'I don't have time,' replied Boyd. 'I'm after a suspect, for Christ's sake!'

The security guard shuffled in front of him, blocking his way.

'For fuck's sake,' grunted Boyd. 'Call your supervisor, but do it quickly will you?'

52

Andrew Hincher's torture-by-James-Blunt had finally come to an end and at last he had a real live human being on the end of the line. 'Okay, sir... we just have to run through a couple of security questions before we can go any further.'

'Okay, okay... fine,' Andrew said.

'Your date of birth?'

'Seventeenth of March 1973.'

'Good. And your mother's maiden name?'

'Jarvis.'

'Very good. And, finally, can you give me an idea of a transaction that you made in the last forty-eight hours?'

Andrew frowned with concentration. His mind was spinning with growing frustration and panic. It was hard to think. 'I... Let me see, let me see...'

'It can be a payment in or out,' the man said.

Last night. He'd ordered a curry. 'I had a takeaway,' he blurted. 'Rani's. I think it was about thirty something.'

The wait was unbearable, but finally the man on the other end of the phone replied, 'That's good enough, Mr

Hincher. All right, let's have a little look to see what's been going on.'

'There should be a lot of money in there,' said Andrew. 'I mean, *a lot*. I need you to freeze the account. I need you to stop it right now!'

'Just a moment, sir...' the man said. 'I'm getting the details up on my screen...'

∽

AUDREY'S PARANOIA was beginning to feel ridiculous. She'd become a criminal over an hour ago. Surely the wheels of justice didn't spin *so* quickly that they'd be after her already? All the same, she felt vulnerable and exposed in the middle of the airport. She spotted a sign for the toilets and headed towards them.

She found an empty cubicle, stepped in, closed the door and sat down on the loo seat, pulling her phone out again and logged into the joint account.

She stared at the screen in a state of shock, her breath frozen in her mouth. The numbers looked impossible, sitting there humbly above a trickle of tiny sums in and out. Just over three quarters of a million pounds.

'Oh my gosh,' she whispered softly.

She navigated to the payment screen and started frantically entering the details of her Revolvo account into the entry fields, her trembling fingers making mistakes and causing her to retype the account number. She switched apps and double-checked the account number, for a second time, then a third and did the same thing again with the sort code.

Her hands were shaking uncontrollably now as she entered the payment details.

Finally, it was all tapped in and her thumb hovered above 'Confirm' at the bottom of the screen. She blew out a breath to settle her nerves, then pressed the button.

~

'GOOD GOD,' said the man on the other end of the phone.
'What?' snapped Andrew.
'I'm looking at your account right now.'
'And?'
'Mr Hincher, can I ask you how much money you *think* should be in your account at this moment in time?'
Andrew had no idea. It could be nothing. It could be a fortune. 'I just won the lottery, mate. My numbers came up, but my wife's gone and claimed it. So I've got no fucking idea how much is there. No fucking clue. It's a *ton*, right?'
'Mr Hincher, according to this, you have just over three quarters of a million pounds in your account. Seven hundred and sixty-seven thousand, two hundred and thirty-seven pounds and thirty-two pence, to be precise.'
'*WHAT?*' Andrew dropped down into the chair at the computer desk. He felt light-headed, dizzy. Almost drunk. The sudden burst of adrenaline shooed away the last traces of his hangover. 'You've got to be joking!'
'No, that's what it says right here. That sum came into your account in the last hour, from a company called Carnivale.'
'YES!' Andrew screamed, drumming his feet against the carpet. He was dimly aware that Liam was staring at him curiously. He pressed a hand over his phone and grinned at his son. 'Liam, I just won three quarters of a million on the lottery!'

Liam's usually dull-eyed face exploded into an expression of astonishment. 'You *what*?'

Andrew whooped. 'We're fucking loaded, mate! We're *fucking loaded!*'

Liam edged across the lounge towards him. 'Are you *serious*?' he asked.

Andrew slapped the phone down onto the computer desk, jumped to his feet and did something he hadn't done since Liam was tiny. He threw his arms about him in a bear hug and spun him round in an awkward, bunny-hopping twirl. The two of them lost their balance and they toppled over, collapsing onto the couch.

Andrew let go of his son, slightly breathless. The moment passed and he extracted himself from the tangle of limbs, ruffling his son's mop of hair before getting up and hurrying back to his phone. He picked it up. 'Right. Listen, mate, what the fuck do I need to do to lock it down? To make sure that money doesn't go –'

'Oh,' said the man on the other end of the line.

Andrew froze. 'What's up?'

∼

AUDREY STOOD at the ticket desk. 'Can I have a ticket to Athens, please?' she asked.

The woman behind the counter smiled at her. 'Of course.' She tapped at her keyboard. 'There's one in an hour and a half, but you'll have to be quick. Check in closes in the next ten minutes.'

'Yes, please – I'll take that,' Audrey said. She smiled shyly. 'Can I go first class?'

The woman behind the counter glanced up, brows raised. 'That's a lot more than economy,' she said.

'How much is it?' Audrey asked.

'Nine hundred,' the woman replied flatly, as if answering was a waste of both their time.

Audrey smiled. 'Fine. I'll take it.'

The woman looked taken aback. 'Are you sure?'

Audrey nodded again. 'And I don't have any luggage to check in. Only this,' she said, lifting her shoulder bag.

'That's small enough to come on board, isn't it?'

The woman nodded. 'So... that's nine hundred pounds, then. How would you like to pay?'

Audrey produced the Visa card for her brand-new bank account.

~

'Uh... your account details have just updated,' the man said.

Andrew almost forgot to breathe. 'What do you mean?'

'Um... well, Mr Hincher, I don't know what's going on but –'

'Just tell me!'

'It's all... *gone*,' the man said. 'Your current balance is now showing as two hundred and thirty-seven pounds and thirty-two pence.'

'*WHAT?*' Andrew roared.

Liam was off the sofa now and standing beside him. 'Dad? What's wrong? What's going on?'

Andrew shoved him to shut him up. 'Check it again!' he snapped.

'I've refreshed it. It's still the same. Just bear with me a second, Mr Hincher... This may be a syncing error. It's the end of the business day and this could well be a –'

'No! She's taken it!' he screamed. '*She's taken my fucking money!*'

'I'm looking at the screen now, Mr Hincher,' the man said. 'I can see a transaction that literally just occurred in the last few minutes. The exact same amount that was transferred earlier has been transferred *out*.'

'Oh, Jesus Christ!' spat Andrew. '*Do something!* Can you do something? Can you stop it? Put it on hold somehow and –'

'Uh... not really,' the man said. 'Once it's been digitally stamped and encrypted, the payment is officially in transit. There's absolutely nothing we can do from this end.'

'Can't it be stopped midway? Can you call the bank it's going to and tell them to stop it going in?' Andrew pleaded.

'We can raise a suspicious transaction enquiry with them, but –'

'Well, *do it*! Do it now!'

'But,' the man continued, 'that's a long drawn-out process. It's also a legal process that can take weeks to resolve.'

'Please do it! I want you to do that!' Andrew said.

There was a pause at the other end. 'Let me put you on hold for second while I check with my advisor.'

Then James Blunt was back on the phone, assuring Andrew that his love was pure, and that he was beautiful.

~

BOYD PACED DOWN the row of check-in desks in the vain hope that Audrey had dilly-dallied before presenting herself with a passport, in order to get a printed boarding pass. But no one ever did that nowadays, did they? Plus, all the nice shops, restaurants and cafes were on the other side.

'You think Greece?' said the terminal's security manager, striding alongside him.

'Yup.' In truth, it could be anywhere with a bit of sun. But Hincher had said they'd been to Greece, so it made sense to start with that.

'Well, these desks are your best bet,' said the manager. 'Air Med, Aegean Airlines, Olympus.' He led Boyd over to counter E3. The Aegean Airlines desk. The lady at the counter was getting ready to close down her terminal.

'One minute, please,' said the security manager. He gestured to Boyd. 'This gentleman wants a word with you before you log off.'

Boyd offered her an apologetic smile. The expression on her face told him that not only was she about to log off the terminal but she was about to clock out from work too. He lifted his lanyard. 'DCI Boyd. I just want to ask you a quick question.'

She nodded for him to go ahead.

'Have you had a passenger under the name of Audrey Hincher check in at your desk in the last hour?'

'Let me see,' she replied, clicking her mouse several times, then clattering at her keyboard with impractically long nails. She looked up at him. 'She booked a first-class flight to Athens. No luggage to check in.'

'Which flight?' Boyd asked.

She pointed at the sign above her: AEE539.

'Ah. When's it due to fly?' he said.

'They should start calling passengers in about an hour,' she told him.

He sighed with relief. He had Audrey. 'Thanks.' Boyd turned to the security manager. 'Would you be able to wave me through the security barriers?'

He nodded. 'Do you want me to alert my team in departures?' he asked.

The last thing Boyd wanted to do was turn this into

some ridiculous spectacle. He could visualise the shaky phone footage on ITV's *Saturday Morning* tomorrow. And, being a Saturday, the news cycle would almost certainly have room for a news story about heavy-handed coppers and security guards 'taking down' a vulnerable woman in the middle of a busy evening at Heathrow Airport.

'Nah, I know which flight she's getting and where she'll be. I think a light touch is the way to go, eh?'

'Are you sure?' the security manager asked.

Boyd shook his head. 'She's not exactly Carlos the Jackal.'

The security manager looked a little disappointed. 'Fair enough. Come along then, I'll wave you through.'

53

Audrey's jangling nerves had finally begun to settle down. The plastic glass of Chardonnay was, of course, helping a little there. She'd discovered it in the cooler cabinet of the WHSmith store in a cute little plastic wine glass with a peel-off cellophane lid... and she'd thought to herself, *Why not?*

She took another sip and gazed out of the observation window at the various comings and goings of small vehicles ferrying bags to and from the parked aeroplanes like worker bees servicing queen bees. She could see 'her' Aegean Airlines plane slowly nudging its way forward and coming to rest, chocks being placed in front of and behind the wheels, before a debarking collar was wheeled forward to lock on and dock with it.

Finally, she mused. *Finally!*

After an extremely stressful eight days of waiting and worrying, it was done. She was forty minutes away from boarding and leaving the country for good. Leaving behind all the rain, the misery, the drudgery... but, most importantly, the miserable life she'd somehow allowed herself to become trapped in.

She felt reasonably confident that she'd be on foreign soil by the time Andy finally figured out that she'd absconded with his winnings. As far as she was aware, he wasn't particularly observant when it came to the household finances. He was good at *spending* money, of course, but not especially vigilant at keeping tabs on it. But when he finally did – in fact, *if* he ever did – spot that such a large sum of money had very briefly hovered in their account, she was certain he'd go straight to the police.

What she wasn't certain about was how seriously they'd take it. Surely they had far more important things to do than arbitrate over whose winning ticket it was? All the same... she was going to have to be super cautious once she landed. She needed to find some remote little sun-kissed Ionian island and access her account sparingly.

She would, of course, give Mum a call as soon as she could, and let her know what she'd done, that she was safe... and, most of all, that she was happy. And *if* the police ever came knocking on her mum's door to ask if Audrey had made contact yet, to please lie to them.

Her mum would do that for her, she was sure. Her mum was well aware of what an awful bastard Andy had been.

Audrey let her mind wander from her list of things that needed to be done as soon as she landed, and onto the more sunlit promise of what lay ahead for her. She was going to find a cosy little *kalyva* perched on a hill, overlooking a marina of sun-bleached fisherman's boats. It would have a veranda, with wrought-iron railings and jasmine weaved through it. Maybe she'd adopt a cat or two. There'd be a bakery just down the road where she'd buy fresh bread and perhaps there might be a cafe by the marina, where she could spend her mornings watching the fisherman bring their fresh haul ashore.

And maybe one day a handsome fisherman with a warm heart might catch her eye...

She was dimly aware that a man had taken a seat beside her, joining her as she wistfully gazed out at the planes.

'Audrey?' he said after a few moments.

Her heart bumped in her chest as she turned to find a middle-aged man in a rumpled suit.

'My name's Boyd,' he said quietly. 'I'm a detective from Sussex Police.'

She felt a sudden urge to throw up. Right there on the corded carpet between their seats.

'Relax,' he said quickly. 'I'm just here to have a chat with you.' He gestured around the seating area and smiled. 'It's just me... There are no other coppers waiting in the wings to swoop in on you, I promise.'

She leant forward and set the plastic glass on the floor between her feet and remained there, hunched over, head in her hands. 'Oh God... Oh God.' The tears came out of nowhere, silently trickling out from between her fingers.

'It's okay,' he said softly. 'I've just got a couple of questions I want to ask you.'

'I did it!' she sobbed quietly. 'If that's what you wanted to ask,' she mumbled. 'I did it. I took the money.'

'I know you've *claimed* it,' he replied. 'I've actually just come from Carnivale.'

She wiped her eyes and nose and then sat up straight again. The other passengers in the seats nearby didn't seem to have noticed that she was crying. Or perhaps they were too embarrassed to make a show of noticing.

'It's actually only one question I have to ask you, Audrey. If you don't mind?'

She raised her damp eyes to meet his. Even though he'd said he was a policeman, he didn't look like one. He seemed friendly. He had kind eyes.

'I'm going to ask you something...' he said, 'and I want you to think very carefully before you answer it. Do you understand?'

He didn't even sound like a policeman, she thought. His voice was soft. She nodded for him to go ahead.

'Was that lottery ticket *yours*?' he asked her.

Fresh tears spilled from her eyes and rolled down her cheeks. 'I'm... in trouble... aren't I?' she whispered. 'If... and if I lie... that means even bigger trouble, doesn't it?'

'I haven't cautioned you.' He smiled again. 'Which means that whatever you say to me right now, I can't use anywhere. Ever. Do you understand?'

She sighed. 'I... didn't plan it, you know? I was just doing what Andrew told me to –'

He raised a finger to his lips to stop her. 'Audrey... I actually know what happened. We have CCTV footage from the corner shop when you first found out. I know you made an impulsive decision. A split-second decision...' He reached out and rested a hand gently on her shoulder. 'And I have a pretty good idea as to *why* you made that decision.'

She was confused. It almost sounded as though he was on her side. But then they did that, didn't they? Good cop, bad cop.

'I know exactly what your husband's like. I know how he's treated you over the years.' His smile faded. 'I know that if I wasn't a copper, I'd happily flatten his nose.'

She felt him squeeze her shoulder gently before lifting his hand away. 'But I *am* a copper, which means I have to ask you this question again. And, as I said, I want you to think very carefully before you answer. Is that clear? If someone later asks me what you said, I have a duty to relay that truthfully. Do you understand? I have to repeat the answer you give to me now.'

She thought she was beginning to understand where he was going with this. He wasn't trying to trick her.

'So I'll ask you again... was that ticket *yours*? Did *you* buy it?'

His eyes met hers, and it seemed to her that he was positively *willing* her to give one very specific answer.

'Yes,' she replied. 'I bought it.'

He nodded. 'Good.' He got up from the seat. 'That's what I thought.'

Was that a sly wink he just gave her? She looked up at him. 'You're not going to...'

'Arrest you?' He laughed softly. 'For what? There's no crime here.' He smiled. 'So I'm all done.'

The tannoy ding-donged and a voice announced that flight AEE539 was now ready to start taking first-class passengers.

'That's you,' he said.

She got to her feet slowly, still feeling shaky and unstable, wondering if there was a last moment 'gotcha' about to descend on her. 'I can... go?' she asked shakily.

He nodded again. 'A word of advice, though... Be very careful about coming back to the UK. If Andrew raises a complaint...'

She nodded, bent down to pick up her bag and shouldered it. 'I don't plan to ever come back,' she replied. She started towards the queue that had begun to form in front of the departure gate, then stopped and turned to look back at him.

Thank you, she mouthed.

He tipped his head at the gate. *Off you go, Audrey.*

~

BOYD EMERGED from the terminal building experiencing a confusing clutter of emotions. He felt guilty and a little angry, no... *disappointed*... with himself that he'd let his heart overrule his head in a police matter. Not once, *ever* in his entire career had he allowed someone he knew to have committed a crime to walk away.

Sure, he'd had crims who he *couldn't* keep locked up because of some procedural gremlin and he'd had to watch them walk away with a smug look on their faces, but never had he actually knowingly *let* someone guilty walk...

But he also felt relief. Relief that with this particular case, this misper hadn't ended up as a cadaver on Dr Palmer's autopsy table, nor had he had to explain to some distraught relative: *Yes, I'm afraid the body we recovered is most definitely your...*

And there was satisfaction too. That even if the wheels of justice hadn't rotated fully, the wheel of karma had. Andrew Hincher was almost certainly going to raise hell about this. Boyd wasn't sure how much credibility Andrew would have, though. It boiled down to his word against Audrey's and it seemed very clear that the people at Carnivale had no real interest in making a big deal out of admitting that they'd handed their money over to the wrong person.

He reached his Captur, parked askance. Luckily there were no wheel clamps and no ticket tucked under the wiper.

Boyd pressed his key fob and the Captur unlocked and blinked a hello in response. He pulled the door open and that was when he realised that the rain had stopped. The heavy grey clouds had cleared, revealing glimpses of blue sky and sunshine.

He closed his eyes and took a moment to savour the warmth on his face and the curiously pleasing smell of wet tarmac. He listened to the sounds around him, the heavy *thunk* of car doors and boot hatches closing, the clattering of suitcase wheels, cheerful 'hellos' and doleful 'goodbyes', and the roar of jet engines revving up as another plane – hopefully Audrey's – got ready to thunder down the runway.

The world was in motion – ever busy, ever circling and ever eager to move on to something else.

54

They had decided to take the dogs up to West Hill this morning. The weather had turned out nice and, given it was April, that was bloody good luck. The beach below, though, was mobbed with DFLs and locals, and the gulls were out in force, picking out tourists to mug on the seafront.

Charlotte was pushing Maggie in her buggy, and the little girl was watching a couple of kids throwing a Frisbee between them across the sloping field, utterly enthralled.

'You're looking rather pensive, Mr Boyd,' said Charlotte.

'Uh?' He shook his head. He smiled at her. 'Just feeling...'

She cocked her head and raised a brow as she hung on for his answer.

'... oddly content.'

'Oddly content is good.' She looked at him. 'Are you going to tell me why?'

The reasons were a mixed bag. It was Sunday. It was sunny. Emma was in a good mood at home, putting together a big roast for them all... and of course Danny Boy was due to move in this afternoon. Boyd had a granddaughter (finally) in a buggy, and a woman he very much loved who seemed equally keen to throw herself into the doting grandparent role. The cancer was behind him (all fingers and toes crossed). But, he realised, it was that snap decision he'd made to let Audrey Hincher vanish into the ether that was the icing on the cake.

It had been highly unprofessional of him to do that, of course, but... *sod it.* He'd given Sutherland an edited version of the truth when he got back to the station and said that he'd arrived too late at the airport.

She was now in Greece. Somewhere.

The DSI had obviously thought about it over Saturday and had texted Boyd this morning with a one-liner: *Oh well. Probably for the best, I think we'll move on.*

He'd told Charlotte the same thing when he'd got home, that he'd just missed Audrey. The way she'd frowned suspiciously at him suggested that she wasn't entirely convinced she'd been given the whole truth. All she'd said in response was 'Good for her' – and that was that.

He looked at her now and smiled. 'Maybe it's just the weather. It's nice to have a bit of sun at last, eh?'

She did that suspicious frown of hers again. It lingered and for a moment it seemed as though she was going to say something.

Then Maggie cooed. They both looked down to see that she was pointing out the Frisbee to Ozzie, one pudgy finger in the air, tracking it as it coasted across the blue sky and descended gracefully into the assured grasp of one of the kids.

Boyd squatted down beside her. 'You like that, eh, Mags? Shall we get one for Ozzie and Mia to chase on the beach?'

Charlotte sighed and then smiled as she watched the

pair of them, heads huddled together, thick as thieves. 'She's got you wrapped round her little finger, Bill.'

55

Audrey opened the shutters and sunlight suddenly spilled into the small guest room, momentarily dazzling her. She stepped out onto the balcony, wrapped her hand round the old iron rail and closed her eyes, savouring the warmth of it on her pale skin. As she stood there, eyes closed, she let all the sounds of the little marina seduce her: the distant clank of halyard against mast, the tolling of a church bell, the insect-like buzz of a far-away motor scooter and the lazy slapping of water against the rocky breakwater nearby.

Finally, she slowly eased her eyes open and let the glinting sparkles of light on the water transform from dancing translucent orbs to perfect flickering clarity.

She smiled.

Breathing in, she could detect the faintest scent of baking bread and fresh coffee.

So, was this a late breakfast or an early lunch? She could call it whatever the heck she wanted, right? None of the locals in the town square below seemed to be wearing a watch or rushing to catch up with the day.

She'd let herself into the guest room late last night. Very late. Athens was two hundred and twenty miles behind her. She'd stayed in a grubby hotel in Levadia the first night, and in a motel by a bus station in Agrinio the second. She'd paid two different – and very grateful – taxi drivers in cash to be here this morning, staring out at the northern Ionian Sea.

Once again, to check that it wasn't some cruel trick, she swiped her Revolvo banking app open and stared in awe at the sum of money in her account.

A voice in her head told her she must be very sensible with it. Three quarters of a million pounds was a lot, yes, but it was going to have to last her the rest of her life.

She had something she needed to do today. Immediately, in fact – it was at the top of her to-do list. She swiped the screen, tapped at it, held the phone up to her ear and waited for the call to be answered.

Audrey gazed out at the blue sea ahead. 'Mum, it's me...'

56

Only a couple of miles away from Mrs Davitt, as the crow flies, somebody else in Hastings received a call at about the same time. It was Samantha Okeke. She stubbed her cigarette out and reached for her phone.

She looked at the screen: Unknown ID. It was her personal phone, not her work phone. Only her brother, her mother, Boyd and Karl had her private number. Them... and, apparently, every sales chatbot in the world.

And of course... Jay.

She swiped to answer the call and paused. The chatbots tended to promptly disconnect if they didn't hear any recognisable words after the first few seconds.

'Babycakes?' Jay's voice rasped softly, quietly. Almost a whisper.

'*Jay?*' she all but screamed. '*JAY!*'

'Yeah... it's me.'

'What the – Where the –'

'Babes,' he cut in. 'I can't talk for long. I've gotta be quick.'

'Jesus Christ, Jay! I've been out of my mind! Worried sick about you! I've been –'

'Babes, shhh... Just let me... speak. I ain't got long.' He cleared his throat. 'I, uh... I... '

'What?' she said, impatient, worried. 'Tell me.'

He cleared his throat again. 'I think... I might be in a spot of trouble...'

THE END

DCI BOYD RETURNS IN

THE FOOL available to pre-order HERE

ALSO BY ALEX SCARROW

DCI Boyd

SILENT TIDE

OLD BONES NEW BONES

BURNING TRUTH

THE LAST TRAIN

THE SAFE PLACE

GONE TO GROUND

ARGYLE HOUSE

THE LOCK UP

THE ARCHIVE

A MONSTER AMONG US

Thrillers

LAST LIGHT

AFTERLIGHT

OCTOBER SKIES

THE CANDLEMAN

A THOUSAND SUNS

The TimeRiders series (in reading order)

TIMERIDERS

TIMERIDERS: DAY OF THE PREDATOR

TIMERIDERS: THE DOOMSDAY CODE

TIMERIDERS: THE ETERNAL WAR

TIMERIDERS: THE CITY OF SHADOWS

TIMERIDERS: THE PIRATE KINGS

TIMERIDERS: THE MAYAN PROPHECY

TIMERIDERS: THE INFINITY CAGE

The Plague Land series

PLAGUE LAND

PLAGUE NATION

PLAGUE WORLD

The Ellie Quin series

THE LEGEND OF ELLIE QUIN

THE WORLD ACCORDING TO ELLIE QUIN

ELLIE QUIN BENEATH A NEON SKY

ELLIE QUIN THROUGH THE GATEWAY

ELLIE QUIN: A GIRL REBORN

ABOUT THE AUTHOR

Over the last sixteen years, award-winning author Alex Scarrow has published seventeen novels with Penguin Random House, Orion and Pan Macmillan. A number of these have been optioned for film/TV development, including his bestselling *Last Light*.

When he is not busy writing and painting, Alex spends most of his time trying to keep Ozzie away from the food bin. He lives in the wilds of East Anglia with his wife Deborah and five, permanently muddy, dogs.

Ozzie came to live with him in January 2017. He was adopted from Spaniel Aid UK and was believed to be seven at the time. Ozzie loves food, his mum, food, his ball, food, walks and more food...

He dreams of unrestricted access to the food bin.

For up-to-date information on the DCI BOYD series, visit: www.alexscarrow.com

To see what Ozzie is up to, click on the instagram link below...

Printed in Great Britain
by Amazon